Joan Fleming and The Murder Room

>>> This title is part of The Murder Room, our series dedicated to making available out-of-print or hard-to-find titles by classic crime writers.

Crime fiction has always held up a mirror to society. The Victorians were fascinated by sensational murder and the emerging science of detection; now we are obsessed with the forensic detail of violent death. And no other genre has so captivated and enthralled readers.

Vast troves of classic crime writing have for a long time been unavailable to all but the most dedicated frequenters of second-hand bookshops. The advent of digital publishing means that we are now able to bring you the backlists of a huge range of titles by classic and contemporary crime writers, some of which have been out of print for decades.

From the genteel amateur private eyes of the Golden Age and the femmes fatales of pulp fiction, to the morally ambiguous hard-boiled detectives of mid twentieth-century America and their descendants who walk our twenty-first century streets, The Murder Room has it all. **>>>**

The Murder Room
Where Criminal Minds Meet

themurderroom.com

Joan Fleming (1908–1980)

Joan Fleming was one of the most original and literate crime writers of her generation. Born in Lancashire and educated at Lausanne University she became the wife of a Harley Street eye surgeon and mother of four, and was already a successful children's author before she turned to crime. She is the author of over thirty novels and won the CWA Gold Dagger in 1962 for *When I Grow Rich* and again in 1970 for *Young Man, I Think You're Dying*. *The Deeds of Dr Deadcert* was made into the 1958 film *Rx for Murder*.

Two Lovers Too Many
A Daisy-Chain for Satan
The Gallows in My Garden
The Man Who Looked Back
Polly Put the Kettle On
The Good and the Bad
He Ought To Be Shot
The Deeds of Dr Deadcert
You Can't Believe Your Eyes
Maiden's Prayer
Malice Matrimonial
Miss Bones
The Man from Nowhere
In the Red
When I Grow Rich
Death of a Sardine
The Chill and the Kill
Nothing is the Number When You Die

Midnight Hag
No Bones About It
Kill or Cure
Hell's Belle
Young Man I Think You're Dying
Screams From a Penny Dreadful
Grim Death and the Barrow Boys
Dirty Butter for Servants
Alas, Poor Father
You Won't Let Me Finnish
How to Live Dangerously
Too Late! Too Late! the Maiden Cried
To Make an Underworld
Every Inch a Lady

The Good and the Bad

Joan Fleming

An Orion book

Copyright © Joan Fleming 1953

The right of Joan Fleming to be identified as the author of this work
has been asserted in accordance with the Copyright, Designs and
Patents Act 1988.

This edition published by
The Orion Publishing Group Ltd
Orion House
5 Upper St Martin's Lane
London WC2H 9EA

An Hachette UK company
A CIP catalogue record for this book is available from the British Library

ISBN 978 1 4719 0199 7

www.orionbooks.co.uk

Printed and bound by CPI Group (UK) Ltd, Croydon, CR0 4YY

There's so much good
    In the worst of us
And so much bad
    In the best of us
That it hardly becomes any of us
    To talk about the rest of us.

E. W. Hoch

CHAPTER I

GINGER stood on the corner where the Rue Servandoni meets the Rue de Vaugirard and looked across at the Luxembourg Gardens. He had come to rest upon the corner as naturally as a swallow upon a wire; any corner was his habitat, any corner from whence his swift uneasy eyes could note danger approaching from the perimeter.

A weak sun shone in a pale sky and one by one the golden leaves dropped from the trees in the park like slow tears.

"Cor!" he muttered, "Gay Paree!" Where his forbears, for even a corner-boy has forbears, would have spat with disgust upon the pavement, Ginger did the modern equivalent, he brought a dirty small comb out of his left breast pocket and ran it through his thick wavy hair.

It was twenty-four hours since he landed at Le Bourget and still he had not found the underworld, that marvellous Paris underworld which he had always understood made London's underworld look like a Sunday school picnic. Where were the what they call 'apackys' throwing their girls about like silk scarves? Where were the gay underground cafés with the gipsy accordionists and the absinthe drinkers?

Within an hour of his arrival Ginger had gone into the dirtiest café he could find; there were no 'apackys' but he had asked for and had been given a large absinthe and the result was that later he had been very sick into the gutter outside the café. The rest of the night he had spent on a seat on the Quai de la Tournelle until a flat-hatted cop had turned him off in the chilly dawn. He felt like all hell now, strewth, he did.

"Gay Paree!"

He replaced his comb in his pocket and crossed over the

1

road and into the Luxembourg Gardens. Close by was a seat of which one end was occupied. Ginger took the other end. He brought out a nail file and began to file his nails.

Some French children with spindly legs and straight hair had tied a length of string between two trees and were playing a primitive form of tennis with many high-pitched cries. Ginger watched them with a dead-eyed lack of interest, then he turned, incuriously, to look at his neighbour on the seat. He was an ungainly looking youth, or was he a man? He had bowed shoulders between which hung a great head with white bulging brow, the head shook very slightly.

Ginger returned to the scrutiny of his finger-nails, biting off that which the file had failed to remove. If it were not for the money which he could feel pressing against his thigh, Ginger reflected, he would be in a very poor way indeed. But he reckoned things couldn't go far wrong when he'd got all that money on board. All he'd got to do was to find a black market where he could exchange his English notes into French money and he'd be all right, he told himself repeatedly. First the black market and then the underworld, and he'd be all right for a cert; he'd soon find a girl for himself and some kind of place where he could doss down. Maybe things weren't too bad.

Bonk! An ill-aimed tennis ball from the racket of one of the children bounced off the hollow-sounding head of the idiot sitting on the seat beside Ginger. The children rushed to retrieve their ball shrieking with laughter and pointing hilariously at the idiot who looked mildly at them with his sad little eyes.

That started it, they abandoned their games of ball in favour of the more amusing sport of baiting the idiot. Joining hands they danced towards him in a semicircle chanting some heathenish-sounding tune, they drew away and again surged forward in the manner of English children playing Nuts-in-May but with evident evil intent.

2

"*Allez, allez,*" the idiot cried, and his voice, yet unbroken, came so shrill and high that they burst into shrieks of laughter and renewed their dance with vigour.

The idiot was almost crying, he turned despairingly to Ginger, who waved his nail file in the children's direction and said:

"B . . . off, you kiddies!"

One or two passers-by now stopped to observe the fun and Ginger began to feel distinctly embarrassed. Far from obeying Ginger's instructions, the children now included Ginger in their mockery, the semicircle increased in number and took upon itself a sadistic quality, inherited, perhaps from progenitors who had mocked at the tumbrils as they drove along the street with the victims for the guillotine. One small urchin, a direct descendant, no doubt, of Marat, stooped down and, picking up a handful of gravel, he threw it directly in the face of the idiot.

"You little devil!" Ginger shouted. Springing to his feet he took the child by one ear and marched him off, shrieking with fear, whilst the others scampered away squealing like mice.

It was all over. Ginger returned to the seat, retrieved the nail file which had fallen in the dust, and went on attending to his nails. A woman was now bending over the idiot, talking in rapid, excited French; she turned to Ginger and continued to talk.

"No parlez Fronsay!" Ginger said.

"*Comment,* you're English?"

Ginger nodded.

"I must thank you," the woman said, "for being so kind to my son."

Ginger felt a bit of a fool, he did not look up from the business of attending to his nails. He had not meant to be kind; though he, Ginger, knew that he 'would not hurt a fly', he had never thought of himself as *kind*.

3

The woman went on talking. "I have had much trouble with the children over Chad," she said. "But for some time past they leave him alone. Now they have started once more I don't know what to do!"

'Well, I'm sure I don't', Ginger thought; he put his nail file away and stood up. 'Couldn't care less'.

"*Attendez, attendez!*" the woman cried.

For the first time Ginger took notice of her. She looked as though some bloke or another had given her a couple of black eyes. No, on second glance they were not black eyes, not that sort of black eye. Strewth, they were marvellous orbs!

"You are English, are you not?"

With eyes narrowed, Ginger was always suspicious when anyone asked him a question, he nodded.

"So am I."

That was a big surprise! English! Never!

"You are surprise, heh?"

Again Ginger nodded.

The woman laughed. "I tease you, boy. My husband, he was English. Sit down beside me," she patted the seat, "and tell me, what is England like? My husband he say nothing except always—bloody. 'England is bloddy!' he say when I ask to go there."

Ginger did not often laugh, but something in the way the woman spoke tickled his laughing strings. He giggled nervously.

The woman smiled. "Bloddy! That is a bad word, yes?"

Ginger went on sniggering until the idiot joined in with a high-pitched "Tee hee! Tee hee!" which made Ginger's blood run cold and he stopped laughing abruptly.

He started framing in his mind the questions he was longing to put: do you know the underworld of Paris? Where do I find it? Where are the apackys and the loverly girls? Where is the black market and where the brothels?

"What is your name?" she asked.

"Ginger," he replied. He must, at some time or other

have had some other name, but he did not remember what it was. Those who comprise London's underworld are not original in their nicknames; the Gingers, the Slims and the Buds number one in five.

"Ginger what?"

"Smith," he said in a burst of inventiveness, "but just call me Ginger."

"How old are you?"

Nervously Ginger rubbed his face all over with his hand. He hated being asked questions. How old was he? "About twenty-two," he answered, truthfully.

"You are a kind boy," she said.

Phew!

"I take you home with me and give you a nice dinner, heh? You look starved to death. When did you last have a meal?"

"I had dinner yesterday at a café on the Great West Road and I've had nothing since."

"But plenty to drink, heh?"

The mere thought of drink made his gorge rise, but the idea of going home with this woman was not unattractive; she was a bit of a scarecrow, Ginger thought, but if she was good for a meal—so what?

Presently she rose, said something in French to the idiot and he, too, rose and slouched after her. "Come along," she said, beckoning to Ginger.

Instinctively Ginger was reluctant to walk beside her, nor was he inclined to walk with the idiot. With elaborate casualness he lined up behind and followed them out of the gardens, up the Rue Servandoni, across the Place St. Sulpice and into the Rue des Quatre Vents. In single file they walked with Ginger bringing up the rear and darting his suspicious glances from side to side. They turned into the Rue des Mauvais Garçons and into an important-looking doorway which led only into a courtyard. At the far corner of the courtyard was another door which

5

the woman unlocked; it led down a flight of stairs into a basement flat.

"Voilà," she said, wrapping herself into a large apron. "I give you something quick, heh? A Spanish omelette, pistolets, coffee?"

Coffee was the only one of the three things which conveyed anything to Ginger. "Do me nicely," he murmured. She hurried to and fro and presently a very delectable smell filled the room.

Though not yet fifty years old, Marie Céleste was a worn-out rag of a woman, her spirit rode her body like a witch on a broomstick; a worn-out broomstick for indeed her body seemed to hang about her spirit in tattered fragments. There was nothing much of her but in her presence no one could for an instant cease to be conscious of her, she sizzled and boiled about one with a restless unease, a burning energy. She talked incessantly as she prepared the meal, telling Ginger the story of her life in which he was patently not interested but which he did not feel the energy to stem. He let her talk away, sitting in a dull stupor and allowing the information to flow over his head.

Her husband had been an artist, a very great artist, in fact, but an unsuccessful one. Look, there were some of his canvases standing against the wall, presently she would show them to Ginger. One day they would be worth a fortune, but for the present—*eh bien*! He had lived in France for thirty years and never once, during all those years, had he gone back to England to see his people. He had loved them not, he loved only Marie Céleste, and she, Marie Céleste, loved only him—or very nearly. When they were both young, ah! what beautiful pictures he had painted of Marie Céleste! They were all there, piled in that corner, every single one of them! She repeated that presently she would show them to Ginger. It was not everyone to whom she showed them, but Ginger, there was something about him —Marie Céleste was sure he would like to see the pictures.

It was over a year ago her husband had died and since then

she herself had not been well. She suffered from bronchitis and shortness of breath, she had been obliged to move from their pleasant attic flat, the apartment they had occupied for over twenty years, and take this basement. The attic had been on the fourth story, you understand, and there had been many stairs; here, though not so pleasant and light there was only one flight of stairs.

When her husband was alive, Marie Céleste went on, she had had to work a good deal harder for, you understand, to maintain a genius of his calibre in comfort it cost money, a great deal more money than he was in the habit of receiving regularly from his father in England. Oh, a great deal more! She had been obliged to go out to work all day, from seven o'clock in the morning until seven o'clock at night, calling, early in the morning on her way to work, at Les Halles, where she had filled her string bag with provisions for her husband and son and carrying it home after the day's work, to prepare the evening meal for them all and to leave food ready for the midday meal on the following day.

But now that, alas, her beloved husband was gone Marie Céleste found that they could manage to live fairly comfortably on the continued allowance from England with the addition of the wages she earned working only four hours in the middle of the day. The difficulty about that was what to do with Chad during those four hours. When her husband had been alive he had kept an eye on Chad, but now she had to manage as best she could and Ginger could see for himself how unsatisfactory it was. During the winter she could leave him sitting by the closed stove in the living-room, playing with pencil and paper, making little wood carvings or modelling with wax; but in the summer he needed to be out in the fresh air. She had to take him to the park and leave him there until she fetched him when her work was over.

At first the children had plagued the poor boy until he trembled and cried and could not be left alone. Then she had

7

enlisted the help of the *gendarmerie;* they had watched that the children did not throw stones at Chad and for a long time now all had been well. She hoped that it was not going to start up again.

By this time she had knocked up an excellent little meal. Ginger had never eaten anything like it, it was queer-looking stuff but it tasted all right. She had some red wine in a kind of water-bottle to which she and Chad helped themselves frequently and after a while Ginger had some too for he never liked to miss anything that was going. Then they had coffee; Marie Céleste appeared to be in no hurry to clear away the meal. "Now you must tell me all about yourself," she said.

Ginger ran his hand over his face. That he would certainly not do, but there was no harm in telling her that he had been in Paris only twenty-four hours and that he had nowhere to go.

"I'm browned-off," he said, "If this is gay Paree give me Southend any day."

"Browned-off?" Marie Céleste repeated, "I have not heard that expression."

"I'm sick of it, it's no go!" Ginger explained.

She might well have asked why, then, he did not return to London, but she did not do so which was as well for he had no intention of telling her why he could not return to London.

They smoked until the room was dark with the blue haze from their cigarettes and the daylight fading.

Chad took no interest in the talk, after he had eaten very heartily he sat on at the table, playing with little lumps of bread which he moulded into shapes. He seemed quite content. Marie Céleste brought more wine, it went pleasantly to Ginger's head. She lighted a shaded lamp and the room looked comfortable and cosy. Ginger experienced a glow which was his nearest approach to happiness.

"I like it here," he mumbled.

Marie Céleste made Chad get up, she marched him over to the sink where she took a soap and flannel and washed his

8

great ears, then she gave him a gentle slap on the face and told him to go to bed; he lumbered off willingly, like a great stupid St. Bernard dog.

When he had gone Marie Céleste went across to the pile of canvases in the corner of the room. "Now," she said, "you shall see. The Naked Beauty!" One after another she turned the canvases round and ranged them along the wall for Ginger's inspection.

Ginger was shaken, he was not only shaken, he was deeply shocked. He had no idea whether they were good or bad, he could only think of them as 'indecent'.

Marie Céleste was greatly amused. "Ah! *Voyons! Le petit bourgeois.*"

She was right. Ginger, the intimate of the dregs of humanity, the pimps, the pansies and the prostitutes of London's underworld had, indeed, a streak of the bourgeois in him. He liked, for instance, to be introduced to a lady before he became friendly and he had a nice social sense; if he were associating in a public house with what he thought of in his own mind as 'nice people', he did not like to be approached by less 'nice people'. Looking at the pictures of the nude Marie Céleste his thoughts of her underwent a great change.

Marie Céleste watched his thoughts change, her great lampblack eyes never left him as he passed from picture to picture. When he had finished looking he took out his comb and combed his hair. Marie Céleste restacked the pictures. "You like them, heh?"

"Can't say as I like them, exactly," Ginger said. "They've got pep."

Pep, Marie Céleste reflected. What would poor Martin think of that? Pep!

It was shock rather than a regard for Marie Céleste's feeling that caused Ginger to refrain from exclaiming that the pictures must have been painted a long time ago. He said stiffly that he had better be getting along now.

9

Where, Marie Céleste demanded, was he going?

Where indeed? Back, Ginger supposed, to the seat on the quay where he had spent last night. Until he had changed some money into French francs there was nowhere else he could go. The bloke who had fixed up his passport and who had run him to the airport in his motor car had stuffed a handful of French paper money into his pocket, it had seemed a lot at the time but almost all of it had gone on that drink last night.

And thinking about drink he drained his glass of the red wine. Ginger had never had wine in his life before, it tasted rough and somewhat sour, but he liked it. You could drink less of it and feel the same kind of elation, though somewhat better, than you felt with beer.

"Some more wine?"

"I don't mind if I do," Ginger said, wiping his mouth on the back of his hand.

"Where will you go?" she persisted.

"Dunno," he mumbled.

"You could stay here, heh?"

"Is there room?" Ginger asked, looking about him.

Then, to his extreme horror, Marie Céleste came round the table and sat herself upon his knee.

"Only in my bedroom," she murmured.

Cor! Ginger looked wildly round. He'd got himself trapped, good and proper he had.

Marie Céleste put an arm round him and ruffled the hair at the back of his neck. Ginger could feel himself slipping.

"I love Englishmen," she told him.

A regular bad woman, Ginger told himself, slipping further. Old enough to be his mother, too! He'd always heard French women were a bad lot, he ought to have watched out for himself, he did!

"Look at me," Marie Céleste said, taking his face in her hand and turning it towards her own. "Your eyes are like mice, they run away from me always. What are you frightened of?"

Ginger was frightened of a lot of things. He had been frightened all his life; right at the beginning he had been frightened of the man and woman who had fought each other and then kicked him. That was the first of a long line of things that frightened Ginger. But right now it was those great black eyes that frightened him, he did not want to look into them because if he did he might not belong to himself any more.

Yet he could not get up and go for there she was, sitting on his knee; she had been very decent to him, he couldn't toss her down like an unwanted parcel. Besides——

"Look at me," she compelled.

He did not want to look at her yet not altogether reluctantly he did so.

What orbs!

"Kiss me," Marie Céleste commanded.

CHAPTER II

For four hours during the early part of the day Marie Céleste worked at a little restaurant called *Le Petit Chevron.* It was, in fact, owned by two English ladies, Miss Taplow, who was tall and dark and handsome, and Miss Field, who was small and fluffy. They seemed very devoted to each other and gave Marie Céleste a free hand in the catering and cooking. Only the midday meal was served, the restaurant being closed in the evening; Marie Céleste knocked off a superbly good menu of the French peasant type in the minimum of time and with what the owners considered to be the minimum of money. In point of fact Marie Céleste was left with a substantial sum for her own pocket and a handsome proportion of the food provided for the customers left the restaurant either in Marie Céleste's string bag or concealed about her person. Nobody at number one hundred Rue des Mauvais Garçons minded very much that the butter, the boiled bacon and the cold chicken were slightly redolent of Marie Céleste.

Miss Field and Miss Taplow, anxious, no doubt, that the 'typically French' myth of *Le Petit Chevron* should be maintained, seldom made a public appearance in the restaurant; they went off to wander hand in hand through the Bois, returning when the last customer had left, Marie Céleste had gone and the larder was bare. Then they would count up the day's takings, congratulating themselves and each other on their treasure of a cook.

It was thus that Ginger found himself housed and superbly fed without being called upon to contribute a sou. It suited him to perfection and though he never paused to consider his good fortune, he was dimly aware that he had done pretty well for himself. Between meals he sloped about the city, acquainting himself with the topography of Paris; a child of the streets, he liked sitting for hours at a table on the streets, a *bock* in front of him, a cigarette hanging from his mouth, hands in pockets, watching the passing to and fro of the city dwellers. He might have been a philosopher studying his fellow creatures, but, in fact, he was not; he was thinking about picking pockets. There was a chap he had met at the Borstal Institution at Hollesley Bay, a certain Chum Harrigan, whose father had been a regular pick-pocket, a topnotcher who had never stooped to petty cash but who robbed big business men of pigskin wallets laden with hundreds of pounds and who, upon one epic occasion, had been known to lift a thousand quid off a bookie at Liverpool. Young Chum was a trainee at his father's hands with no mean share of his father's skill. His father, Chum recounted, had taken the braces off a cop whilst he and the cop had been sitting side by side in a pub; once you'd got hold of the principles of the thing, Chum said, it was a matter of practice; as Ginger and Chum lay in the cool grass under the big elms, ostensibly watching the cricket, they had practised removing articles from each other. Chum had said it would take years

12

of practice before they were any good, but Ginger was itching to try out his skill on his own.

No sooner had he left Borstal than he was off to the dog racing at the White City and the very first bloke he tried had caught him at it, had hailed a cop, and Ginger had had to leave the scene with the utmost speed. It was undignified and Ginger had decided that he would leave the game alone until he had further practice. Now, however, that there was no other immediately apparent means of making money, Ginger was toying with the idea of starting again. For hours he sat in the cafés, soothed by the noises of the city, and contemplated the prospect of making money, without, of course, working for it.

Presently he had the idea of making Chad his stooge.

"Leave Chad with me," he threw off casually one morning as Marie Céleste was wrapping a scarf round her son's neck preparatory to taking him into the Luxembourg Gardens where she would leave him until her work was done.

"Oh, how you are kind, Ginger," Marie Céleste smiled. "You will take him out for me?"

"Sure."

"O.K. my dar-rling," Marie Céleste exclaimed, putting her arms round his neck and kissing him affectionately. Ginger was immensely embarrassed by Marie Céleste's demonstrativeness, he considered it indecent in broad daylight, but accepted it indulgently because she was 'Fronsays'. So, when Marie Céleste had gone Ginger would put his own wallet into Chad's inside breast pocket, then he would take off his own jacket, roll up his shirt sleeves and proceed to remove the wallet from Chad's pocket. The idiot, however, annoyed him very much; he seemed to think it was some sort of tickling game and would double up with laughter until tears were streaming down his idiotic face. Ginger amused himself by calling him all the foulest names he had ever heard, using language which had been thrown at himself when he was a child. Chad was delighted, he thought they were terms of endearment and would chuckle

13

and push Ginger playfully until Ginger lost patience and stamped out of the room and Chad's huge face would change completely, it would crumple up like that of a baby, and he would follow Ginger whimpering and demanding attention.

"—!" Ginger said. "You——! Now look 'ere, get this into your big fat loaf——" and Chad, not understanding a word, would beam and smile once more, glad that the quarrel was made up and the game renewed.

But it was not a lot of fun to pick the pocket of an idiot. Almost instinctively, certainly without any plan being formulated in his mind, Ginger began to look out for what he considered to be posh folk and here he was seriously puzzled because he saw women emerging from the meanest houses looking as posh as you please. As for the men, you'd see a bloke getting out of a white Hispano Suiza and, honest to goodness, you'd wonder; he'd look like a lot of Ginger's own friends in London, nicely dressed, mind you, with all the trimmings, but away from his car you couldn't be sure if he'd have a wallet worth pinching.

And so the sad leaves fell and soon the autumn became winter, an icy wind blew so that Ginger could no longer stand comfortably upon the corner of the Rue des Mauvais Garçons and the Rue des Quatre Vents. Marie Céleste gave him money to buy himself an overcoat and he bought a very posh one at the Printemps, a sort of ginger brown felt with a mottled pattern and with a belt like a sash, but even clad in this it was still unpleasantly cold upon the corner.

Marie Céleste lighted the stove in the living-room and now Chad sat beside it all day long. "I hate the winter," she said, "we must feed well for only so can we all keep well."

But Marie Céleste did not keep well; with the first cold wind she began to cough and shiver and to worry about what they would do if she were in bed again, as she had been last winter.

"What did you do then?" Ginger asked roughly.

"I had to send Chad away, to a home," Marie Céleste

14

replied, "But never again, oh, never again. Poor boy, he was so miserable, and when he came back to me, so thin! They starved him."

Ginger looked at Chad dispassionately. He did not consider it would do Chad any harm to starve, as it was he ate a great deal too much food.

One evening Ginger came in late, Marie Céleste had been writing, she was clearing away the writing materials and upon the chimney piece was propped a letter.

Major General Sir Matthew Quest, K.C.B., C.B.E.,
Rivington Court,
Gloucestershire.

"Strewth!" Ginger whistled through his front teeth, "What the hell?"

"Mon beau père," Marie Céleste tossed off casually.

"What?"

"My father-in-law, my little cabbage," she said, flicking the end of Ginger's nose. Ginger clutched the back of a chair to give himself a feeling of security. What the hell was she talking about?

"I have told you many times I am English, my husband was English, therefore I am English. But you never listen, my little Ginger, you are not really interested in other people, are you? Are you?" she repeated, after a little pause. "You have been here now for four weeks, you have never once ask me a question."

That was quite true. Ginger was incurious about Marie Céleste as about almost everybody and he expected that other people would feel the same lack of curiosity about himself. Marie Céleste had been aware of this. "You ask no questions, and you want none, eh? That is how it is, *mon petit*?"

Ginger blustered. But this letter, he meant to say, that was a bit much. What was it all about?

15

Marie Céleste chuckled. "Ah, you are interested now. When you hear my *beau père* is an English milord, that interest you, heh?"

"A lord!"

"A knight, you call it."

"Strewth!"

"Chad's grandfather. And I, Ginger, 1 am Mrs. Martin Quest. Martin was my husband and I am Madame Quest. Marie Céleste Quest! Does it not sound silly? So I am Marie Céleste to everyone, anyway, French people find it difficult to pronounce Quest, they like to put in a V, like this, *Qvest*!" She shrieked with laughter and then was taken with a violent paroxysm of coughing. When it was all over Ginger sat down at the table opposite to her.

"Look," he said, "I'd better hear it. You tell me everything, Marie Céleste. I never thought you was a dark horse, strewth, I didn't. You of all people, I thought I could trust you."

"And so you can," Marie Céleste said, wiping her eyes. "That you didn't know does not mean I kept it from you. I tell you all you want to know. I keep nothing from you, Ginger. How can you think I deceive you!"

But Ginger was not to be mollified. He felt the ground had slipped from beneath his feet, he needed reassurance. He waited, tapping his long white fingers on the table top. Marie Céleste blew her nose, tucked her handkerchief into her belt and lighted a cigarette.

"My husband was the eldest son of Sir Matthew Quest. I met him thirty-one years ago, when I was young and he was not so young. He had left home, you understand, because he quarrel with his father and mother. They wanted him to be a soldier like his father but Martin, he wanted to be an artist. He was very frightened of his father, you understand. Oh, make no mistake, my Martin was a very brave man, but his father, oh . . ." Marie Céleste blew a thin stream of smoke

16

into the air above her head. "Martin call him a—what was it —a 'Holy Terror'!"

Ginger was dimly aware of a fellow feeling for the dead Martin Quest.

"Well, Martin, he took an *atelier*, how do you call it—a studio, here in the city and we live there, very happy, oh very happy." But here Marie Céleste's face clouded. "*Eh bien*," she tempered, "perhaps not always so very happy but we love each other very much." There was a long pause and at last she said: "I tell you all, Ginger. You understand that my Martin was a great genius, but," she threw out her hands expressively, "nobody know it; nobody buy his pictures—pouf, my poor Martin. Because he was so—so—disappointed, you might say, he drank a great deal. I don't blame him, Ginger, and you must not blame him. You don't understand how the genius feel, right here, deep down inside himself."

Marie Céleste pressed her hands against her flat chest and, after another long pause she went on: "Martin became very ill with the drink, it was not wine and beer he drank, like you and I, but *les fines*, you understand, *Calvados* and *Pernod*. He was in hospital for a long time and when he recovered a little he found he could no longer work very much. So I had to work for us both. I have always been able to do the *cuisine*, a good cook, you would say, and I go out working. But then money was hard to earn and there was no money left for Martin to buy drink and without it, you understand, he could not live. So Martin wrote to his father and told him he had been very ill, and asked for an allowance."

Ginger sneered. Allowances! He had heard about the sons of rich men receiving *allowances*!

"It wasn't a lot, you understand, but——" words failing her she shrugged, leaving it to be understood that the allowance was sufficient to provide ample drink for Martin. There was another long pause; Marie Céleste's face, as she dreamily watched the smoke rising from her cigarette, wore a singularly

17

sweet expression. "We were very happy," she murmured at last, "Until, suddenly, *voyons*! *J'etais enceinte*! I was having a child! Oh, how shocked we were!" Marie Céleste laughed in happy reminiscence. "My poor Martin, it was the last thing he expect, I assure you. A child! When at last we both realize that indeed our child was coming for here was my stomach, out here, Martin said he would marry me!" A look of almost childlike delight transfigured Marie Céleste's face. "And so we were married, and by a priest, at l'eglise de Saint-Séverin, just along the road there. I had a new dress and Martin wore a collar and tie——"

Ginger stirred uneasily, he was not in the least interested in what they wore.

"—and Martin wrote to his father and told him he was married and going to have a child and asked for more money. And he got it!"

He would! Ginger lit up another cigarette from the stump of the old one. Of course he would!

"And then the baby came, and Martin wrote to his father and said that he had a son and I had a letter from Martin's mother. *Moi! I!* She said how happy they were that Martin had a son and she hoped he could be christened in a church and that we would call him Matthew after his grandfather and St. Chad after his great-grandfather."

Marie Céleste, wrapt in her reminiscences, rocked herself to and fro. This was evidently a happy period in her life, it might have been some time before Chad's defects became evident. "He was such a lovely baby," she said. Then her face became sad again and with a deep sigh she dismissed a great many years of pain and sorrow. "It was bad whilst the war was on, you understand, and during that time the allowance ceased. Yes, it was very bad. But it was all over after a long time and once more we heard from Martin's father. The war was sad for him too for he had lost his two other sons. He asked that Martin return home to Rivington and bring his wife and son.

That," Marie Céleste pointed out, "that was *me* and *Chad*!"

Ginger stared at her. Even he realized the tragedy of the situation.

"The only son, returning home," Marie Céleste said, and her voice was a little hoarse, "with me and Chad! And Martin himself, you understand, he was a wreck!"

"Well, I don't know!" Ginger ejaculated, "Did you turn down the offer?"

"Of course!"

"I call that silly."

"It was impossible," Marie Céleste said firmly, "quite impossible. So then Martin wrote, he had a terrible time writing, you understand, his hand was very unsteady, it had been a long time since he wrote anything and his hand would not form the letters. So at last he went to a typing bureau and told them what to say and they wrote to his father and he signed the letter. He showed me the letter, oh, it was beautiful! He said he had a wonderful wife and a son of whom he was proud, and that he had made a place for himself here in Paris and that he could not tear us up by the roots and—how was it he put it—*transplant* us. Was it not beautiful?"

Ginger grunted.

"Then his father wrote, very, very sad. He said they were getting old and lonely and Martin was their only son left, could Martin visit them? And poor Martin! Oh, Ginger! My poor Martin! He cried! You understand, he was very weak. We had a very bad scene that time. He didn't go, of course. They wrote to ask for a photograph of Chad and Martin bought in a photographer's shop a photograph of a boy of five and sent it and said that it was Chad when he was five and that we had not had a photograph taken since. So Sir Matthew arranged through his *banque* to pay for the rent of an *appartement* for us but everything cost so much dearer now that we had nothing over for the drinks which Martin had to have. So

19

Martin let a friend have the *appartement* and he received money for it and this he spent on himself. He became very ill, he was always in and out of hospital. Then one day a telegram came to say his mother had had a bad—what do you call it— stroke. Martin must go to her bedside. But Martin couldn't!" Marie Céleste's lips were now forming a thin line. She remembered how she had gone out to look for Martin and how she had found him, at last, face downwards in the gutter outside his favourite café, how she had shaken him and dragged him upright, how she had tried to get the information into his head, how impossible it had been and how, at last, Marie Céleste had taken the matter into her own hands and wired back to the Quests that Martin himself was too ill to come.

Lady Quest had died without seeing her only surviving son for the first and last time for thirty years and Martin himself had died some weeks later.

"—and that is how it is," Marie Céleste said, and wept a little.

"Well, I don't know——" Ginger pronounced, picking his teeth reflectively.

"There is the house," Marie Céleste murmured, wiping her eyes and indicating a photograph which Ginger had not noticed hanging over the chimney piece.

"Gaw' strewth!" he exclaimed, "It's a bloomin' palace!" He studied it for some considerable time whilst Marie Céleste coughed. At last she said: "Chad is heir to all that."

Ginger said nothing; he was surprised to the point of being deeply shocked, words failed him.

Marie Céleste coughed again and took a deep draught of red wine. She said: "Chad's proper name is Matthew St. Chad Quest. His great-grandfather on the other side, you understand, was Lord St. Chad; Matthew's mother was an Honourable before she was married, and after, too. Her husband was knighted because he was a good soldier in the 1914-18 war. The present Lord St. Chad is Chad's great uncle, and he is the fourteenth milord, Ginger, the fourteenth Lord St. Chad, and his own son will be the fifteenth!"

So what? It was the dough at the back of the set-up which impressed Ginger. If he were fiftieth Baron of his line Ginger couldn't care less, the whole lot were Tories and therefore stank, but the hard cash implicit in the whole affair was very impressive indeed.

"Chad's a damn silly name," he said, to show that he did not attach any weight to all this information. "They'd split their sides laughing at that name over there. There's a Mr. Chad, with a long nose, looking over a wall and saying 'Wot, no——' whatever it is. You see it drawn in chalk on privy walls. You couldn't call anyone Chad over there, they'd laugh you off the streets."

"*Tiens!*" Marie Céleste commented politely.

"Are you still getting any money from this b——?" Ginger asked.

"*Mais oui!* He send me an allowance still but it is not so great, you understand. Things cost so very much more now. It is enough to pay the rent of this place but there is nothing over."

"Why ever don't you get more?" Ginger asked, astonished.

Marie Céleste shook her head firmly. "*Mais non*, that I could never do."

Ginger made a sound denoting disgust.

"After Martin died his father wrote me a beautiful letter, I still have it, as I have all the letters, you can read them all if you would like to, Ginger."

But Ginger would not like to. Read through a lot of old letters? No, ta very much, it was too like work.

"Oh, well—he wrote this beautiful letter and said he would like me to come to Rivington with Chad but that he would quite understand if I did not want to. He said he would try to continue to send the allowance as he had done when Martin was alive but he was not very happy in his money affairs; since the last war finish, he told me, things have become very bad for

21

him. But even if he had to reduce it, he said, he would try always to send me something each month. And so he does and each time I write him a letter and thank him and tell him—" Marie Céleste paused, "—and tell him——"

"Tell him what?" Ginger said impatiently.

"Oh, never mind," Marie Céleste snapped, "I write him a nice little letter."

Ginger eyed the missive upon the chimney piece.

Later he went quietly into the little slice of a room at the end of the basement passage and looked down at the sleeping form, illuminated from the light in the passage, of Matthew St. Chad Quest. He was snoring loudly, a stream of saliva, like the track of a snail, ran from the corner of his slack mouth on to the pillow.

There was a lack of variety about the more polite of Ginger's exclamations. He simply said: "Strewth!" and left the scion to his noisy slumber.

Later still, when Marie Céleste lay tossing in her uneasy sleep, Ginger crept from her side and returned to the living-room where he put the kettle with very little water in it on the gas stove. When a vigorous stream of steam was coming from the spout he applied the back of the envelope to it, the flap peeled back easily and Ginger took out the letter, handling it carefully with the tips of his long white fingers. He unfolded it and read:

Mon cher beau père,

I have to thank you for the money order from the banque *which came safely. Chad and I are thankful for it for times are still very dear. Chad continues in fine health. I think you would be pleased to hear that he is interested in birds, that is your hobby, too, is it not?*

He watch the birds in the gardens for many hours and then he come home and tell me so interesting things about that kind of bird. With what money he can save up he buy little books

22

on the Quay d'Orsay and read about his birds. He grows up
to a fine man, so big and strong. I hope you shall be proud of
him.

Chad sends you his thankful remembrances,
from your affectionate
daughter-in-law
Marie Céleste Quest.

"Strewth!" Ginger exclaimed out loud, "Some imagination!" He put the letter carefully back and resealed the envelope. He regretted the trouble he had taken to get up and to open the letter; it had not been worth it.

CHAPTER III

STRONG drink did not agree with Ginger, it made him feel ill; in theory he could drink anybody under the table but in actual fact after a couple of *fines* he was invariably violently sick. This had its advantages in that it was a great deal cheaper to drink beer; Ginger spent very little money.

He strutted about the streets of Paris changing an occasional pound note from time to time but keeping his wallet satisfactorily full. He had received one hundred pounds in English notes in one of his curious 'business' deals which had been the cause of his leaving England so hurriedly.

Two of his acquaintances had stolen a lorry parked outside an all-night café on the Bath Road. It was loaded with tobacco on its way from a wholesale tobacconist in Bristol to a firm of cigarette makers in London. The tobacco had been disposed of by his two cronies and Ginger's part in the affair had been to dispose of the lorry. This he did and received the notes in payment. But the two thieves had been caught, a particularly astute piece of work on the part of the police; they had subsequently given information as to Ginger's undertaking in the robbery and if it had not been for another acquaintance of Ginger, a crook who had found Ginger quite useful in the past, he would by now have joined his friends in the remand prison and be awaiting trial at Winchester Assizes. As it was, he was bundled out of the country with a forged passport on a charter plane.

The wallet of notes gave him satisfaction and a feeling of security. He supposed that, somehow or other, in due course he would hear the result of the trial and once the informers were safely inside he might venture back to England, perhaps dye his hair and change his habitat from that of Kilburn to Camden town. One thing only about his future was certain, Ginger considered, and it was that once Slim and Buck were out again, which might not be for some years, he, Ginger, would seek them out and give them the hiding of their lives; he was always able to beat his opponents to pulp—in anticipation.

Honour among thieves is an outworn adage, vestiges of it may remain, perhaps, amongst the few aristocrats of the underworld. But amongst the gutter-rats, the cheap crooks, of which the greater part of the underworld now consists, there is very little loyalty and no honour. They may mouth high-sounding phrases which they pick up in the cinema but when it comes to a show-down they turn Queen's evidence without the slightest qualm.

"Sauve qui peut"; though Ginger did not actually repeat the words, that was his general gist of thought; he congratulated himself on his fortunate and clever escape. As for his companions—well, they'd got it coming to them!

So he loafed about the streets of Paris, to all appearances exactly as he had loafed about the streets of London. There was, however, an immense difference; in London his loafing concealed 'business', he would invariably be engaged in some curious form of business, acting as a go-between of some kind, on the look-out for one person or carefully avoiding another but at the same time keeping a watch, sure of some ultimate monetary gain. But in Paris he was on holiday, that is, his mind was more of a blank than when he was in London, and though he still eyed every *gendarme* that he passed, he did not bolt down a side street when he saw one approaching.

He planned to remove, sooner or later, something of value from the pocket of one of these Frenchies, but he intended to wait until a good opportunity occurred and one which he was sure would succeed, not end in dismal failure as had his first serious attempt.

In the meantime Marie Céleste appeared to become increasingly ill. Her illness did not manifest itself in pallor, lassitude and pain, but now her body seemed to cling about her spirit like a few worn-out rags. Her great eyes, always like beacons, now had an unnatural light in them; there were two bright patches of colour high on the cheek bones of her skeletal face and she was possessed of a burning restlessness as though there were little time left in which to get done all that she had to do. She did not sleep for more than an hour at a time; she would wake shuddering, in a damp perspiration and would pace restlessly up and down the icy basement corridor. At last she made up a bed for Ginger in the living-room, assuring him that she did not love him any less but that she loved him too much to wake him up continually during the night.

"What's wrong with you, Marie Céleste?" Ginger asked irritably.

"It's *la grippe*, my cabbage, I get it every winter. If only I can keep going and do not go to bed I shall be all right, you shall see, in the spring. Ah, the spring! I shall go down into the country and you shall see where I played in the fields when I was a little girl. We shall walk through the buttercup fields and you shall make love to me beside the stream, heh?"

Ginger thought it a macabre idea but did not say so.

After Christmas it became very cold indeed; at the street

corners the wind lay like a wild beast, ready to leap up and tear at the flesh of one's face as one turned the corner. Marie Céleste hurried off to work whatever the weather, clad in the most odd assortment of garments, an old moleskin coat, a balaclava helmet and a muffler which was a genuine antique in that Martin Quest had worn it at Eton as captain of Oppidans, and high-heeled Russian boots of the 1928 type. Before leaving the flat she would make up the stove, kiss her menfolk affectionately, check over with Ginger the food she had left for them, hang her inevitable string bag over her arm, clasp her worn purse tightly, and trot off with an *"au revoir, mes enfants!"* leaving Ginger and Chad as silent fireside companions.

But one morning Marie Céleste did not appear as usual in the living-room. Ginger awoke and lay waiting for his early morning cup of tea. Marie Céleste did not have early tea herself but she knew what English gentlemen liked and she proudly brought the weak brew to Ginger every morning.

But not this morning.

She lay in her bed in a pool of blood, feebly calling for Ginger.

When at last he came he shrieked with fear and rushed from her room in horror. He pulled himself together sufficiently to fetch the *concierge* who, in turn, fetched his wife and, after a great deal of hurried talk, Ginger was sent to the doctor whose name and address in the Place St. Sulpice, were written for him on a slip of paper. The doctor was out but Ginger left the message, writing laboriously on the doctor's appointment pad: Quest, 100D, Rue des Mauvais Garçons, *urgent*.

He stayed out all that day; at first he was determined never to return but as the day wore on his urge to return grew stronger. No. 100D, Rue des Mauvais Garçons was the nearest thing he had ever known to a comfortable home; he slunk back late in the evening.

The good wife of the *concierge* had been busy. Chad had

been fed, the stove had been kept alight and, above all, Marie
Céleste had been attended to. She was now lying flat on her
back between clean white sheets; she looked strangely at peace
and almost beautiful. Her voice was feeble. "Oh, Ginger, why
did you run away all day?"

"I couldn't face it, honest," Ginger muttered. "What's wrong
with you, Marie Céleste?"

"I had a hæmorrhage from the lung. I had a little one last
year, that time I told you about, when I had to go to hospital
and Chad had to go away to a home. And now I have another
—much worse."

"Must you go to hospital again?"

"I should go, but you must understand, they want me to go
to a special hospital, for lung disease. They will not now accept
me in the ordinary hospital. So I must wait for a—what do
you say—vacancy."

She reached out her hand and took Ginger's hand; her own
was hot and dry. "Oh, Ginger, how I am glad you are here!
You can help me now, my little cabbage."

"Who—" Ginger cleared his throat, "—who cleaned up
all that blood?"

"Madame Duflos. A very kind woman."

"Did—did you cough it up, Marie Céleste?"

"I woke up feeling something warm in my mouth—and
behold, *voyons*! It was blood. Streams of blood!"

Ginger shuddered. Then, as Marie Céleste looked at him he
felt a curious emotion, the same sort of emotion that he had
felt when he went for the children in the gardens because one
of them threw gravel in Chad's face. He knelt beside the bed
and put his arm round the top of Marie Céleste's head.

"I think I shall die, Ginger," Marie Céleste said, almost
casually.

"Not you."

"I shall die, like my poor Martin. Perhaps he wants me
and I must go."

27

"But I want you," Ginger said, to his immense surprise; he had never said anything like it in his life.

Marie Céleste smiled, there was something immeasurably sweet in her smile. She now had three menfolk and they all needed her. Though Martin was dead he was a great deal more alive to her than he had been at the end of his life.

"You want me to get better, Ginger?"

"You must."

"Will you look after me and Chad, so that I need not go to hospital?"

Ginger was startled but he kept calm.

"Of course."

"Madame Duflos has many children, she cannot do much for me. Can you go out and buy the food for us all and can you cook it?"

"I can try," Ginger said dubiously.

Marie Céleste pressed his hand.

"I can tell you how to cook; I shall lie in the bed in the living-room and can tell you everything to do. Oh Ginger, if you do this for me, we shall all be happy, for I shall not need to go away and Chad will be safely with us. Then I shall get better, I promise you. I shall get better for you and Chad. Oh, Ginger, how you are kind!"

Kind! There it was again!

* * * *

Ginger was sure he was not kind, he did not want to be kind, he did not intend to be chivvied into being kind. What wide boy, what super crook, what Ace of the underworld is *kind*? To hell with kindness. What he ought to do was to walk out on Marie Céleste and her idiot son, leave them cold, taking with him any oddments of value upon which he could lay his hands. That, he told himself, was talking sense.

He talked sense to himself whilst he awkwardly performed

28

menial tasks, brewing tea for Marie Céleste, cutting hunks of bread and slabs of meat for himself and Chad, making up the stove. He wasn't going to wash up dishes, not for anybody he wasn't; he and Chad ate with their fingers, crouching over the stove. Chad was disturbed by the changed state of affairs, he spoke very little but his eyes were unhappy like those of a monkey and if Ginger spoke roughly to him, telling him to get out of the b— light, he whimpered and cringed until Ginger felt like hitting him.

Marie Céleste fretted about her employers. What would they be thinking of her? Would Ginger go along to see them and explain that she was ill but that she was hoping to be back at work before long? With the utmost reluctance Ginger folded himself up in his new overcoat and shuffled off.

There was a notice on the door of *Le Petit Chevron* —FERME. Ginger, following Marie Céleste's instructions, tapped on the door which was immediately flung wide open by Miss Taplow who might well have been standing behind it waiting for a caller. Ginger was so startled that he recoiled in a great lurch, like an overbred spaniel, and, tripping backwards and stepping on the hem of his over-long coat, he landed in the gutter to the sound of a boom of laughter from Miss Taplow. She surged out and pulled the cursing Ginger to his feet, brushing him down and begging him to come inside, all in *'la plume de ma tante'* type of French. Ginger told her to cut the cackle, he was English and he had come with a message from Marie Céleste: her laugh rang out resonantly. She took him inside and gave him a glass of red wine, calling loudly for "Maisie, darling!"

Maisie was Miss Field; in spite of the bitter cold she was wearing, beneath two or three gaily coloured cardigans, a summer frock with a frill round the hem, and what appeared to be one or two flying buttresses of the same material; she was rather pretty but she looked like a sickly cake.

29

Ginger was dazed and sullen, not so much from the appearance of the two English ladies, which would have dazed anyone, but from the ignominy of his arrival and he harboured a sullen resentment against 'the two old scarecrows'. Curtly he told them of Marie Céleste's illness and then, whilst the booms and the twittering cries of the Misses Field and Taplow raged round his head, his eyes ranged round the room. He was not interested in the tables with the peasant-checked table-cloths, the fancy wine bottles used for flower decoration, the rustic baskets of fruit, the thick cheese board, but he was very interested indeed in a black painted metal box that he discerned upon a small table by the door.

Miss Taplow hit him heartily upon the shoulder, it was like a blow from the swinging boom of a yacht. "And who may you be, m'boy?"

"Me? Oh—I lodge there."

"D'ye know, Marie Céleste has never given us her address; otherwise, of course, we should have sent round to inquire. Where does she live?"

But he wasn't going to tell them the address, no fear. He thought hurriedly. It was quite beyond him to make up a French address. His eyes slid about the room. He jerked his head: "The other end of the town."

"Over the river! But we always understood she lived quite near!"

Ginger stood up. "I must be getting back. It'll take me half an hour on the Metro." He could not tear his eyes away from the black japanned box.

"Maisie darling, could we find something to send dear Marie Céleste?"

Miss Field spread out her hands prettily. "The cupboard was bare!" she quoted. "We've nothing in the place. We can't get on at all without Marie Céleste."

Miss Taplow thought. "We could send her a couple of bottles of Sauterne, perhaps. I'll go and get them." Rattling some keys which she brought from the pocket of her suit she left the room.

Ginger turned to Miss Field. "I'll give you Marie Céleste's address," he said. "Have you got a pencil and paper?"

Squeaking distractedly Miss Field tapped herself here and there with both hands. "Dear me, no. Where is there a pencil and paper, I wonder? I'll never remember it if I don't write it down."

"Run and get something to write with," Ginger said urgently. Obediently she trotted out.

There was plenty of room in Ginger's coat above the belt, for the box. It rattled noisily as he put it inside and, staying not upon the order of his going—he went.

It is not easy to describe the manner in which rats move from place to place, they do not walk, they do not run, nor do they glide; they move so swiftly that one is only aware of a dark shadow, with a shudder of disgust.

* * * *

Marie Céleste kneeled beside her bed and said her rosary. She had heard the bells of Saint-Séverin ring for the *Angelus* and, remembering the days of her youth, she reached for her long-neglected rosary. She had heard the bells of Saint-Séverin ringing many times a day for a great many years but only now, when there was so little time left to her, did she take any heed.

Ginger found her praying, she continued self-consciously to do so, not turning round as he opened the door. Ginger retreated with an inevitable "Strewth!" He was, indeed, so upset that he postponed the opening of the tin box. People, he knew, did not pray unless they were going to die. Was there, perhaps, truth in what Marie Céleste had said? Was she going to die?

Ginger looked across at Chad. He was slowly chipping away at a piece of wood which bore some resemblance to a donkey.

His head was shaking continuously as though, having no control over it, he were being driven along a cobbled street in a crude cart.

"I couldn't care less," Ginger told himself over and over again.

But it was not true.

CHAPTER IV

Was she getting better or was she not? It was hard to tell.

The doctor came daily, he stayed for a long time, talking a great deal, only ceasing to talk, in fact, when Marie Céleste herself was talking. Ginger, listening outside the door, was surprised at how much Marie Céleste in her weak state could talk. At times the discussion would reach altercation pitch. Ginger would feel sure that they were having a fearful row, but by the time the doctor left he would be smiling and shaking his finger at Marie Céleste, pouring out a stream of French which even Ginger could tell was not abusive.

The doctor could speak a little English. He told Ginger that Marie Céleste was not to get up but that for the time being she might lie on the bed in the living-room because, when Chad was not under her observation, she worried about him. He said that he was making arrangements for her to go away to a sanatorium in the Languedoc but in the meantime, they must all do everything they could to make her happy. "She is a lady with what you English call a strong will, *hein*?" the doctor said smiling; he went away shaking his head and saying: "I admire her very much."

Being wholly French, Marie Céleste was far from oblivious of the question of money. Indeed, she thought a great deal about it. Like all French women, she was thrifty, she had a small store of money which she had saved during the many years

32

in a *bas de laine,* or woollen stocking which is the French equivalent for putting aside for a rainy day. There had been a great many rainy days in her life but nothing that Marie Céleste had considered warranted more than a mere picking at her little hoard. She decided that the time for a discussion of finance with Ginger had now arrived. She approached the subject in her own forthright and energetic way.

"*Voyons,* Ginger, *mon ami.* Now that I am not working we have no money coming in, on what are we going to live?"

Ginger was shaken. "What about the cheque from his lordship?"

"Tch! Ginger, you silly boy. He cannot send me money, like that."

"Well, you told me——"

"Oh, I get an allowance from him but it is paid through a *banque,* you understand, no money actually passes. The *banque* pay for the rent of this flat."

"You mean you don't get the cash?"

"Well, of cou—r—rse not, stupid boy! The English are not allowed to send money out of their own country. It is a business arrangement made by Sir Matthew Quest with his *banque* in England, you understand."

"Of all the rotten ideas!"

"It is not a rotten idea, I assure you. If the rent of the flat was not paid for me I could not afford such a nice place. Chad and I would have only one room in some dirty street. After all, Rue des Mauvais Garçons is very nice, do you not think?" She went on hurriedly, "But now I am ill, on what do we live?"

What indeed? Ginger could go out and get himself a fairly inexpensive meal, but there was always Chad to feed, and he needed stoking almost with a shovel. Ginger looked at Chad with distaste. Great useless hulk, forever chipping away at his wooden animals, smiling to himself, head on the move.

"You must work, Ginger. Get yourself a job." She folded

her pitifully thin arms and lay back against her pillows looking at Ginger with her great lamp-like eyes.

Work? Ginger shied visibly. Work! The very word was abhorrent to him. He was as deeply shocked as a man who has just been told that he has contracted leprosy. Did she not know that Ginger would be very upset indeed if he had to work? And as to working under an employer, that would upset him psychologically! Ginger knew a lot about psychology, having been in the hands of psychiatrists for a long time in his earlier youth. They, being clever doctors, had understood how very deeply Ginger would be upset by having to work for anyone.

But he did not want to distress Marie Céleste. He left the room and went to the end of the basement passage, into the cupboard under the stairs where, under a loose floor board he had concealed the cash box he had stolen from *Le Petit Chevron*. He counted the notes. If he had counted out the equivalent amount of notes in English it would have been a lot of money, but he reckoned it was not more than twenty pounds or so. He went back into the living-room and tossed them on the bed with a gesture.

"*V—wa—lar!*" he said humorously.

"*Voyons!*" Marie Céleste exclaimed, delighted, "*Les choses se sont arrangées!*" Things had arranged themselves!

Nothing could have done Marie Céleste more good. She was delighted. Wisely she refrained from asking Ginger where he got the money.

Marie Céleste never put a foot wrong in her dealing with men; she praised and flattered Ginger in such a way that he felt a very fine fellow indeed, ten feet high. Pressing home her advantage, she passed, quite painlessly, to the question of a meal for them all, purchased and cooked by the very splendid Ginger with his own very fine hands. She picked a note out of the bundle he had given her and handed it to him, telling him exactly what to buy in the market and to hurry back with the goods. He went off happily, carrying the string bag and Marie

Céleste lay darkly hoping that he would pay attention to her last injunction and really hurry back, for only when he was in this fine mood of elation could she set him to work to cook the meal.

They had fillet of veal and fried potatoes, with small braised onions and a thin gravy.

"You see, how it is easy!" Marie Céleste cried, *"Mon brave chef de cuisine!"*

Ginger was childishly delighted. For several days now he and Chad had eaten only bread rubbed with garlic and cold meat or salami; this meal, cooked under Marie Céleste's detailed instructions, was a banquet. They opened a bottle of wine and Ginger, in a burst of bonhomie, made himself a paper hat resembling a chef's hat which caused Chad to choke with laughter so that he had to be heartily beaten upon his great bowed shoulders until he recovered.

It was a party, they were all infected a little by the febrile excitement of Marie Céleste. Though Ginger did not laugh, nor even smile, for he did not often do so, he did give his occasional snigger and was aware of a curious sensation within himself that he did not recognize.

It was happiness.

*   *   *   *

It is certain that amongst Ginger's forbears there was a first-rate cook. Ginger liked cooking, he took to it naturally as a young bird flies; what was even more important he did not consider cooking to be work. His talent was undoubtedly inherited, for cooks are born, not made. It was strange that anyone who had lived on the poorest quality of food all his life, starting as a child with white doughy bread and synthetic jam three times a day, should now be able to distinguish readily between good food and bad and be able to enjoy a meal that he had prepared, whilst noting, as he ate, that next time

35

he would put a little more of this or a little less of that in order to improve the flavour.

"My poor Martin," Marie Céleste lamented. "How he did enjoy his meals years ago. He used to say, when we were young: 'Marie Céleste, how I am lucky! I have a splendid lover and a superb cook! What more could a man want?' But, alas, when he drank more and more it spoiled his palate, he could not enjoy his food like he used to. The taste, you understand, did not affect him. One day I put, by accident, you understand, one spoonful of salt into the tomato soup instead of sugar. It was *terrible*—but Martin, he supped away, noticing nothing. I cried very much afterwards, when he was out," Marie Céleste said simply.

Ginger was often embarrassed by things that Marie Céleste said. He now looked at her reflectively. Her love-making, like her cooking, had, indeed, an unforgettable flavour. He dimly perceived that it was for this reason that he stayed on at 100 Rue des Mauvais Garçons, looking after Marie Céleste and Chad. It was for this reason that, whilst Marie Céleste was ill, he did not range the streets looking for a girl. That was the nearest he ever got to analysing the situation.

When his thoughts cohered at all, they took the form of captions such as he read when he studied his favourite comic strips. His latest caption was 'Crook turns Cook,' and as he stirred the sauces or tossed the frying potatoes in their pan under the watchful eye of Marie Céleste he was, as he would have phrased it himself, 'tickled pink'. In spite of the fact that Marie Céleste took sole charge of the notes, instructed Ginger in detail when he went out for food and, on his return, demanded an exact account of what he had spent, together with every centime of change, the money went. It was not very long before Marie Céleste warned him that they only had a few thousand francs left. "But perhaps we can manage," she added, "For next Monday I shall go back to work."

Ginger was doubly perturbed. He was as determined not to

relinquish any of his private reserve as was Marie Céleste of the contents of her *bas de laine.* He kept his pound notes very safely in the inside breast pocket of his jacket. He could, by pressing his elbow against his side, always feel the presence of his wallet and gained, therefrom, immense moral support.

He was, however, worried about where further money could be found. He was also concerned to hear that Marie Céleste intended to return to her old employment. The Misses Taplow and Field would undoubtedly have informed the police of the theft of the money box. Though Ginger was aware that Paris was a big place and that it was easy for anyone to hide in its crowded streets, he thought it possible that the police were keeping a watch out for him and, if Marie Céleste were to return to *Le Petit Chevron,* she would certainly be questioned about the theft.

One could see that Marie Céleste was still very ill but from the way she spoke and the light in her great eyes Ginger would not have been at all surprised to find her up and out one day. In order that she would not impulsively get up and go back to *Le Petit Chevron* when he was out, he invented an untruth to restrain her. He told her that he had accidently met the English ladies. He said he had been sitting at a café in the Rue des Ecoles when they had passed by and had seen him. They had stopped and had come up to him and asked him how Marie Céleste was and if he would give her a message. The message, he said, was that they had succeeded in finding a *cuisinière* and, though they hoped Marie Céleste would soon be well again, they did not wish her to return to *Le Petit Chevron.*

Marie Céleste wept bitterly but she soon recovered. "I understand," she said philosophically. "*C'est la vie,* heh? They believe me to have an infection of the chest, *phthysie,* we call it over here, and they are afraid to catch it. That is it, ah, but yes, I understand it very well!"

"It's a pity," Ginger commiserated, "But there it is."

Marie Céleste found the fact that she was not to return

to the employment of the Misses Taplow and Field at least bearable, but she was greatly worried about money.

"We should be better off if we were to move to a smaller flat," Marie Céleste said. "But I do not wish to do so. The arrangement for my father-in-law to pay the rent here was made but a year ago, I do not want to upset that so soon. Besides—if we had a smaller flat there would be no room for you, Ginger, and what would I do without you now?"

"Don't worry, Marie Céleste," Ginger said, awkwardly, "perhaps something will turn up." Marie Céleste piously said that perhaps *'le bon Dieu'* (Whom she had for so long neglected) would provide for them.

Ginger was sceptical about *'le bon Dieu'*. He knew that if you wanted anything in this world, you had to get it yourself and he had a pretty good idea of how he was going to get some money. He had at last found an *estaminet* which was frequented, if not by the Paris underworld, for he could not be sure of that, at least by people with whom he felt very much at home. Though he had not yet found any 'apackys', and had begun to think that they only existed in English stage shows, he had found certain French bookmakers and wide boys who sat about all evening and half the night in this *estaminet*. They had regarded Ginger with suspicion and curiosity at first but after a little time he came to be regarded as one of themselves. Occasionally one of them would speak a few English words to him but in the main Ginger sat with them and listened to their rapid French, understanding little of the talk, but feeling comparatively at ease. There was one chap, Ginger could not make out whether he was a bookie, or a bookmaker's clerk, or what he was, but he went to race meetings and seemed to be on good terms with everyone; they called him Paul and he frequently stood a round of drinks. He could drink an extraordinary number of *fines* and, late at night, he was often drunk, though not helplessly so.

Ginger was attracted to the man Paul; there was something

so slick, so assured, about him until he began to show the effects of drinking and even then he had a noisy boisterousness and could still cause his drinking companions to roar with laughter at his jokes. Ginger discovered that he had a motor car of his own which he kept in a mews near to the café. In the early hours of the morning he would stagger along to it and would sleep slumped in the back seat. Then, when he woke up in the morning, he drove himself back to his home in the suburbs.

Ginger was not sure that he had money, but once or twice he followed him back to the motor car and had observed it to be a costly make. After a little time Ginger decided that he had money actually on him for he used to come to the *estaminet* straight from a race meeting. For several evenings Ginger sat close beside him on the leather-covered bench against the café walls. He knew that if he waited long enough he would see his wallet.

When at last he saw the note-case and noted exactly whereabouts on his person Paul kept it, Ginger made up his mind to relieve him of it; he reckoned it would be easy, late at night. After close proximity to Ginger all evening Paul would not be able to feel Ginger's predatory fingers creeping into his breast pocket.

This time Ginger did not act on impulse. The stealing of the money box from *Le Petit Chevron* had, he considered, been a stroke of pure luck, the sort of thing that might only happen, he knew, once in a lifetime. Four factors in that robbery had turned out well for him; the actual presence of the money box, the success of his ruse to get rid of Miss Field, his rapid departure from the restaurant and, lastly, the actual presence of money amounting to about twenty pounds in the box. It might well have been empty.

So Ginger was cautious. It might well be that he was going through a spell of good luck but nevertheless he couldn't reckon on it. He was not going to be in any hurry to relieve Paul of his wallet, he would wait until the opportunity arose.

But in the meantime Marie Céleste's funds were getting lower. If only they did not have to eat! And if only Chad did not have such an enormous appetite. He ate as much again as Marie Céleste and Ginger together. It was disgusting!

Marie Céleste began again: "Ginger, *mon petit chou,* we shall all starve if you do not earn money soon." She refrained from using the word 'work' again but she looked at him pitifully.

"It's that great hulk!" Ginger replied angrily. "Couldn't he earn a few francs, Marie Céleste?"

Marie Céleste's eyes filled with tears. She never as much as mentioned Chad's deficiencies but now she showed that she was at least aware of them. "How could he earn?" she asked Ginger, "Who would employ him?"

"He could get a job in a car park, watching the cars," Ginger said, knowing that this was far-fetched. "Or he could sell bootlaces, or matches."

"Bootlaces! Matches! You are joking, Ginger."

Even Ginger realized that he had gone too far, but he felt irritated to a point of anger. "What's it all in aid of?" he shouted, working himself up into a fine state of irritation. "Two whacking big meals a day and what does he do? Sits by the fire or shuffles out to the gardens and there he sits and sits. But he's always ready for the next meal."

Chad realized that he was being talked about; anxiously he looked from his mother to Ginger and back at his mother.

Marie Céleste shrieked. When it came to a display of temper she could wipe the floor with anyone. She burst into a furious cataract of spitting French. Ginger felt as though he had had a blow in the face. He put on his overcoat and wrapped his muffler round his neck and still Marie Céleste raged.

"I'm going," he said, tying the belt of his coat with a final furious jerk.

"Go," she screamed, "We'll do without you. We'll manage somehow. Go, and never return!"

So Ginger left with all the accompaniment of banging doors and stamping of feet on wooden stairs of a man leaving for good.

CHAPTER V

BUT he was not really angry. Ginger had no violent temper, he had, indeed, very little temper at all. He felt strong irritability which rapidly gave place to a burning resentment. He was always a victim of other people's injustice. Smarting with vexation he hurried along the street to the café he had frequented of late.

After a time the man Paul arrived, he nodded to Ginger who immediately joined him on the bench against the wall. The place became fairly crowded and Ginger pressed more closely to his companion awaiting his opportunity.

Somebody threw down a set of poker dice, heads drew closer together round the marble-topped table, the air clotted with the reek of garlic, blue smoke from Camels and the fumes of *Calvados*. Notes were shuffled back and forth across the table according to the toss of the dice.

Ginger did not take a turn at throwing the dice but he watched acutely, his white face sharp with interest. Paul had a handful of small money loose in his jacket jocket, he pulled out franc notes and pushed back his winnings without taking out his note-case. Whilst the play was in progress Ginger knew that he could not take the case but the more Paul won the more he drank; Ginger knew that he had only to wait patiently. One by one the players fell away, either slipping from the table to doze against the wall or shuffling off into the bitter night outside, singly or arm in arm. Ginger lost count of the number of *fines* Paul ordered for himself but it was after two o'clock in the morning before Paul showed any sign of wear. He slumped back against the wall, the dice lay neglected upon the table, washed up in a swamp of cigarette ends, ash, pools of alcohol, crumbs of potato crisps, sodden scraps of paper.

The owner of the *estaminet*, in a hideous state of undress, switched off some of the lights, collected the dirty glasses and slapped at the table tops with a dirty cloth. He said something to Ginger which Ginger took to mean it was time to go. Someone was sitting on Paul's other side, he shouted a rude retort at the landlord and, during the rapid exchanges which took place Ginger insinuated his long thin hand inside the jacket of the man Paul, closed his fingers over the wallet and removed it, all within five seconds. He put it in the breast pocket of his jacket beside his own. He had kept on his great coat all evening, to his discomfort, and now he drew it closer about him and retied the girdle.

All the time Paul looked as peacefully asleep as a baby, replete at his mother's breast. After more shouting and abuse between the landlord and his clientele, Ginger and the man who had been sitting on Paul's other side left the *estaminet* with Paul hanging between them, feet dragging along the pavement.

The other man was talking in voluble French the whole time but Ginger made no attempt to understand him, he was congratulating himself upon a very neat piece of work. The practice he had had with Chad had helped him and he was considerably elated by the success of his venture. He was anxious now to rid himself of his burden and to get into a quiet corner alone where he could count the contents of the wallet. Circumstances, of course, had favoured him; never, for instance, had he seen Paul quite so drunk as tonight; his instinct was to leave the man slumped against the wall but the third man was showing all the energy and enthusiasm of the regular drunkard's friend. Unwillingly Ginger assisted in the conveying of Paul to his motor car. He did more than assist, two or three times Paul slipped to the ground, his legs like lengths of rope and he took his turn in dragging him upright as a mother picks up her fallen child, all to the accompaniment of encouraging noises from the third man, mainly unintelligible to Ginger but undoubtedly enthusiastic.

They reached the garage where the motor car was parked. His companion took the key out of Paul's pocket, unlocked the doors and he and Ginger together thrust him inside on to the back seat. Ginger did not wait to see whether the third man stayed with him or went his own way, he slipped off, out again into the night and the icy cold air, hurrying along as though he knew where he wanted to go.

A motor car slid quietly up behind him and gave two rapid 'poop-poop's' on its horn. Ginger looked up. In the light of the street lamp on the other side of the road he saw who was driving the car; it was the man Paul and beside him sat the companion who, with Ginger, had just carried him away from the *estaminet*. He raised an arm in greeting then pressed his car into speed and disappeared from view, turning out of the street into the Boulevard Raspail and away.

Ginger clawed frantically at his breast pocket.

It was, of course, empty.

Not only had Paul's fat wallet gone—but his own too.

The ferocious beast that was the north-east wind tore at Ginger's ears and threw a handful of dust and omnibus tickets in his face.

Weak with frustration and an irritability about which he could do nothing, Ginger cried. He drew into the shelter of a street doorway and cried. Then, like a small boy who had fallen and hurt himself and runs to find his mother, he turned and headed for the Place St. Sulpice and No. 100D Rue des Mauvais Garçons.

'Les choses s'arrangeront' was one of Marie Céleste's favourite remarks. Things had, in fact, arranged themselves. Ginger returned to 100 Rue des Mauvais Garçons because he

43

had no money at all and the alternative to doing so was to sleep on a seat on the Quay Montebello and to starve to death.

*   *   *   *

It did not matter at what time of night one returned; one rang the bell at the big gates and waited, putting slight pressure upon one of the gates. Duflos, the *concierge,* would stir in his sleep, would roll over and reach for the lever which released the lock.

Ten seconds was all he allowed for ingress. That was on a normal occasion; tonight however, he and Madame Duflos were busy upon errands of mercy. Ginger had to ring many times. He was, in fact, about to turn away in despair when, miraculously, the gates opened. Madame Duflos was standing in the courtyard and showed every sign of satisfaction at seeing Ginger. She was joined by her husband and together they made Ginger understand that they were glad he was back, that Marie Céleste was dying and that she was not content to die unless she had seen Ginger for she was afraid he had left the house for good.

It seemed that the rage into which Marie Céleste had worked herself and which had driven Ginger from the flat had also caused her to have a hæmorrhage. The doctor had said that another hæmorrhage would undoubtedly kill her and indeed it had seemed that she was already dead when Duflos had gone out to fetch a priest from the presbytery beside Saint-Séverin.

But after the priest had administered the Last Unction, .Marie Céleste had rallied. They had fetched the doctor who had said that Marie Céleste would die but that he could not say when. She must lie absolutely flat and still and must suck small pieces of ice.

But Marie Céleste refused to lie still, she asked continually for Ginger and when they told her comfortingly that presently

44

he would be back she had cried and shrieked that it was not so, that she herself told him not to return, that they must go out into the streets and search for him.

Poor soul, the good couple felt, she was not herself! It was unlike her to make trouble of any kind. Chad had been distracted with worry and grief, the doctor had given him a strong sleeping draught and now at last he was asleep. The Duflos themselves had had no sleep at all, they were more than glad to see Ginger home. They would retire and leave him in charge.

With what slow steps Ginger descended to the basement room!

*   *   *   *

Whether it was the administration of the last rites or Ginger's return to her that gave Marie Céleste a renewed hold on life it is impossible to state. Her spirit, which was very much alive, refused to leave her body. It inhabited the rags of flesh and bone and shone out of the deep hollows of her eyes like a great beacon light. Ginger was like a lost traveller in the darkness who moves towards the light for warmth and comfort.

"I am not afraid to die," Marie Céleste said. "Now that I know *him*."

By *him* she meant her friend Death.

It was no longer *'les choses s'arrangeront'* but she, Marie Céleste who must arrange *'les choses'*, she would not die until *'les choses'* were suitably *'arrangées'*.

For several days she lay recovering. She lay on her back staring up at the ceiling whilst Ginger kept the stove going, went out to buy food with the money which remained from the cash box he had stolen from the Misses Field and Taplow. He cooked meals for himself and Chad and he made vegetable soups and milk drinks for Marie Céleste. He did everything meekly, almost automatically, cowed by events. The doctor had said that Marie Céleste would die; Ginger knew that he would stay with her until she died.

But it looked very much as though the doctor were wrong. Marie Céleste was getting better.

The icy wind brought snow in its wake, for a day it snowed heavily; then a soft wind blew over the city, melting the snow to slush and the slush to dirty water and presently the weak sunbeams of early spring thrust their way into the basement room.

"Now I shall get up," Marie Céleste said, and did so. She wrapped herself in a great many clothes and walked about the rooms. She went up the stairs to see the Duflos who exclaimed in incredulous wonder but when she returned she was greatly exhausted. She slumped down into a chair beside the table and drank the black coffee he gave her to revive her.

"It's not really any good," she said. "Ginger, what shall you do when I die?"

He shrugged his shoulders.

"Will you take care of Chad for me?"

"Me?" Ginger's mouth hung open. "Come off it!"

"What is going to happen to Chad?"

What, indeed?

"The last of the Quests," Marie Céleste said, looking at Chad. "Poor Martin! How often he would look at Chad and shake his head and say that." There was a long pause. "I shall take him to England. I must take him to his grandfather."

"Do they, does he know—" Ginger jerked his head, "Does he know about Chad?"

"Know about him?"

"About him being loopy?"

The pause that followed was a great deal longer. Marie Céleste was having a struggle with herself. There was no longer any virtue in not admitting Chad's defects. She gave in.

"No," she said, humbly. "They were never told that he is not normal. At first, when we first realized it, Martin said there was no point in telling them. Then Martin heard that first one brother was killed in an aeroplane accident and then the other one, he heard when the last war was ended, had been killed in a bombing raid over England. He said he hoped his father would never know that Chad was not normal for now he, Chad, was the old man's only heir and that it would be sad for him to know. For, you understand, though at one time Martin feared his father, as he became older I think he felt some love for the old man; Sir Matthew must be a very old man now."

"Wait a minute, wait a minute," Ginger said, brow wrinkled, "I don't get it."

"He will leave all his money, his house, everything he has, to Chad," Marie Céleste told him. "There is no one else."

"How do you know?"

"There is nobody. All are dead. His wife, his three sons. There is only Sir Matthew left."

"The sons may have some children."

"One was not married. The other married but his wife died in childbirth and the child as well. A very sad family. When Martin died Sir Matthew wrote to me that he hoped to die first so that Martin would go to England to live at Rivington. He said that now Chad was the only Quest left and that he hoped that when he himself died, Chad would come over and take his place. He said he would very much like to see Chad. But of course——"

Marie Céleste shrugged her shoulders sadly.

It took a few minutes for the full implication of all this to break over Ginger and when it did he became brisk and business-like.

"But look," he said, "Chad might be a ruddy millionaire."

"Sir Matthew isn't *so* rich!"

"But look at the house, a ruddy palace. You say when the old man dies Chad'll be the owner of it all."

"Possibly. Possibly."

"And you Marie Céleste. You're his mother. You could have been living there too, all this time, like a bloomin' queen."

Marie Céleste smiled, a mere twisting of her over-red lips.

"You could have lived on the fat of the land. Bloomin' servants waiting on you hand and foot. Cars and chauffeurs when you wanted drivin' about. Fur coats, diamonds, feather beds. Cor! Ever heard of your luck? What's wrong with you? Why haven't you gone after what's yours by right? Strewth, Marie Céleste. I thought you'd got some go but, honest, what are you sitting around in this mucking hole for when there's all that *yours by right*!"

Again Marie Céleste smiled implacably.

"You're daft, woman," Ginger exclaimed.

"But I told you all this some time ago——"

"I didn't realize—honest——"

"Ginger. Do you not see? I can do nothing. If Chad had been like other people I should have gone to England long before this. I should have taken him when he was yet a boy, when things here were so bad with Martin. I should have taken him then to Sir Matthew and say: 'Here is your grandson, bring him up as an English gentleman.' I'd have come back here to Paris, to my poor Martin, and then I could have given him all my attention, instead of dividing it between him and Chad. But how could I? Look!" Marie Céleste's voice rose slightly hysterically: "Look at him!"

Ginger looked at him. Chad's great head was bent over his hands as they worked, chipping away with a knife at his crude wooden donkey; his head almost always hung forward as though it were ill balanced by his high bulging forehead and his great hanging lips. He was smiling to himself because he was happy again that his mother was no longer ill in bed, he was making small rhythmic grunts and, as always, his head shook slightly from side to side.

"It would be cruel," Marie Céleste said, very low now, "To take Chad to Rivington and hand him to his grandfather. 'Here is your grandson,' I would have to say. And he would look at him——" Marie Céleste buried her face in her hands, "It would be too cruel."

Ginger rubbed his face all over with his hand. Then he got up and went across to a small looking-glass hanging on the wall. He peered at himself, taking his comb out of his breast pocket and combing his hair back several times. Then he turned and faced Marie Céleste:

"You could take me," he said.

Marie Céleste raised her haggard face. "*You?*"

"Well—I'm not such a bad-looking bloke. At least I'm not loopy."

"You." Marie Céleste repeated, uncomprehendingly.

"It'd do everyone a spot of good," Ginger declared. "You, the old man and me."

"How?"

"Well—he'd be pleased he'd got a grandson—see? You'd be pleased because you'd be treated like the Queen Mother—see? And me? Well—stands to reason I'd be doing meself a bit of good—see?"

Marie Céleste was aghast. "You say poor Chad is what you call loopy," she stated. "But the poor boy would never, *never* have an idea half so silly—so stupid—as that idea of yours, Ginger."

CHAPTER VI

NEVERTHELESS, quite evidently something had to be done and done quickly. Marie Céleste accepted the fact that Ginger could or would not go out to earn regular money. She had never been used to a man who worked for her and, indeed, Ginger was a great improvement upon Martin; at least he did not drink, at most he was certainly a help to her in that he prepared food with some success.

But everything was so finite; if Marie Céleste lived to see the summer, on what were they going to exist? What was going to happen to Chad if Marie Céleste could not continue

49

to live? How much longer could Marie Céleste's indomitable spirit continue to beat up the finished material it inhabited?

Ginger grumbled a great deal, he also continued to harp on his idea. He reproved Marie Céleste constantly for what he said was her 'pigheadedness,' deploring the fact that she would not even discuss the possibilities of his idea; if she would only consider it they could talk it over and plan accordingly. She was unreasonable.

And Chad ate and ate. He went out into the fresh air for a stroll, into the Rue des Quatres Vents and round the Place St. Sulpice and came back with an appetite bigger than ever.

"Doesn't he ever get ill?" Ginger grumbled. "Has he always been like this?"

"He is very healthy," Marie Céleste said, with a touch of pride.

"Well, I wish he'd die!" Ginger burst out irritably.

"S—sh!' Marie Céleste admonished. "You must never wish people dead. That way you may die yourself."

There was a long pause. Ginger was peeling potatoes at the sink. Marie Céleste sighed heavily. "Sometimes I wish myself Chad could die. When he was small and we realized that he—he was not quite normal the doctor told us that such boys grow up delicate and often die before they are twenty. But Chad is over twenty and look how he is strong, my poor boy." There was another long pause. "If he were to die," Marie Céleste said dreamily, "all his troubles would be over."

"They would," Ginger put in. "The children in the park would not laugh and make fun of him——"

"—or throw gravel in his poor face."

"—or shout after him in the street."

"—there would be no need for him to go to an institution if—when——"

"—ever!" Ginger concluded triumphantly.

"He would be always happy. 'Happy ever after', as you English say."

"And the old boy over there——" Ginger jerked his head in what he considered to be the direction of the English Channel, "Wouldn't ever know he was a softy."

"He would only know that his heir was dead, like his wife and his sons and like he himself will one day be."

Ginger banged the pan of potatoes on to the gas stove.

Thus it went on, hour after hour.

Marie Céleste was by no means amoral, simply her morals were as unstable as water, they fluctuated from hour to hour, like the stock market. No one would have been more shocked than herself to be told quite plainly that what they were planning was murder and large scale fraud.

And Ginger, he was a small-time crook, neither a successful pickpocket nor a daring confidence trickster nor an intrepid thief in his own right; he would become all three if he received sufficient backing.

They went on from the supposition that Chad was already dead.

Marie Céleste would spend the contents of her *bas de laine* on fares for herself and Ginger to England. They would proceed to Gloucestershire where they would go at once to Rivington Court. There Marie Céleste would ask to see milord. When she met Sir Matthew Quest she would produce the evidence of her identity, all the letters, and there were many of them, that had accumulated over the years, the few personal possessions of the late Sir Matthew Quest, her marriage lines. Sir Matthew Quest would remain in no doubt at all that Marie Céleste was his daughter-in-law. He would treat her like an honoured guest, ordering the best guest room to be prepared and bringing out a bottle of his favourite wine. He would show Marie Céleste all the kindly friendship that was evident in his infrequent letters. Marie Céleste would lie in a superb bed (certainly a four-poster) in the splendid bedroom and look out over the trees of the great park. A lady, at last!

And her son, Ginger——

Here Marie Céleste's imagination faltered slightly. She could see herself at Rivington Court far more clearly than she could see Ginger. Sir Matthew must understand that Ginger was a French boy, he had been born and brought up in the circumstances of the French bourgeoisie and he must understand that he was not like his own sons had been. Ginger must not, of course, on any account speak a word of English. He would have to learn English gradually, just as though he were a French boy. It was a pity, Marie Céleste thought, that she had had to sell Martin's clothes; they were considerably different from Ginger's own clothes and might possibly be more in the English taste. His clothes had been of the most simple, but good, you understand. It was, again, a pity that Marie Céleste could not afford to buy other clothes for Ginger, but there it was.

She would have to get a passport, and what about Ginger? Was his passport in order?

Ginger preferred not to discuss his passport with her. It was in one of the outside pockets of his jacket where it had been since he arrived in Paris. It was one which would not survive scrutiny. Undoubtedly details of his appearance and of the passport with which he had been hurriedly presented by the friend who had helped him out of the country, would have been circulated to all the English ports of entry and a quiet watch would be kept for him for a long time to come. It would be better if he were to apply for a French passport along with Marie Céleste, in the name of Matthew St. Chad Quest.

What would be better still would be for Ginger to have his hair dyed black. He had no doubt that he would have been 'gazetted', that is that his photograph would have appeared in the English Police Gazette in connexion with the tobacco robbery and he might easily be recognized by his distinct hair. Fortunately Rivington appeared to be in what Ginger considered 'a very outlandish' part of England, he would have to take the small risk of being recognized in the wilds of Gloucestershire.

All day they talked over their plans. The bells of Saint Séverin rang out over the city, they rang for the Angelus, for Benediction, for Vespers, for Compline; Marie Céleste's rosary hung unheeded beside her bed. She had made her peace with her God; there was now a great deal to be done before she joined Him for ever.

Ginger staggered to bed in the early hours, exhausted with the vigour and vitality of Marie Céleste's planning. At the back of his mind, he knew, there was just one little thing which had not been settled; whilst caught up in the machinery of Marie Cèleste's organization he could not remember what it was.

Only in the quiet moment before he dropped off to sleep did he remember what it was and marvelled that he could have forgotten.

It was that Chad was not dead. He could hear him now, the sound of his snoring in the next room coming to him quite clearly. He was very much alive.

* * * *

There was a small barber's shop off the Boulevard Raspail where Ginger had had his hair cut more than once. He lost no time in returning there and, with many gesticulations and a few French words that he had picked up, indicating that he wanted to have his hair dyed black. When it was finished the effect was not bad, it had been quite cleverly done with a dye that had not entirely removed the natural shine and the cost was little more than that of a few packets of cigarettes.

"So that is why you wanted the money!" Marie Céleste observed when he returned. "You are not so good-looking, my boy!"

"Maybe not," Ginger said, peering at his reflection in the looking-glass, "But a lot less noticeable!"

"Will you come into the country with me today, Ginger?"

"The country! Blimey, what next?"

"You shall see why I want to go to the country. I cannot go alone, you must come to support me, Ginger."

"O.K. O.K. Anything you say goes."

Marie Céleste was not fit to do anything but lie in bed but she prepared for the trip into the country with a fierce determination. She was like someone carrying an over-heavy parcel. She would frequently stop and put her burden down, and hold her side where she had a pain. She put on a great many clothes and finally her moleskin coat and the woollen muffler. Then she hung a black oilcloth bag over her arm.

Though it was only a step to the Gare d'Orléans from the Rue des Mauvais Garçons they took a taxi and then a train southwards into the *villégiatures,* the region of nondescript little villages that lies around Paris.

Marie Céleste had been born in one of these villages, the illegitimate child of the wife of the postmaster. She had been sent to an orphan's home but each summer, during the time that the postman took three week's holiday in Dieppe, Marie Céleste returned to the place of her birth to stay with her mother. Those three weeks every year meant a great deal to the child Marie Céleste and as she grew up the memory of them remained with her. Even after her mother and her stepfather were dead Marie Céleste continued to visit the post office, making a friend of the post-woman who took over her stepfather's work. In time the postal work became too much for the woman, she became old and almost blind. She was allowed to remain in the post office cottage, with its small garden at the back, and a new post office was erected farther down the street. Now the old woman lived alone on her small pension and was visited from time to time by Marie Céleste who would bring her small gifts of food.

It was no great surprise to her when Marie Céleste arrived. This time she bore no gifts; Ginger waited outside. After quite

a short chat with her friend, Marie Céleste got down to business.
Could she take a few roots of primroses from the back garden
to grow in the window boxes of her flat in the Rue des Mauvais
Garçons?

But certainly.

Marie Céleste took up an old trowel, beckoned to Ginger
Could she take a few roots of primroses from the back garden
She knew exactly what she wanted and exactly where it grew.
She dug out three trowelfuls of earth and then, plunging her
hand into the soil brought out a small whitish root.

"What is it?" Ginger asked.

But Marie Céleste did not know what it was called in
English. It had a pretty blue flower in the summer. She dug
again into the earth and brought out more roots. Altogether
she took six, then she took three primrose roots and put them
into her oilcloth bag to cover the roots. There was nothing
remarkable about what she did; she was just like any witch-
like woman gathering herbs and simples to take home for
medicinal uses. Ginger stood watching her, he might have been
an attentive son waiting to carry her bag. He knew better than
to ask what she was up to. Neither then nor at any other time
did Marie Céleste say anything at all about her actions. She
simply acted and Ginger watched carefully everything she did.

They walked very slowly back to the station. Marie Céleste
coughed a great deal and Ginger had to put his arm round her
to support her. Going back in the train Marie Céleste threw
the primrose roots out of the window. "We shall not need these
now," she said wistfully.

When they got back to the Rue des Mauvais Garçons Marie
Céleste hung the black bag on a hook behind the door of the
living-room. It hung there for two days. Ginger did not refer
to it but he began to wonder if her mind was wandering and if
she had forgotten about it.

But this was The Pause.

Poisoners have one thing in common, there is one idiosyncrasy intrinsic in them all; having procured their poison they never use it immediately, they keep it for a day or two, perhaps for weeks, months or even years.

Marie Céleste, even though she had so little time to spare, kept it for two days. On the evening of the second day she brought down the oilcloth bag and went over to the sink with it. She took out the roots and scrubbed them quite clean. They had a gnarled white appearance. She dried them carefully on a cloth. Then she sent Ginger out to buy a piece of horse flesh which she showed him how to cook as a pot roast with vegetables piled around it in the iron saucepan. When it was ready the smell was very savoury. Chad, sitting by the stove, raised his great head and sniffed appreciatively. As usual he was hungry.

Ginger, sprawled beside the stove, remarked: "There he is, hungry again."

"Eating is the only pleasure the poor boy can enjoy," Marie Céleste observed. Then she did a curious thing, she went over to Chad and, taking his great head in her hands, she cradled him against her lean bosom as though he were an infant. She murmured endearments to him and kissed the top of his head. Ginger turned away sickened—or perhaps a little jealous, but when he turned back the expression on Marie Céleste's face had altered completely; it was a little frightening.

She went over to the sink and grated one of the roots finely on the grater. She flavoured it with sugar, mustard, pepper and salt and, finally, she added vinegar and stirred the mixture It looked rather unpleasant, being of a greyish colour. She added a dessertspoonful of milk from the top of the milk carton and stirred again. It still looked unappetizing. She tasted it and immediately went to the sink and spat.

"It will not do," she said, "I am mistaken."

During the meal Marie Céleste was silent, a deep frown between her brows. The excellent meal she had prepared was demolished, Chad having by far the greatest share.

Next morning Marie Céleste asked Ginger to go out shopping. "You will buy the same food that we had last night," she told him, "and *this*." She handed him a piece of paper on which was written a single French word: *Raifort*.

"What is it?"

Marie Céleste did not know the name in English but she described exactly the stall at Les Halles where Ginger would be likely to find it.

He thought that he had bought the same root that Marie Céleste had dug up on her visit to the country but when it was scrubbed and placed before the root Marie Céleste had prepared he saw the difference immediately.

Sprawling, as usual, beside the stove he watched covertly as she cooked the meal. He saw her grate two of the little roots he had bought and add it to the mixture she had made the previous evening. Again she tasted the result and made a slight grimace, though this time she seemed more satisfied. When the meal was served Chad, as usual, promptly drew up his chair to the table, grinning in anticipation; though he was not actually dribbling like a spaniel when a tasty morsel is held up to it, he looked as though he might at any moment do so. Marie Céleste gave him a large plate of food and added, at the side of his plate, a spoonful of the unpleasant greyish mixture. Chad immediately dipped the end of his knife into the sauce and tasted it.

"Oh, you naughty boy!" Marie Céleste exclaimed in French, "*Mauvais garçon*! How often have I told you never to eat with your knife!"

After which Chad sedulously avoided the sauce. He ate everything else on his plate and left the little island of sauce, as lonely as a cloud. Ginger did not blame him, he, personally would not have touched it, it looked like a cat's vomit.

It can never be said of Marie Céleste that, having put her hand to the plough etc., etc. She was like a small dynamo, having decided upon her goal she pressed on so that it would seem that her frail small body was simply motive and nothing but motive.

She devoted the next day to the problem of obtaining passports for herself and for her son Matthew St. Chad Quest. This involved the filling-in of forms, the taking of a taxi-cab to a cheap photographer where she and Ginger were photographed separately and a visit to a second-hand clothes shop where an endless conversation evidently on the subject of passports took place between Marie Céleste and the owner, who, apparently, was persuaded into witnessing the documents necessary for the obtaining of French passports. Ginger, lounging about, apparently bored, would have liked to know the gist of the conversation but it was not divulged; all that was asked of him was that he should sign his name as Matthew St. Chad Quest, along the dotted line and keep his mouth shut. This he found easy.

When the transactions were over and the forms forwarded to the necessary quarter Marie Céleste looked even more worn out than usual, but as soon as she and Ginger returned to the Rue des Mauvais Garçons, she put on her cooking apron and set to work to prepare a meal exactly identical to the meals they had had on the two previous evenings. She had thrown away the remains of the sauce but Ginger, again watching her intently, saw her get two more roots out of her black mackintosh bag and clean them. Then she took the two remaining roots of *roifort* that Ginger had bought and scrubbed them clean. Then she grated them all together. Ginger, fascinated, slouched over to the sink and stood beside her. Again she stirred them together and flavoured the mixture with mustard, pepper, salt and sugar; again she added vinegar. The expression on her face forbade questioning but Ginger wanted to know the name of the ingredients she was using.

"Look it up in the dictionary," she snapped.

Ginger looked up *raifort* in Marie Céleste's shabby little

58

pocket dictionary. "Horseradish," he said. "But what's the other?"

"I have told you, I do not know."

"Let me taste it?"

Marie Céleste had a small double saucepan, she was now pouring her mixture into the top half. She swung it out of Ginger's reach. "It is not for you," she returned.

Nervously Ginger bit his thumb nail. "But he won't eat it," he said, at length. "You won't get him to touch it."

There was now boiling water in the bottom half of the pan and Marie Céleste was vigorously stirring her mixture in the top half.

"It is pleasanter when hot."

In fifteen minutes or so the meal was ready. The sauce looked a great deal better, it had a creamy consistency that it had not when uncooked. Marie Céleste tasted it and seemed to find it to her liking. As on the previous evening she served Chad with a large plateful of food and added two tablespoonsful of the sauce at the side of the plate. But this time Chad was not going to be had. He did not even dip the tip of his knife into the sauce, he ate round it.

Ginger avoided Marie Céleste's eye for a few minutes but when he realized that she was eating nothing he looked directly at her across the table. There were great tears rolling down her face. Ginger felt a sudden irritation, he turned towards the great cumbersome mass of Chad who was now eating his meal with both feet in the trough, as it were.

Ginger put out his own fork and dipped it into the sauce. "Look," he said. Marie Céleste gave an exclamation but Ginger took no notice. The sauce tasted sharp but it was not unpleasant. Ginger had heard vaguely of horseradish sauce, he had seen chalked upon boards in cafés he had frequented in England: *Roast beef and horseradish sauce*. The horseflesh they were now eating strongly resembled roast beef, the sauce had a strong mustard-like tang which blended favourably with the meat.

"Nice," he said, nodding to Chad.

Chad, arrested with this manœuvre, looked up attentively.

"Very nice," Ginger said, "yum yum!" He made the motions of gobbling up the roast meat and horseradish sauce. But Chad, understanding, shook his head. Ginger got up and went to the stove for the pan, he brought it over to the table and poured a little of the sauce on to his own food. "Look," he said, he pressed some of the vegetable and potato into the sauce. "Like this!" He took a forkful of the mash and raised it to his mouth. He had had no intention of swallowing it but the demonstration was entirely realistic. Marie Céleste gave a small shriek and, jumping up from the table she snatched Ginger's plate away from him. Chad was delighted, he thought it some kind of game and turned his attention at once to his own plate. He followed Ginger's example exactly, squeezing his potato and vegetable into the sauce with the back of his fork. The result was to his liking. His plate was soon empty and he waved it about in the air, asking for more. Marie Céleste served him with the few remaining vegetables, there was no meat left, but she poured the rest of the sauce on to the vegetables and Chad set upon it with relish.

Ginger avoided Marie Céleste's eyes.

At mealtimes Chad often propped the little wooden donkey he was carving in front of him. It was there now. There was no mistaking it for any other animal, Chad had evidently inherited a modicum of his father's talent, it was quite a whimsical little creature with hanging head and drooping tail. He looked at it appreciatively from time to time, grunting slightly.

Ginger's eyes slid uneasily about the room, he was suffering from one of the sudden revulsions of feeling to which he was prone.

There was an air of brazen despair about Marie Céleste.

Having forced herself to believe that what she was doing was for the best she hung on desperately to that belief. She watched, dry-eyed now, whilst Chad scooped large forkfuls of food into his mouth.

CHAPTER VII

GINGER did not undress and get into bed. He sat on the edge of his bed; he felt sick with fright.

Four hours later, when Chad began to feel ill, Ginger went to his aid. He began by moaning with pain and pointing to the inside of his mouth and throat. Ginger brought him cold water to drink and he seemed to recover. He lay back against his pillows, groaning, and Ginger sat at the foot of the bed watching him. An hour later Chad appeared to be very ill indeed. His eyes kept rolling upwards, so that half the pupils were beneath his lids, his hands were icy cold. Then he vomited into a bucket which Ginger brought.

Ginger held his head and rubbed his hands and pulled the bed clothes over his shoulders. In a panic he went to fetch Marie Céleste but she refused to come. She lay huddled in her bed in the living-room with her hands pressed to her ears and would not stir. Ginger hurried into his great coat. Marie Céleste was evidently not oblivious to everything. "Where are you going?" she snapped.

"To fetch the doctor," Ginger said.

"You fool. Are you mad?"

Ginger thought he probably was mad but it had suddenly become extremely important to save Chad's life. He who had so often declared Chad's life to be useless now desired more than anything to preserve it. He whose attitude was one of contemptuous indifference to everything and everybody was now frantic with anxiety lest Chad should die. He tore out into the night, down the Rue des Mauvais Garçons, across the Rue

61

des Quatre Vents and into the Rue de Saint-Sulpice. It did not take the doctor long to dress and come out; Ginger almost dragged him along the streets. "I don't know what's the matter with him," he kept saying, "I don't know what is the matter with him!"

Nor did the doctor know what was the matter with Chad. He died within a few minutes of the doctor's arrival. There was a sound in his throat like the rattling of dice in a dry box, the pupils of his eyes showed as tiny recumbent moons, his mouth hung open.

As the doctor closed the eyes Ginger said once again, quite automatically: "I don't know what is the matter with him."

"Marie Célèste sleeps?"

Ginger nodded.

"I shall come again in the morning."

*   *   *   *

With clammy hands Ginger prepared the coffee. When it was ready he took a cup over to her, standing beside her bed. "Come on, you'd better drink this." She was so still that Ginger wondered for a moment if she were dead, too. But she was not, presently she sat up and took the cup from him.

"The doctor is coming. Chad—" Ginger cleared his throat, "Chad died in the night." He looked down at his hands, which were trembling. He looked at the hands of Marie Célèste; they were quite steady.

"Will you go out and leave this to me?" she said.

That was exactly what Ginger intended to do, but the doctor arrived before their coffee was drunk. Ginger opened the door for him, the doctor beckoned to him to close the door of the living-room.

He asked, first, how Marie Célèste was. Ginger couldn't say. Nor could he tell the doctor how Marie Célèste had taken the news of Chad's death.

"She is a mother very devoted," the doctor said. There was a pause. Then the doctor shook his head. "It is a merciful providence," he said, "that boy is dead."

Ginger stared at him open-mouthed.

*   *   *   *

Marie Céleste made all the arrangements. Chad's body was removed to the undertaker's, Marie Céleste sent Ginger along with the death certificate, upon which the doctor had described the cause of death to be acute gastro-enteritis, and arranged for the funeral. She unpacked, from amongst a great many moth-balls and much tissue paper, a complete outfit of mourning, together with a widow's veil. She hired an automobile to follow the hearse and she bought a wreath of white flowers and tied to it a card bearing the words in French:

For my darling son, from his mother.

There was no one other than Ginger and herself to mourn at the funeral. They drove to the Cimetière d'Ivry in absolute silence. Chad's body was committed to the earth amongst other apparently new graves.

Ginger wondered just how big Marie Céleste's nest egg could be, she was certainly not economizing over the obsequies, she gave money to the priest who said the prayers at the grave-side and driving back from the cemetery she began to talk about a grave stone. It would, unhappily, she said, have to be of the smallest. She could not afford one more than a foot high but it should be of the best stone and she would have the name inscribed thereon in large letters.

"Wait a minute," Ginger exclaimed. "You'll have to be careful about the name. That is if we're going to do what we've planned." There must not be two Matthew Saint-Chad Quests, he pointed out, one below the ground and the other at his grandfather's house in Gloucestershire, England. But Marie Céleste was adamant, whatever else she had taken from her son she would not take his name. His grave would not be that of an *'inconnu'*. Ginger thought of the thousands and thousands of head stones, of the long avenues of the dead along which they had walked at the Cimetière d'Ivry and decided that it was not worth bothering about.

Now that it was all over, now that Chad was not a victim of suffering before his eyes Ginger did not give him a thought. They went ahead with their plans for going to England. Marie Céleste did not want to give up the flat. The rent was paid for a month in advance, they could walk out and leave it as it was. If they found that things did not go well for them in England there would be somewhere to which they could return. If, on the other hand, things did go well, the flat would simply revert to the owner and the furniture, which was of small value, could become the property of the Duflos who had been so kind that they deserved anything which came their way.

Marie Céleste gave some thought to Martin Quest's paintings, standing forlornly with their faces to the wall. It was clear that she could not arrive at Rivington burdened with the canvases; she decided to leave them behind and presently, if all went well, she would ask the Duflos to pack them and dispatch them to England where—but even Marie Céleste's fertile imagination stalled when she envisaged their ultimate fate.

With two exceptions Ginger complied with everything that Marie Céleste arranged; hers was the master-mind, he would do everything she required of him. He did, however, object to her plan to go to Gloucestershire in deep mourning. "You didn't ought to go on wearing all that palaver," he told her, "It's not nice. We're never going to make a success of this if you go all tricked out in deep black for the son you've brought along with you!"

But mourning was something about which Marie Céleste was very sensitive. She broke out into a great deal of exclamatory French, the issue being that either she would go in her mourning or she would not go at all, Ginger must bear in mind that she was still virtually in mourning for Martin Quest. Was she not his widow? It would, in fact, be unseemly for her to visit his old home in any other clothes.

Then something else upset Ginger, so much so that he declared he had thought better of it and could not go through with the arrangements.

"Come," Marie Céleste exclaimed, "What a little mouse you are! You have lost your nerve, my cabbage!"

"Nothing of the sort," Ginger grunted. "It's just I've remembered something."

"Well, what is it you have remembered?"

"That bloke, Sir Matthew Quest. He'll be a Tory!"

"A Tory! Heh, what does that matter?"

"What does it matter? See, Marie Céleste, I'd rather have a snake up the leg of me trousers than have any truck with a Tory!"

Marie Céleste laughed, it was the first hearty laugh she had had for some time; that kind of remark was very much to her taste. She made various comments of a bawdy nature but Ginger continued to glower glumly.

"Is it really as bad as all that, my cabbage?"

"I'm not having nothink to do with Tories," Ginger declared, "I know what they are, thanks very much."

Tories! They were, indeed, according to her Martin, the Root of all Evil and, though she herself had no feelings about them one way or another, she could quite well see that Ginger had a stubborn streak in him that would make a permanent stumbling block of this fact. She thought the matter over for a few hours and then she put the situation to Ginger like this: *"Voyons, mon petit,* you do not like Tories we agree. But you do not go to Rivington Court to do them a favour, heh?"

"Well, I don't know. It wouldn't be doing them a favour

65

to have taken Chad along to his highness and told him it was his grandson!"

It was a remark which hurt Marie Céleste, it took her a few moments to recover. At last she said:

"Think, Ginger. Why are we making this plan?"

"To do ourselves a spot of good, I suppose."

"Exactly. I do not for one moment suppose that you will stay at Rivington Court. It is *you* who will take *me* there. You are taking me there because I am ill and can no longer support myself."

Ginger cheered up. "I get you. I'll dump you there, leave you lying in your feather bed, living on the fat of the land, and I'll get meself off, taking anything I can lay a hand on."

Marie Céleste looked pained. "But of course not! Oh, Ginger, how—how simple you are! Indeed I think stupid. How would it be for me if you went off with the family jewels? No. It shall be done well, this thing. We do this for our mutual benefit, Ginger, do you not understand? You shall take me to Rivington and you shall appear to be my son, the son of Martin Quest. You are not a bad-looking boy and I shall teach you how you must behave. I shall wait for a few days to see how Sir Matthew likes you, if you play well he *shall* like you. Then I shall ask him if he will make you a provision, an allowance, or what you call it. Is the *endowment* the right one?"

Ginger couldn't say.

"Anyway, he shall give you an allowance, the same, perhaps, that I have had all this time, or a grand total of money and you shall say thank you, very nicely, to your old grandfather and shall depart. You can do what you like then, Ginger."

Ginger rubbed his hands together and then rubbed them all over his face. That was more like it.

"What a child you are! It was you who had the plan in the first, and it is now I who develop it."

"I didn't think it out in detail."

"Well, I did. I thought it out so very carefully. Then you can leave me there, Ginger, as I say, and you can go where you like, do what you like. Return to London if you please——"

"No, I can't do that!"

"You must write to your grandfather from time to time——"

"I can't do that neither!"

"Rubbish! You can write a perfectly good letter from a French boy just beginning to learn English. Never forget you are that! Then I shall arrange it that when your grandfather die he shall leave you his house and money. You can be sure I shall do that for you, Ginger. You can leave it to me, I promise I shall not fail you."

Ginger went on rubbing his face.

"So you see! He is a Tory, yes, but you are the master."

Yes, he saw that. He would, nevertheless, have to live in the house of a Tory, eat at table——

"But for how short a time!" Marie Céleste exclaimed. "Really, Ginger, you look for trouble."

"I'll do it if it's for a short time," he said, "but I wouldn't live there. Not for anyone, I wouldn't. Even for you, Marie Céleste!"

"Who is asking you to live there? Not me, silly boy!"

Marie Céleste was suddenly serious. Neither, she realized, was she going to live there, the most she could do would be to die there.

She raised a glass of red wine to Ginger.

"Here is to the old Tory's downfall. You will come, Ginger, will you not?"

He raised his own glass and looked at her over it. Yes, he would come.

*　　*　　*　　*

Marie Céleste insisted on taking her fur coat, she hid her decent black beneath the incredibly old moleskin. Ginger protested but she was quite adamant. "Who knows?" she said, "They may turn us off so that we have to sleep in the hedge, my fur coat would be very useful then." Her own personal luggage consisted of a wickerwork portmanteau, two oblong baskets one of which fitted right down over the other and was secured by a strap.They also took an old leather case fastening along the top, which Marie Céleste called 'Martin's Gladstone bag'. It was with this bag, she said, that Martin had left home thirty years before, taking with him nothing but what the bag contained. She put into it all the letters, documents, mementos and small possessions of Martin Quest together with the photograph of Rivington Court, everything, in fact, which would prove her to be Martin Quest's widow. She was leaving nothing to chance. When all these things were packed the bag was not full, Ginger was able to put the few possessions he had acquired on the top.

"A tooth brush and tooth paste you must take," Marie Céleste said. "The English are very particular about toothbrushing." Remembering that Ginger was also English and was not fussy about tooth brushes she added: "I mean English upper class."

Ginger sniffed.

"And pyjamas you must take. I bought you two beautiful pyjamas, Ginger, one pair you have never worn. You must never go to bed without undressing and wearing pyjamas in England." That had been one of the things that Martin Quest had told her many years ago and she had often thought of it with a sigh when later on, night after night, Martin had fallen on to the bed and gone to sleep fully dressed.

Ginger sniffed again.

"And handkerchiefs," Marie Céleste went on. "You must take these handkerchiefs which belonged to Martin, *and use them*!"

She looked at his shoes. "And your shoes must be clean. English gentlemen have always very clean shoes." Martin's shoes shone like newly fallen chestnuts when she first married. Towards the end the soles of his shoes flapped and slapped against the pavements as he shuffled along and the uppers looked like something found by a beachcomber.

"And," Marie Céleste went on, "you do not pick your teeth with a fork. You shall take a bundle of tooth picks and use them, but not a fork or your finger, remember. You shall also have a cold bath every morning——" But she had gone too far. Ginger exploded. Cold bath every morning! He'd rather be back at the Borstal Institution in Hollesley Bay!

Marie Céleste retracted. "Well, a warm bath every night. Come, Ginger, that is luxury. The bathroom will be like a palace, with big silver taps and a shower and mirrors all round so that you can see yourself! Oh, *quelle luxe*! Certainly a warm bath every night."

Marie Céleste looked at Ginger wondering how much further she could go.

"Your hair," she ventured, "Must not be combed during meals——"

Strongly as Ginger resented her adjurations he paid them some heed, realizing that hers was the master mind.

The packing exhausted Marie Céleste, she was obliged to lie down on the bed for some time, complaining of great pain in her side. Ginger, unused to catching trains, was anxious to be off. He fidgeted nervously about the room. "Come on, let's get cracking!"

"I must have a taxi to the Gare du Nord. I cannot get there," Marie Céleste whimpered, "And I have so little money left, so little! Go and fetch a taxi, Ginger."

When he returned with the taxi Marie Céleste was standing by the door, she was quite ready but she was looking round the living-room as though she were leaving it reluctantly. As she moved to go she looked back and exclaimed. Like a predatory jackdaw she swooped down upon a small object lying neglected beneath the table.

It was the wooden donkey that Chad had been making.

*　　*　　*　　*

"Stop the taxi beside the doctor's house in the Rue Saint-Sulpice, Ginger."

"But we haven't time."

"Only for two seconds. Do as I say!"

When the taxi stopped Marie Céleste fumbled in her reticule and brought out an envelope with the doctor's name written on it in her own hand. "Slip this into his letter box," she said.

"But what is it?"

"Never mind what it is, Ginger."

"It's money, Marie Céleste. It's a bundle of notes, I can feel it."

"Perhaps."

"You're never going to give him this!"

"Please mind your own business!"

Marie Céleste, still holding the envelope looked down at Ginger. He was staring down at it, almost dribbling, and she knew just what he was thinking: he could take the envelope and dart off with it into the Paris crowds and never be heard of again.

"All right," he said. Avoiding Marie Céleste's eyes he put out his hand for the envelope, "I'll do it, if you want."

"Mais non," Marie Céleste snapped, "I will do it myself."

She pushed past him and was out of the taxi and across the pavement before he could do anything to prevent it.

"What on earth did you do that for?" he said angrily when she returned after slipping the envelope through the letter box.

"The doctor has been kind, very, very kind. I do not want him to think I am ungrateful."

"Damn silly waste of money I call it."

"You can call it what you like. You can have all the money

70

I have left, Ginger. You can change it into English money on the boat. It is six thousand francs, it will have to pay for our meals on the journey and our fare from the English port into Gloucestershire."

"But that's only about six pounds, Marie Céleste. It's not enough, it'll barely pay the fare."

"Well, it is all I have."

"Do you mean that?"

"I have not another centime."

"Well, of all the damn silly things—to give the doctor all that money! You're mad!"

Marie Céleste leaned back, exhausted.

"Sometimes I think you are mad, other times you say I'm mad. Perhaps we are both mad, Ginger, both mad."

CHAPTER VIII

IT was an interminable journey. It would have been a great deal easier if Ginger had been willing to cross London. But in spite of the fact that he now had a fine crop of black hair and a perfectly good French passport in the name of Matthew Saint-Chad Quest with a photograph of himself, rather than of someone whom he vaguely resembled, Ginger would not take the very small risk of being recognized by someone in London who knew him, if not one of the underworld then a particularly astute London policeman.

So they crossed England by devious paths and mossy winding ways, spending one night in the waiting-room at Reading station. Rivington was on a small branch line, the train stopped at each station with a weary finality. Marie Céleste grew very tired indeed, reaching the stage when she called in French upon the name of a name of a god of a kind.

When they finally reached Rivington they were not the only

passengers to alight. There was a man and two youths, one of them bore a quite horrifying resemblance to Chad, he had a huge head, with a bulging forehead and a shuffling walk. The other youth clung timorously to the arm of the man. Ginger was glad that Marie Céleste did not notice them, he kept her occupied with her possessions, bags, fur coat, umbrella and reticule, and was glad to see that they left the station quickly. More slowly he and Marie Céleste walked towards the barrier, Ginger carrying the luggage.

"There's less than a pound left," he said. "We can't get a taxi, they cost something in England."

"I cannot walk," Marie Céleste moaned.

"Maybe you won't have to," Ginger said. "Maybe it isn't far."

They gave up their tickets and came out into the station approach. It was empty of vehicles and people, a small bus was turning out into the road beyond. The old porter followed them out.

"For God's sake remember you do not speak one word of English," Marie Céleste hissed.

"Where are you for?"

"Rivington Court."

"Ah!" A look of understanding crossed the porter's face as he looked at Ginger and back at Marie Céleste. "You've gone and missed t'bus. They sent t'bus down for two new arrivals, they've just gone. The driver ought to have waited. Do they know as you're coming on this train?"

Marie Céleste seemed very French, so foreign, in fact, that she might have come from a great deal farther away than the other side of the channel. She stood there, her widow's veil blowing about her head, her preposterous moleskin coat wrapped round her spare figure, expostulating in rapid French.

"I'm afraid you've 'ad it," the porter said kindly. "It's round three miles to the Court. I could phone for a car from the village."

But he quite understood that Marie Céleste did not want that.

"You'll have to hitch hike," he said, illustrating his meaning by a jerk of his thumb.

So they stood out on the road and Ginger jerked his thumb a great many times until at last a lorry driver, anticipating a tip, stopped. He was immediately sorry he had stopped for, on closer inspection the couple looked more like gipsies than ordinary folk. Good naturedly, however, he took them up beside him on the front seat. The lorry was laden with nets of Brussels sprouts.

The driver set them down at a pair of great iron gates hanging from two stone pillars which were surmounted by a pair of very fine lead eagles. Ginger's spirits began to rise. This was a great deal more like it.

"That's the lodge," the lorry driver said, indicating a small white house. "The gates aren't ever opened," he explained. "Delivery vans go down a lane to the back entrance but it's a long way round to walk, you get in through that small gate at the side and follow the drive right up to the house, you can't miss it. So long."

They looked at the lodge. It was a pretty little white house. It was, in fact, a cottage orné, with pointed gothic windows with lead lights and a frill of toy battlements round the edge of the roof. An old man in corduroy trousers tied with twine below the knee, was hoeing the ground in a vegetable patch in the garden at the side, they could see him over the low stone wall. Ginger picked up the luggage and Marie Céleste pushed open the small gate beside the big ones. She had just about reached the end of her resources, she was panting for breath and coughing with short hard little sounds. The sight of the great gates, however, gave her new courage and hope.

They set off up the drive which was covered with a soft green moss. On either side rhododendrons grew thickly and above them great elms arched their bare branches over the driveway.

"If you speak one word of English," Marie Céleste gasped, "all is lost. For remember, you do not speak like someone French who learns English!"

Ginger was aware of that, he was aware of a great many other ways in which he did not resemble a French boy coming to England for the first time. But there was no going back now. He was in it good and proper, for better or for worse. And if it was for worse he could always snatch up a silver cigarette box (or something) and run for it.

At the top of the slope the drive emerged from the trees into the open park which fell away in soft green undulations. Ahead of them, in the centre of a gentle green saucer lay the house.

"It's a bloomin' palace," Ginger exclaimed, as he had done when he saw the photograph.

Where the original Rivington Court, broad-browed and serene, had lain in its glorious setting the modern Rivington glowered sullenly. It was a very splendid house indeed but its splendour had a spuriousness which makes the word splendiferous more apt. It had all the nonsense about it that the most abandoned of late Victorian architects could think up; it had tall narrow windows and bay windows with cast iron railings around and a great many turrets surmounted by slate witches' hats; everything, it seemed, that could be used in the building of a house had been used and the effect was uncomfortable. From a distance the house seemed resentful: what the hell am I doing here? it seemed to say; as one approached its expression changed to a malicious sneer: what the hell are *you* doing here? it seemed to ask.

But to Ginger and Marie Céleste it was the Mecca of their hopes, the Promised Land. With lighter hearts and quickened step they went down towards the house, so heartened was Ginger that he scarcely noticed that he was carrying baggage which, coming up the drive, had seemed an intolerable burden.

There was an entrance porch as big as a church; it had tall, narrow stained-glass windows in a geometrical pattern and a dazzlingly varied tiled floor, so sacerdotal was it that Marie Céleste almost fell to her knees with something more than mere fatigue. At the east end, where the altar should have been, was the front door, or rather two gigantic oak doors studded with great iron bolts which would not have looked out of place at The Traitor's Gate in the Tower of London. There was an iron rod hanging beside the door, it had an elaborate handle. Ginger pulled it, half expecting a great clamour of ringing bells to break out. Somewhere, a long way off, they heard a mean little ping.

They waited.

Marie Céleste, pushing aside her enveloping veil, looked up at Ginger and smiled. The smile and the light in her great eyes was as grateful and comforting to Ginger as the warming rays of the sun on a chilly April day.

"It will be all right," she whispered, "you shall see. The only thing that can go wrong is if you forget, for one moment, that you are a French boy and you cannot speak one word of English. Your name is *Chad,* remember."

"I'll remember," Ginger whispered back, "I won't let you down."

Unaccountably he reached for her hand in its black cotton glove and squeezed it, and then he blew his nose to hide his embarrassment.

"That's right," Marie Céleste appraised, "You are using a nice clean handkerchief." In French she told him to ring the bell again. "From now on," she whispered, "I shall always address you in French, you understand more than you think."

They waited.

"Why do they not come?"

They came, but not through the front doors, which were never used. One of the attendants came round the side of the house to see who was playing the fool with the front door bell.

Rivington Court was no longer the home of Sir Matthew

Quest, K.C.B., C.B.E., it was a State-owned school for mentally deficient boys.

*   *   *   *

Marie Céleste made a frightful scene. She was as angry as she had been on the night she turned Ginger out of the flat. He was terrified that she would bring on another hæmorrhage. The attendant, however, was used to scenes, thoroughly enjoyed them, in fact, and this one made quite a pleasant change, it was more exotic than the scenes to which he was accustomed.

He dealt with her admirably, handling her firmly yet gently and himself keeping as steady and unmoved as a rock. Ginger was so shocked by the events that he remained quite motionless beside the baggage, his face the colour of rationed cheese but when the attendant finally turned to him and said: "Who is it you wanted to see?" he remembered to shrug his shoulders uncomprehendingly.

"Your Mum's worked herself up into a fine state," the attendant said, "but she'll be all right now, I'll go and get her a drink of water."

He returned quickly with the water and another attendant. Revived more by the interest of the two men than by the water, Marie Céleste began to explain in English.

One attendant seemed at a loss to know what she was talking about, but the other repeated the name. "Sir Matthew Quest," he said, "Quest. That's the folk that lived 'ere before the government. They're all dead except the old boy."

"They are not all dead," Marie Céleste pointed out, "I am Mrs. Quest and this is my son Matthew Quest."

"Fancy," the attendant murmured, he was in the process of picking up Marie Céleste's gloves and reticule which she had thrown down at the height of her fury. "You'd best go along and see the old man, I reckon."

"But certainly," Marie Céleste returned, perking up. "Where does he now live?"

"At one of the lodges. Which way did you come?"

Marie Céleste pointed.

"That's right. The lodge is by the big gates, that's 'im. Why, you passed it, didn't you know he lived there?"

"He writes to me from Rivington Court," Marie Céleste pointed out.

"That's right. It's all Rivington Court, the whole estate, three lodges and home farm and all. And a bloomin' great white elephant it is! The house is as cold as the grave, Burrr! You'll get your deaths standing around in this draughty porch. You'd best get yourself back to the lodge, pronto," he added unexpectedly: "M'am."

*   *   *   *

It was unbearable, it was impossible, it hadn't happened.

And yet it had, for there they were, walking away from the house, back along the drive, Marie Céleste half dead yet scuttling along like a mole, and Ginger making heavy weather of the baggage, dragging along a yard or so behind. The attendants watched them, laughing a little sheepishly before they returned to their *non compos mentis* charges and the house watched them narrowly, derisively until they disappeared over the brow of the hill.

The cottage orné, of which there were three, one at each entrance, had been built in the days of the Prince Regent, when the house was still a house and not a frowning monster. A latter-day Quest who had married the wealthy heiress whose money had rebuilt the house, had intended to tear down the cottages and rebuild them in a style in keeping with the great house, but the vast resources of his wife had not run to it after the extravagance of rebuilding the house. He had had to leave them as they were, unwittingly leaving three little gems of the Gothic revival to posterity. Two of the cottages had had to go with the house when it was taken over by the State, they were occupied by the matron and the bursar respectively, but the third had a charming garden and had been retained by and for a gardener.

The gardener was Major General Sir Matthew Quest, K.C.B., C.B.E.

Again they rang a front door bell and again no one answered. But this time Marie Céleste did not look up and smile at Ginger, nor did Ginger reach affectionately for her hand. He stood nervously biting his nails. The front door bell was the sort you wind up, it made a common noise, the sort of sound you would expect to hear if you rang the front door bell of a bungalow at Jaywick Sands.

They waited.

They rang again.

They waited.

There was a shuffling noise round the side of the house. An old man appeared, he was distinctly soiled, as opposed to dirty, that is he was covered with a thin coating of soil, the good red earth of Gloucestershire.

"Yes?" He did not want any wooden pegs, nor any knives sharpened and was about to say so when Marie Céleste asked for Sir Matthew Quest.

"I am he," he answered, very correctly, "is there anything I can do for you?"

Ginger thought Marie Céleste would promptly have another attack of hysterics, or a hæmorrhage, or, at the very least fall into a fainting fit. She did none of these things, she rose superbly to the occasion.

"Yes," she nodded, "I see you are Sir Matthew Quest. You are very like Martin. I am Marie Céleste." She held out her hand and looked up into his face. "How do you do?"

"Marie Céleste," the old man repeated seriously. He took her hand formally and, looking down at her he said: "How do you do, Marie Céleste."

You could have knocked Ginger 'down wiv a feather'.

Marie Céleste was quiet and restrained, gone was her excitable manner and the pea-hen edge to her voice. Only her great eyes shone out of her worn-out face as the sun shines gratefully into a prison cell.

They held hands and smiled at one another for an embarrassing length of time. 'Hey,' Ginger thought, 'she's forgotten me.'

"So very like my poor Martin," Marie Céleste repeated.

Through Ginger's mind flashed the thought: she needn't have brought all that junk along, all the papers and documents, she's Marie Céleste all right, anyone would know that. It was only when the old man turned from her and looked at Ginger that Ginger felt heartily thankful they had lugged the Gladstone bag full of proof along with them.

"And this is Matthew, or Chad, as you call him," he stated.

Marie Céleste had not said so and for one ghastly never-to-be-forgotten moment Ginger thought she was going to repudiate him. She could so easily have said: No, this is a young man who has carried my bags from the station. It was a shocking moment, a wave of sweat broke out all over Ginger's back and his mouth went so dry that he couldn't have opened it if he had tried. Not that he did try. He said nothing but took the general's hand and bowed a little forward, avoiding his eyes and thus, involuntarily, making an oddly French gesture.

"So this is Chad!"

Marie Céleste looked away, turning her back, and Ginger felt with dreadful unease that she would have given anything to undo that which she had done.

*   *   *   *

In anticipation Marie Céleste had felt that their main difficulty would lie in convincing Sir Matthew that she was, indeed, Martin's widow. In her inmost being she had never ceased to bask in the glory of being the wife of Martin Quest.

79

Even when Martin lay, a sodden evil-smelling travesty of a man, vomiting his heart out into the gutter, deep down the glory was still there, and that was why she never deserted him. Now she dismissed all the horror of the latter days as Martin's wife and remembered only the early splendour; pride shone in her eyes and she took on a dignity which proved her, indisputably, to be Martin's wife.

There was no glory, nor pride, nor dignity, or any other virtue in the demeanour of Ginger and Marie Céleste was quick to perceive this. She was, indeed, momentarily uncertain as to whether or not to repudiate Ginger. But her instinct overruled her reason and she decided to go forward with their scheme in the face of what she saw to be a very grave difficulty. She knew now that whereas she might make a good impression Ginger would invariably make a bad one but she concluded, for better or for worse, that it was preferable for Sir Matthew Quest to have Ginger for a grandson than for him to have no grandson at all.

Immediately Marie Céleste asked Sir Matthew whether he spoke French and, no doubt, his answer turned the scale. He could not speak French and that fact, of course, gave Ginger an enormous advantage for if he had addressed Ginger in French the game would have been over.

Sir Matthew took Ginger's hand, a little shyly, and searched his face for some sign of resemblance. He said: "Well, my boy."

It might have been a big moment but it wasn't. Sir Matthew was too old, it had been too long since he saw his eldest son, disappointment and resignation were too deeply ingrained in the old man's soul for it to be a big moment. His eyes crinkled at the sides and he looked at Ginger not too curiously, but merely a little quizzically.

"I must go at once and ring up Mildred," he said.

* * * *

Nothing could be done without Mildred.

"Who the hell is Mildred?" Ginger hissed as soon as the old man was out of ear-shot.

Marie Céleste's thoughts flitted about bat-like. Surely Mildred was not the surviving child of the wife of the third son? Marie Céleste understood that she had died in childbirth, her child with her. Surely Sir Matthew had not a grandchild of whose existence Marie Céleste was not aware?

They listened. Sir Matthew was speaking on the telephone. "Is that you, Mildred? I would like you to come round at once. Yes, indeed, it is urgent. No, I am quite well. No, I should prefer not to tell you on the telephone." (Pause) "A very astonishing thing has happened. You will come then? Good."

In moments of crisis, Marie Céleste had heard, the English always made tea. If atom bombs were to rain upon London, she understood, they would all make tea. So now she was not at all surprised to see Sir Matthew go into the small kitchen, light the gas and put on the kettle for tea.

He explained: "I have a Mrs. Angel who comes in during the mornings. She cleans the cottage and cooks my main meal, and for the rest, I look after myself. Unfortunately Mrs. Angel's daughter is having a baby at the moment, she hasn't been in for several days. I'm afraid there isn't any cake or anything, Marie Céleste."

Cake? Why was he talking about cake? Marie Céleste had no idea. She felt very exhausted and badly wanted to sit down and until he invited her to do so she must continue to stand.

Sir Matthew put out plain white pottery cups and saucers upon a solid silver tray of the period of George I. "Did you have a pleasant journey?" he asked.

Ginger looked round. The cottage was not as small as houses that he knew but it gave the impression of being poky. The furniture was too big and too grand for its surroundings. The sitting-room had a miserably thin carpet (it was a valuable Aubusson), there were some hideous ornaments (two Adam marble torchères, a quantity of *Capo di Monte*) and ghastly-looking pictures on the walls (still-life by Landseer and two Stubbs) but there were some valuable trinkets lying about.

Ginger, hearing Sir Matthew and Marie Céleste talking amiably in the kitchen across the little hall about the weather and the slowness of trains, was able to take his time and make a careful choice. There were a number of small coloured boxes in a display table with a glass top. It was not locked. Ginger examined the contents through the glass top, then having made his choice, deciding finally upon a golden snuff box with a small miniature in the lid painted upon ivory, he raised the top of the table and slipped the trinket into his pocket. He would have taken another were it not for the idea that the disappearance of two might be more readily noticed.

The whole operation took rather less than a second of time but time is only a matter of relativity. In that immeasurable period Ginger was aware of someone passing the window. The awareness was no more than that of the angler who knows that a trout is lurking there in the shadows beside a stone; no more—and no less. Someone had passed the window and had looked in as they passed.

Ginger went into the kitchen for a nice cup of char—he needed it.

CHAPTER IX

THERE was a noise outside like an iron bedstead being thrown down a fire-escape.

It was Mildred's car driven by Mildred.

Mildred belonged to the school which believes that to display any emotion at all is bad form. The result was that she felt things possibly more deeply than the average person. There was a spurious gaiety about her, a kind of bouncing Captain-of-the-hockey-team cheerfulness which wore better than did

Mildred herself. She was in her fiftieth year but she looked older.

Ever since Mildred was born she had belonged to someone else. First to her mother and father, later to her Aunt Quest and later still to a fractious and ailing husband. Then Ivy had claimed her attention and now Ivy and Sir Matthew together were wearing her out. She was always at the beck and call of someone.

Someday, Mildred told herself, she would go abroad, make herself a patchwork quilt, paint pictures, read books. It was always someday; Mildred's life had already held a great many days and not on one single day had Mildred done just what she wanted to do, for herself, and all day long.

Her expression of pleasure at the arrival of Marie Céleste was probably quite genuine for here was a ready-made daughter-in-law to take over the care of Sir Matthew Quest, or at least share it with Mildred who had borne the burden ever since the death of her Aunt Quest. It was true that the ready-made daughter-in-law looked rather more dead than alive, a storm-battered sparrow of a woman who would appear to be a great deal more in need of care than Sir Matthew himself but she was, indeed, more nearly related to Sir Matthew than Mildred who was his only niece by marriage. She smiled at her and Marie Céleste, looking into the wrinkled prune of a face, liked her because she saw nothing to cause her to fear.

"And this is Chad!" Mildred exclaimed.

It was a quibble, of course, but Marie Céleste was comforted that on neither occasion had she introduced Ginger as Chad.

"He doesn't speak any English," Sir Matthew told her.

"*Ah, sa ne fay riang!*" Mildred exclaimed, *"je purr parlay froncay avec Chad, n'est par?"*

Ginger looked dumbfounded.

Marie Céleste immediately addressed Mildred in rapid French, saying that she observed that she could speak French, had she been to France? But Mildred, never having been to

France, or indeed, out of England, could not reply. All the French she knew she had learned at her Ladies College and she had 'kept it up' all these years because 'some day she hoped to go to France which she had heard was such a beautiful country'.

So that was all right.

No Frenchman could be expected to understand Mildred's French, Mildred herself would be the last person to expect it. Marie Céleste sighed with relief; she might almost begin to relax. Name of a name but she was tired!

And then Ivy came into the room, after which no one could be expected to relax.

* * * *

When Mildred had accepted the fact that she would never have any children of her own she had decided to adopt a child, a little girl for preference. She had taken all the usual steps and her name had been put on to a 'waiting list'. Like waiting for a new refrigerator, by the time her turn came for the required article she had adjusted herself to doing without it. However, she was informed that there was a suitable baby girl in need of a mother at a Bristol Orphanage, would she kindly go along and inspect same at the earliest opportunity. By this time Mildred's husband was almost a permanent invalid and Mildred had little time to spare for a baby.

However, one look at little Ivy sufficed; Mildred instantly claimed her for her own.

Little Ivy was the prototype of the perfect little girl. She had everything: golden curls, fat rosy cheeks, chubby hands, round blue eyes, a cherub mouth.

"We thought you wouldn't hesitate," the matron said approvingly as Mildred took the baby in her arms. "Little Ivy is the favourite of us all. She's a little angel, isn't she?"

"Do you know anything about her parentage?" Mildred

asked, and, seeing the look which passed between the matron and the sister, instantly wished she had not asked.

"Only," the matron said, "that she was a little unwanted. Her mother was an unfortunate; she brought little Ivy to us when she was only three weeks old. She was a pretty girl, the same golden hair and blue eyes. She said her name was Ivy Smith but she left no address. Actually, we've never heard anything from the mother since. So we called the baby Ivy Smith, too."

"Poor little mite!" Mildred pressed a kiss on to the top of the baby's shining head, she felt as though she never wanted to let her go but there were a great many formalities before she was able to take little Ivy home. By that time Ivy was over two and had ideas of her own. Mildred had her baptized again, she was called Stella Mildred Rollright but the little girl insisted that she was Ivy, she always referred to herself as Ivy, the maids called her Ivy, the gardener called her Ivy, the milkman, the butcher's boy and the men who emptied the dustbins called her Ivy. So in the end Mildred and the Quests called her Ivy too.

And Ivy flourished after the way of ivy.

She flourished exceedingly.

Little Ivy was almost immediately replaced by medium-sized Ivy, who rapidly became a great-deal-bigger Ivy. By the time the Ladies College had finished with her she was a very-large-Ivy indeed. Her sojourn at school was an essay in retrogression; if Mildred herself had not at one time been Head Girl, Ivy would have been given the sack several times over.

Ivy, now nineteen, stood not upon the threshold of glorious womanhood but in it up to the neck. She looked about thirty and a very splendid specimen indeed of every man's idea of the perfect barmaid. The owners of the most popular bar in Newmarket would have taken her on at sight.

But she was not destined for the bar. Mildred was a great believer in careers for women. Ivy had had a secretarial training in London and was now waiting for the secretarial college to find her a job, which they seemed in no great hurry to do. In the meantime Mildred was making tentative efforts to have Ivy presented at next summer's court. Mildred herself had missed the opportunity of being presented because of her mother's illness and now she was anxious that her adopted daughter should not be similarly deprived. The trouble Mildred was experiencing was in her friends, though many of them would do anything for Mildred, absolutely anything, they all drew back sharply at the suggestion of presenting Ivy to the Queen. Recoiled is perhaps the word.

So Ivy ranged about the countryside, in something of the manner of the original Piltdown woman, determined, so far unsuccessfully, to lose her virginity. That she was unsuccessful was not, perhaps, due to the men of Gloucestershire being particularly chaste, but merely that they are more moderate in their requirements.

It had been evident, from the start, that Ginger had it coming to him but at the moment, between Ginger and his fate, there was Marie Céleste and, though Marie Céleste had been more than once given up for dead, one look at Ivy redoubled her determination to live, if necessary, for ever.

What Ivy thought about Marie Céleste was evident upon her expressive features. 'Just look what the cat's brought in!' her face cried, but her mouth simply said how-do-you-do nicely.

And when she turned to Ginger, Ivy's face cried: 'Just look what Father Christmas has put in my stocking!'

Until he went to France Ginger had never shaken hands in his life except upon the embarrassing occasion when he left the Borstal Institution and had been obliged to shake hands with the principal. But in Paris, he discovered, you shook hands with everyone, the barman, the *concierge,* the doctor, the undertaker. Even so Ginger had never been able to do so comfortably. Ivy took his lean, mastic hand and held it in her own hot one for a long time whilst Mildred explained that

'Chad' did not speak English and here was an opportunity for
Ivy to practise her French. Ivy smiled at Ginger, it was by no
means a simple smile, it was intended to assure Ginger that
language between himself and Ivy would be redundant.

*　　*　　*　　*

It is no good pretending that Marie Céleste was not disappointed. She was bitterly so. The great Rivington Court, the
Mecca of her dreams, had turned out to be a small ornate
cottage, the great English milord an elderly gentleman living in
comparative poverty.

Two things which she had not expected, however, of the
existence, of which, indeed, she was scarcely aware, never
having experienced either, she received in good measure, kindness and courtesy.

The cottage had three bedrooms, one was occupied by Sir
Matthew, the second was used as his dressing-room and the
third was the spare room. It was decided that Marie Céleste
should occupy the spare room, and that Sir Matthew's things
should be removed from the dressing-room in order that
Ginger might sleep there. Mildred at once went upstairs and
made up the two beds with worn linen sheets which had once
been very fine.

Marie Céleste's philosophy, *les choses s'arrangeront* was
all very well for her native Paris, she was far from sure that
things would arrange themselves here at Rivington. She needed
time to think things over. She therefore retired to bed for three
whole days and whilst she was in bed, things once more did
arrange themselves.

Mildred and Sir Matthew were by no means surprised at
her retirement to bed; Sir Matthew, indeed, belonged to a
generation the ladies of which always took some time to recover
from a journey.

The whole structure of English upper-class country life

now rests upon the (probably) bent back of Mrs. So-and-so who comes in daily to do the housework and some cooking. Single-handed she keeps the flag of gentility flying, if only at half mast. When the last Mrs. So-and-so has packed up, the flag will be run down, probably for ever.

Thus it was that the fate of Marie Céleste and Ginger hung upon the non-appearance of Mrs. Angel whose daughter had developed complications in the form of an interesting (to Mrs. Angel anyway) condition called 'milk-fever'. Mrs. Angel could find time to rush into the Lodge and report on the latest manifestations of milk fever but not to do any washing up or preparing vegetables. In the ordinary way Sir Matthew would have gone to stay with Mildred, who lived some two miles away, until such time as Mrs. Angel was able to return to work, but, as there were now two guests in the house, this was impossible.

It began by Ginger making some black coffee for Marie Céleste and from there it advanced with rapid strides, Ginger preparing an omelette for Sir Matthew and himself, making toast and milk coffee for breakfast and a rabbit stew for luncheon until at last it was evident that the corner boy had turned chef. There was no way out of it—Ginger was hungry and the food was there, it was simply a question of cooking it. Mildred, with a lively display of dumb charade showed him where everything was kept, though he would, in fact, have had no trouble in finding the things himself.

"You're a brick, Chad, you really are," Mildred exclaimed, delighted. "Isn't he a brick, Uncle? *Vous êtes un—un bon garçon!*"

Sir Matthew looked steadily at Ginger for a few moments, then looked away. He went out into the garden to hoe, leaving Mildred to chat merrily, undaunted by Ginger's stolid silence.

Marie Céleste lay in bed, between the very fine linen sheets, and stared at the ceiling. She was suffering from, amongst other things, mild shock. The shock of finding Rivington Court

88

an institution and the almost legendary figure of Sir Matthew Quest, of whom her husband had been frightened and whose shadow had hung over their whole married lives, like that of a tyrant, turning out to be a fragile old man.

"The Holy Terror," she whispered to herself over and over again and, resting on her elbow she was able to see through the net curtain into the garden where 'The Holy Terror' was placidly forking over the earth.

Then there were the lesser shocks; that, for instance, of seeing Ginger in these surroundings. Being quite honest with herself Marie Céleste realized, with a sick feeling, that Chad himself would have fitted better into the setting. They would have been kind to Chad . . .

And then that awful blonde girl!

At the time of planning, it had seemed so very right to bring Ginger over to Rivington as her son but in the plain light of facts it now seemed a dreadful thing to have done.

Lying there, staring up at the ceiling, Marie Céleste decided that Ginger must go, sooner rather than later. But if Ginger went she must go too for now she and Ginger belonged together. And Marie Céleste did not want to go. She could see that there was a place for her here. She could live with Sir Matthew and look after him, and though the cottage was by no means splendid, it was a great deal better than anything to which Marie Céleste had been used. And what was more—she was in her own place for, if this was not her rightful place, where was it?

Marie Céleste and Ginger had not been lovers since she was ill, she wanted very much to get better; she was proud to have a young and handsome lover. Marie Céleste knew that to have a roof over one's head was the most important thing in life but very close behind that came love, so close, in fact, that they became inextricably mixed from time to time.

That was her quandary.

On the third day Marie Céleste got up and dressed herself

carefully. She asked Ginger to carry the Gladstone bag down into the living-room and she took out all her papers and documents and arranged them neatly, waiting for Sir Matthew to come in from the garden. When he did so she showed him everything, the photographs, all the letters, the little mementos of Martin. He seemed disappointingly unmoved.

"My dear," he said gently, "why are you showing me all these?"

"You should see them. You should make sure I am not an impostor!"

"But, my dear Marie Céleste, what an extraordinary notion!"

"I could very easily say I was Mrs. Martin Quest," Marie Céleste pointed out. "How could you prove it?"

"I shouldn't need to, I should know at once."

"I wonder," Marie Céleste's eyes narrowed. She paused. "You know, you are so very different from that which I expected."

"In what way?"

"Martin talked of you very much. He was frightened of you, do you know?"

"Yes, I think he was. But, you forget, I am an old man now. I wasn't always an old man, Marie Céleste, a shabby old boy digging in the garden. I suppose that in my time I have been as good an Army officer as any. But on the whole—" words were not coming easily, he hesitated a good deal but eventually got out—"everything I cared about has gone out of my life. First my three sons and then my dear wife." He sighed heavily. "The trouble is, I've lived too long. There's no one left now but Mildred."

'When I am better," Marie Céleste pointed out, "I can look after you."

"That's what I have begun to hope," Sir Matthew said and added, a little uncomfortably: "I must confess to you that even the small allowance to you was causing me a little embarrassment, my dear. It would be more economical for me if you were to live here with me."

Marie Céleste's great eyes were now as soft as those of a fallow doe. "There is nothing I should like better. Martin used to say I could cook like an angel."

"Not like Mrs. Angel, I hope," Sir Matthew said stiltedly. "That boy has turned out a few excellent meals, by the way."

Marie Céleste's lips tightened slightly. "Ah, good. He has been making himself useful."

Sir Matthew nodded. "You know——" he said, and stopped.

"Well?"

"About Chad—has he been earning anything?"

"But yes."

"Good. I've been a bit worried about it. You never mentioned it in your letters. I began to wonder——"

"Wonder what?" Marie Céleste asked sharply.

"I wondered if, perhaps, he was a bit of a wastrel."

"But no, indeed. Why should he be?"

"Like his father."

"Martin was not a wastrel, as you call it," Marie Céleste began in instinctive loyalty, and then subsided. After all, it was ancient history now.

"I thought you might have told me if he had got some sort of job and was helping to support you. You wrote such excellent little notes every month, Marie Céleste. I have been grateful to you for that. But I read between the lines, or at least I thought I read between the lines. You told me all sorts of charming details about Chad but you never once said that he was a good son to his mother. I gathered that you were having trouble, probably the same sort of trouble that my wife and I had with Martin. So I never pressed that you should bring him over here. I thought it best to let well alone."

Unaccountably Marie Céleste burst into tears. For the first time since Chad had died she cried for her son, hot tears gushed out of her for Chad. Great gentle soul that he was, what harm

91

had he ever done to anyone? He could be here now, nodding and smiling placidly, chipping away at his little wooden donkey. Sir Matthew might even have liked him. Scalding tears of almost unbearable remorse flowed down Marie Céleste's tired face.

Uncomfortably Sir Matthew patted her bowed shoulders.

When at last she began to recover he went on: "I think you should know," he said, at last, "that after my dear wife died I had to remake my will. I had left such possessions as I still have to her, you understand. But when she died I had to reconsider how my property was to be left. I considered it for a long time, Marie Céleste, because I realize that much unhappiness can be caused by a carelessly made or thoughtless will. I must tell you that my property has been greatly reduced in value owing to—well, all sorts of things which you wouldn't understand, mainly connected with the social revolution in the midst of which we live. I sold Rivington outright, retaining only this lodge and the garden surrounding us for myself. The money was invested and, together with certain investments I already had, I have an adequate income for modest living. You must understand that to live on income one needs a large capital sum these days."

Marie Céleste was listening with great attention now, her frame shaken occasionally by a dry sob which was an aftermath of her breakdown.

"I could live in better style and in greater comfort if I lived on capital and there is, in fact, no reason why I should not do so. But I belong to a generation which did not live on capital. It is something we did not do, like secret drinking. And so, when I do actually shuffle off," he smiled, "I mean, die, there will be quite an appreciable amount of capital to dispose of. About —well, something in the region of thirty thousand pounds."

Marie Céleste was now perfectly still.

"And I have left it like this. The allowance I made to you was to continue until my death. When I die an annuity is to be purchased out of the capital to bring you in a reasonable allowance. The residue of the estate, that is, what is left, is to be divided equally between Mildred and Chad."

"Chad!" Marie Céleste exclaimed sharply.

"Mildred is my dear wife's niece. My wife loved Mildred dearly and, indeed, so do I. She has been like a daughter to us."

There was a long pause.

"I think it is only right that I should acquaint you as to how things stand exactly, Marie Céleste. After all, you and Chad are now my nearest and dearest," the last was said a little whimsically. "With regard to your allowance now, Marie Céleste——"

"I don't need any whilst I live with you," she said quickly.

"I take it that you have no other means? Well, I must certainly continue to give you, perhaps, half of it. You can't be penniless, my dear. You will need 'pin money' as we used to call it. Well, to hark back, I made this will after my dear wife died. I thought at the time it was a prudent one but of late I had begun to wonder whether Chad were turning out to be a wastrel and, if he were, whether it was not extremely unwise to leave half the remaining capital for him to do what he liked with. I was actually wondering whether I could put my problem to you in a letter. You do see my point, Marie Céleste, don't you?"

"But yes."

"Nothing could be worse for a boy with any of poor Martin's propensities than to receive a lump sum at the age of twenty-two."

So Chad might have been all right after all; there would have been no need for him to go to the State Institution when Marie Céleste was no longer there to cherish him, provided, of course, that Sir Matthew had died before Marie Céleste. But there was no profit to be had in such agonizing thoughts.

"I really do not know," Marie Céleste said, "why I should have given you the idea that Chad was an unsatisfactory son—"

93

she must remember that it was Ginger of whom she was talking— *"is* an unsatisfactory son," she corrected herself. "He is not at all a bad cook after my instruction."

"What sort of job did he have in Paris? Was he a cook?"

"But yes."

"Ah, I begin to see light. You didn't want me to know he had a menial job, that was it, wasn't it?"

"Menial job, what is that, please?"

"In a kitchen."

"Oh, but yes." Marie Céleste nodded vigorously. "That was my idea."

Sir Matthew took her hand. "My dear," he said, "when I was young I should have been profoundly shocked at the idea of my only grandson being a cook in a Paris café. But I assure you that I have by now learned a great deal from life. Now I am only too thankful that he has a job at all. You see, he might have ideas about being a painter and that would be unbearable; I couldn't stand another would-be artist in the family. Not again in one lifetime!"

Then, to his very great discomfort Marie Céleste held his hand to her face and kissed it.

"I think," he said uncomfortably, "I had better leave my will as it stands."

CHAPTER X

GINGER was a graduate of the 'so-what' and 'I-couldn't-care-less' school of thought, his manner seldom varied. At present his face wore a look of slightly contemptuous indifference but beneath the surface he was deeply perturbed. In what way had he bettered himself? After Chad had—had died, why did not he and Marie Céleste stay on in the Rue des Mauvais Garçons? They had a roof over their heads even if they did not know how the next meal would be paid for. And life in Paris was a great deal more to his liking than the taste he was now having of life at Rivington.

With some effort Ginger was honest with himself, they had given up the life in the Rue des Mauvais Garçons for what appeared to be something far better, for luxury and rich monetary rewards in one form or another.

And look where they had landed themselves!

Ginger experienced no difficulty at all in remembering not to speak. He had no desire to speak, he had nothing to say to this pack of Tories. The only temptation he had to speak was to tell little Ivy to go to hell; she got into his hair. He badly wanted to tell her that if she had so much time to stand about watching him she could do the cooking herself, but Ivy had a happy disposition in that she believed herself born to be served, nothing that had happened in her life so far had caused her to believe otherwise.

She popped into the lodge on the slightest of pretexts, or no pretext at all. When Ginger was sitting on a Louis Quinze settee in the living-room, with his feet up on a brocade-top stool, biting his nails and studying racing results, she burst into the room, stepped over Ginger's legs and plumped herself down beside him; Ginger coldly removed his feet from the stool and withdrew into as small a space as possible. Ivy, undaunted, snatched the newspaper from him, and said that as he obviously could not understand what he was reading, she would read it for him, teach him English in fact.

Ginger found it deadly dull; in so far as he loved anyone he was in love with Marie Céleste; he could never forget the days when they had been lovers and he looked forward to a renewal of those happy times. He had no desire for Ivy. He knew her type.

Ivy read happily on whilst Ginger nibbled at his fingernails and wondered how long it would be before Marie Céleste's wonderful vitality was renewed.

When Ivy had gone and the evening meal was over Sir Matthew sat beside the fire and read *The Times*. Ginger did not return to the settee; he felt distinctly uncomfortable when he was alone with the general. He wanted to go out into the cold wet evening to locate a public house but he was in the ridiculous situation of having no money with which to buy a drink. He reasoned that to take money from Sir Matthew was a different proposition from removing a gold snuff box from a show case; the disappearance of the snuff box had not yet been discovered but the disappearance of money would certainly be discovered and Ginger realized that he was in no position to be kicked out of doors.

He went up to Marie Céleste's room to see if by any chance she had a couple of shillings to give him.

He was in a mood of nervous irritation.

"Look," he began angrily, "we've been here four days now! Isn't it about time you got up?"

Marie Céleste raised herself on her elbow.

"S—sh! Do lower your voice, are you mad? He may hear you!"

"So what!" he exclaimed but in a much lower tone.

"Ginger! It is not right that you are here. I see now that we have done very wrong."

"So what!" he snorted.

"So you must go."

"Go! But that's all very well. You've got us into this mess——"

"It was your idea and your idea alone."

"But you didn't half catch on!" Ginger gave vent to an oath which Marie Céleste very much disliked.

"Be quiet!" she snapped. "I am Sir Matthew's daughter-in-law, he is pleased to see me. He is delighted that I have come. And now that I have come I shall stay and cherish him."

Ginger sneered. Cherish! What a word.

"It is you who are the impostor. We did what we did because

96

we thought it was for the best. But it was not so. It would have been quite well for me to have brought Chad here. It would have been all right because he is not a great English milord but just a kind old man. He is not a 'Holy Terror' either. Poor Chad could not help being as he was. Sir Matthew would have been very sad but he would have understood." Marie Céleste leaned back. "Can you understand how much I suffer now, in my mind?"

But Ginger did not understand anything about suffering ot the mind.

"Look, have you any dough at all? I haven't had a drink in four days and I can't stick it much longer. My nerves are all to pieces."

"Exactly. It is evident that you must go. We have made a mistake and we must do our best to put right that mistake."

Ginger sat down and placed an arm awkwardly round her shoulders now covered with her best nightdress.

"What say we both go, and cut our losses? What about you and me, old girl?"

Marie Céleste smiled, the special little smile she kept for moments of love. *"Les choses s'arrangeront!"* she said, "but in the meantime you must go from here. You are sure to be discovered. You cannot keep silent for days, for weeks. One time you will be taken by surprise and say something in your English which is very different from that of Sir Matthew. Then all will be over and I shall be turned out as well as you for that I have aided you."

"You should have thought of all that before."

Marie Céleste was silent. It was only too true.

"Look, I don't mind getting out of this hole. Make no mistake about it. I've no desire to stay in this dump. We were a lot better off in the Rue des Mauvais Garçons, you and I."

"No we were not. We had no money to buy food. I could not work. You would not work."

Ginger gave her a dirty look.

"I am a great deal better off here. I am *chez moi*—at home."

"Aw—hell!"

"It is true."

"Well, say I go——"

"Keep your voice down, if you please."

"Say I do what you want and go."

"Yes?"

"What do I live on?"

"What did you live on before the day I first met you in the gardens of the Luxembourg?"

"See here, don't bring up all that! You know very well I was down and out."

"But then you were in Paris. Now you are in your native country. Can you not return to—to the occupation you held before that?"

"Hell," Ginger said again. "I thought you'd got all that clear. I'm on the run, see? You know what that means, Marie Céleste. The police want me. You know that perfectly well, why do you think I had my hair dyed? Don't come over all innocent, s'welp me Gawd! It'll be months before I can go back to London. If I stay away a year it might be all right, but I'm not going back there in less. I don't want to get myself inside again, no fear! Six months was quite enough for me."

"Inside—gaol?" Marie Céleste said thoughtfully.

"Of course, and don't pretend you didn't know it. Cor, Mrs. Martin Quest, this is rich, this is!" Ginger said bitterly.

Marie Céleste continued to think. Then she said, "I have had a long talk with Sir Matthew."

"Yes, and by the by, what were you up to, gassing away to him in the room with the door shut? If that girl Ivy hadn't been hanging round the kitchen I'd have been listening at the door. What was it all about?"

"About—money."

"Now you *are* talking."

98

"Ginger—he has left half his fortune to Chad."

"Fortune? He hasn't a penny to scratch himself with!"

"Hasn't he? He's rich. Very, very rich."

Ginger took out his comb and combed back his thick black hair.

"Says you!"

"I tell you he is rich. You must understand; people like this—I can't explain it—but he has much money invested. That is he would not spend the money, it lies in some bank or with some firm and they pay him so much each month, or year, and it is upon that money that he now lives."

"Well, what a damn silly idea!"

"Is it not." Marie Céleste agreed.

"They're crazy, Tories."

"Very crazy but what will you? Perhaps you do not think it so crazy that he leave half of his money to Chad when he dies?"

To Chad. Ginger suddenly realized what this meant.

"To Chad?"

Marie Céleste nodded slowly, her great eyes fixed on Ginger's face. She allowed a few moments for the information to sink in.

"So that is why it is important that you must go away. Do you see?"

Ginger was gnawing his finger-nails almost ravenously.

"You see, Ginger? If you stay even another week you will certainly be found out. But if you go now, just quietly slip away, you will simply remain the good son who has brought his mother home. The will shall remain in your favour for there shall be no reason why it should not."

"That's all very well," Ginger argued, "but there's always the question of ready."

"Ready?"

"The cash. It might be months, years before the old man dies. He doesn't look ill to me, he's out in all weathers digging in the garden. He looks a lot healthier than most. What am I going to use for money till then?"

Marie Céleste thought. "He says that I must still have some of the allowance he gave me."

"Some of it?" Again the oath. "What was it at best? About two quid a week, eh? Wasn't that about it? Halve that and what do you get? What do *I* get?"

Absurdly little, of course.

Marie Céleste began to be impatient. "Surely, Ginger, surely you could find means to live until—until he dies. You must. Think of it. You will have a lot of money coming to you when he dies."

"How much?"

"I don't understand English money very completely. I remember the sum he mentioned. It is divided between you and that Mildred. That Mrs. Rollright, or whatever her name is. His niece by marriage."

"Well, how much?"

"Thirty thousand pounds!" Marie Céleste said, with due respect.

"Gawd 'strewth!" Ginger dropped his comb and stooped to pick it up, his face had flushed a rich scarlet.

"Only half of that will be yours. What is 'to buy an annuity'?"

Ginger was stricken apparently dumb.

"First the money he leaves must buy an annuity for me. I have no idea what it means but I do know I would continue to have a small allowance. Out of that thirty thousand pounds must come the money for me, and after that what is left will be for you and Mildred."

Never having dealt in large sums of money a thousand pounds seemed a vast fortune to Ginger, whether it was a thousand, ten thousand or fifteen thousand was not important but he liked the sound of it.

"Fifteen thousand pounds!"

"So you see, *mon cher*, it is worth waiting for."

In the light of this staggering news Marie Céleste's request that he should leave at once seemed the only feasible one. Away from here, there was not much chance of his being proved an impostor, but here, there was no chance at all that he would not, sooner rather than later.

"All right, I'll go."

"We must think where you should go that I may come and see you."

"There's a city about twenty miles away, Birmingham."

"Oh yes, I have heard of it. A very big city. You can find employment there?"

"And there's Bristol, that's not so far away either——"

"*Tiens!*"

"And Bath—look have you got ten bob for the fare?"

"Maybe, in my purse. There is two large silver pieces and some coppers."

Ginger looked in her purse. There was exactly five shillings, eleven pence and a threepenny bit.

"Not enough for the fare."

"But surely—what is it, Ginger?"

Ginger had not remembered the gold snuff box, but his hand, thrust into the pocket of his trousers, had encountered it. There were always pawn shops, second-hand jewellers. He ought to be able to nose out a reliable fence . . .

'Nothing," he said but there was the shadow of his curious wintry smile on his face. "Look, I'll go tomorrow morning. I'll take this five bob, Marie Céleste, and in the meantime you can find out how you get to Birmingham, what bus or where the train goes from and so on. You can put it out that I—that I'm anxious to find a job of work and I'm going after one. You needn't say I won't be back, but later on I'll send you a wire, eh? How's that? I'll say I've found a job and I won't be back. And then, when you're better, you'll come and see me in Birmingham? It'll look like the perfect mother and son, eh?"

"That is right. You must do nothing that will cause them to wonder, or think you do not know how to behave. That is a very good idea, *mon brave*."

"Say—how much did you say it was, the money?"

"Thirty thousand pounds."

"Half of that I get, is it? That's fifteen thousand pounds!" Ginger licked his thin lips. "Fifteen thousand pounds. It's wurf doing anythink for that. That's money, that is!"

Marie Céleste closed her eyes. She was exhausted. She had worked hard and she had won. All would now be well. She took Ginger's hand: "You are my good boy, my little cabbage," she said, with a sigh.

CHAPTER XI

IT was by no means a coincidence that Ivy was going into Birmingham to have her hair done.

No journey, however small, could be undertaken by a Quest without reference to Mildred. Marie Céleste made it known that Ginger would like to go into Birmingham and Sir Matthew at once telephoned to Mildred who always knew the times of trains and buses. Yes, there were at least two morning trains but the journey involved changes and a slow cross-country ride. There was a bus which went directly through the village, stopping to pick up passengers at the War Memorial at midday. If Chad were to catch the bus he would be able to get himself a return ticket without any difficulty of language arising.

But Mildred hesitated; Ivy was standing beside her trying to say something.

"Are you there, Uncle? Ivy has a hair appointment in Birmingham, she could go with Chad. What was that, Ivy?"

Ivy was pointing out that as Mildred had her Women's

Institute that afternoon she could spare the car to Ivy who had not yet passed her driving test but was occasionally allowed to drive Mildred's car with the 'L' tied on to the back, provided someone who could drive went with her.

Mildred did not leap at the idea but if Ivy were to take 'Chad' into Birmingham in the car Mildred would, at least, know that she was satisfactorily employed. She concurred, a little reluctantly.

Marie Céleste was in her room when Ginger went in to say goodbye. She gave him the remaining money and then she kissed him. Holding his face between her hands she kissed him good and proper; it was not the kiss of a mother bidding farewell to her son. Then, looking round hurriedly, she seized upon one of her few, and possibly one of her dearest possessions, Martin's Etonian muffler. She tied it round his neck and tucked the ends in beneath the lapels of his overcoat.

"Voyons!" She kissed him again. "I shall not ask you to write to me soon. I know you will."

Write? Ginger had never written a letter in his life. But he wouldn't lose touch with Marie Céleste, that was certain. He didn't want to leave her, it was only sheer necessity that was causing him to do so.

Men did not leave Marie Céleste.

"You've been a good boy," she said, "you remembered all the things I told you and you won't forget them now that you are no longer with me?" She didn't say: you won't forget me. Men did not forget Marie Céleste. She kissed him yet again, they were torn apart by a peevish bark from the horn of Mildred's car which Ivy blew vigorously.

Marie Céleste watched the departure through the net curtain of her bedroom window. She would have preferred Ginger to go on the bus but reluctantly admitted that it would be of advantage to save him the fare. She could not see Ivy from her position but she watched Ginger go out and get into the car.

103

His lovely new overcoat, of which she had been so proud, somehow did not look quite the thing.

Sir Matthew, standing at the gate to wave good-bye, was dressed in incredibly old clothes. He looked old and bent and shabby. And lonely.

Marie Céleste dragged herself downstairs, she would cook him a splendid luncheon; he would bring her vegetables from the garden and she would make a *pot au feu*. But, name of a name, how tired she was! How her bones ached! She wished that she could quickly become used to the warm damp climate.

Ivy was in full fig. Mildred insisted on well-cut tweeds for the country and Ivy's tweeds were, in fact, very well cut; stuffed with Ivy, however, they looked as though they had been bought off the peg in Berwick market. A velour beret, the colour of autumn leaves, was the correct wear with well-cut tweeds; Ivy wore hers well forward over her face, perched upon her golden curls with the abandon of a bunch of grapes worn by a young lady in the chorus at the Windmill theatre. She wore well-bred low-heeled brown leather shoes but when driving the car her skirt rode up to such dizzy heights that nobody could be expected to spare a glance for her shoes.

Every time she saw Ivy ready to go out, Mildred's poor heart was rent with anguish. Though she did not put it in so many words she wondered how it was that with all the thought, care and money she had put into the dressing of Ivy, her adopted daughter unfailingly turned herself out looking like a cheap tart. But that was only one of the lesser things about Ivy that rent Mildred's heart.

With some dignity Ginger drew the voluminous skirt of his overcoat round him and averted his eyes from Ivy's legs. He was not interested in Ivy's legs. He was, in fact, still tingling from Marie Céleste's kisses and he wanted to go on tingling without any interruptions from Ivy.

Ivy's driving was equal to everything else she did. The

examiners who had failed her in her driving test had called it 'sloppy'. They rattled and banged along the highway whilst Ivy hummed, threw her gears in and out, jammed on her brakes so that they both swung forward with heads against the windscreen, and blew the horn long and loudly when driving along the straight.

But Ginger was indifferent, he only wanted to get there. He became a little uncomfortable, however, when she turned off the highway into a side turning and drove down a country lane, finally turning into a gateway and stopping. He looked round for bushes into which the young woman might intend to retire, but they were surrounded by bare fields, and whilst contemplating this fact Ginger felt suddenly as though he had been hit with a large feather bed, and hit hard. He struggled but the feather bed pressed down upon him until he felt that he could not get a breath. With such air as was left to him he let fly a string of oaths including Marie Céleste's least favourite one and with a superhuman effort he heaved the feather bed off him and sat back glowering, as breathless as an Olympic runner.

"I thought there was something funny about you," Ivy said also, sitting back and taking a cigarette out of her case.

Funny? What the hell did she mean?

"Are you a queer?"

Never was there a more awkward moment. Ginger had always been a man of very few words but now he was simply itching to tell her what he thought of her. He bit his lip and looked out at the grey lowering sky.

"You do look funny," Ivy said, she spoke with an educated accent but her voice was tainted with a painful shrillness, a sharp cutting edge like a newly opened tin. She took out her pocket handkerchief, licked it and proceeded to rub the lipstick off the corner of Ginger's mouth which was as close as she had got to that goal. The moment was, perhaps, the nearest Ginger had ever come to real suffering. He was not going to be

105

caught swearing in English again; he couldn't even exclaim irritably; he simply had to put up with it.

"There!" Ivy said tenderly. "Your girl friend won't find anything wrong now."

She backed the car into the lane and presently they were again on the main road.

"You know, if only you'd come off it and be friends it would save you a lot of trouble. You aren't a queer, are you? I was only teasing. I know your sort. You're slow off the mark but once you get going, wow! I know you're out to pick up some girl. You're browned off with Rivington, aren't you? It's too slow for you, isn't it? So am I. I like towns and lights and people. But what's the good of my talking—you can't understand me, can you?"

She gave him a side-long glance of such mockery that Ginger's blood ran cold. Had his involuntary cursing given him away? He realized now that there was not the slightest chance that it had not. Ivy was sharp, you had to admit that, very sharp.

"Well, here we are," Ivy said at last. They had reached a car park in the centre of the city. "What time do you want to be going back?"

But Ginger had had quite enough. All this pretence, all the care not to speak his native language, all the constant mental vigilance had, he told himself, worn him to a shred. He would get to hell out of it and Ivy could think what she damned well pleased. He slipped out of the car almost before it had stopped, slammed the door without a look round, and was off.

The car park man approached with maddening slowness, breathing heavily and fumbling with a book of tickets. Ivy swore but she knew that if she didn't park the car properly and wait for her ticket there would be difficulties later on. By the time the attendant had laboriously fixed one half of the ticket under the windscreen wiper and handed her the other half Ginger was out of sight. Ivy sped like a swallow in the direction he had taken. There were a great many people about, people who didn't seem to be bent on any errand, simply cluttering up the pavements.

If it hadn't been for his overcoat she would never have seen Ginger again. But that overcoat stood out, even over on the other side of the square.

Having put what he considered to be an adequate amount of space between himself and Ivy, Ginger came to rest upon a street corner, still breathless. Hands in pockets, eyes sliding to right and to left, lips nervously fidgeting with a cigarette, he was in the state which was his nearest approach to meditation. He stood there for a long time mentally 'Cor-ing' and 'gawd-strewth-ing' until hunger drove him into a nearby 'dining-room' for 'gravy soup, sausage and mash, baked college pudding' which cost one of Marie Céleste's half-crowns.

After the meal he took to the streets again, passing from jeweller to jeweller, standing in front of each shop and studying it with great attention. Instinct should have guided him to the right jeweller but it did not, it simply led him away from the wrong ones, that is, the jewellers in the main streets whose windows were decorated with gleaming new silver and jewellery.

After a long and careful survey he turned off the main streets and ranged about the poorer-class district. He saw one or two pawn shops and hesitated for some time outside each. He knew pawnbrokers of old, however, and he had never found them to be soul mates. It was something half way between the first-class jewellers and the pawnbrokers that he wanted and only after a lot of walking about and doubling back on his tracks did he find what he considered to be a suitable establishment.

It was a small second-hand jeweller's shop, one third of the window was covered with a wire on the inside. Behind the wire were grubby pieces of jewellery carelessly arranged. There were notices saying: 'All on this tray 30/-' or 10/- or even 5/-. In the remaining two thirds of the window there were second-hand cake baskets, entrée dishes and candelebra of Sheffield plate and a number of small boxes of imitation Bow enamelware. It was the boxes which decided Ginger more than anything else. He went inside.

There was no one else in the shop, the owner of the shop rustled out from an inner office, he wore a black alpaca coat and thick glasses. Ginger handed him the snuff box. The jeweller held it in the palm of his hand, feeling its weight. In the dingy little shop it was a thing of beauty, Ginger was proud of it. The jeweller examined it carefully, turning it round and round before a small magnifying glass which he held in front of his glasses. Drumming his long fingers impatiently on the counter Ginger looked round. When he turned back the jeweller was not looking at the box any longer but looking at Ginger. "Look," he said, "I don't want any funny stuff. See this?"

This was a revolver.

To say Ginger was affronted was an understatement.

"Single-handed I can't afford to deal with customers without I've something to protect myself with."

"You must have some funny customers," Ginger returned rapidly.

"I have," the jeweller said, he was looking past Ginger and out into the street. "Shut the door, there's a good chap."

Ginger, swallowing his irritation, did as he was asked. There was no point in quarrelling with the shop-keeper.

"How much do you want for this?"

They always asked that. Ginger had the answer ready.

"Twenty-five."

"Twenty-five what?"

"Quid, of course."

The jeweller put the little box down on the counter, directly in front of Ginger. "Don't try and be funny."

Ginger picked up the trinket, weighing it in his hand as the jeweller had done. "It's solid gold."

"Don't make me laugh."

Gawdstrewth, what a phoney lot the Quests were! Ginger had not heard the expression that 'all their geese are swans' but his mind struggled with a similar analogy.

Once more the jeweller was looking beyond Ginger. The bottom half of the door was of frosted glass with the jeweller's name written obliquely across it in clear glass.

Ginger himself examined the snuff box, not that he had any idea as to whether it were gold or not but to give himself time to think.

"Solid gold," Ginger repeated, "been in the family ever since I can remember."

The jeweller treated the information for what it was worth.

"Solid pinchbeck," he corrected.

Ginger had never heard of pinchbeck, all the confidence he had regained from his sojourn on the street corner once more receded.

"How much will you give me for it?" he asked huskily.

"It's an old piece all right," the jeweller temporized, "but I couldn't sell it in this district. There's nobody as would want it. You're in the wrong part of the world for selling a thing like that. Live here? No, I thought you were a stranger in these parts. We make things like that in this city, boy. Turn 'em out in droves. Not pinchbeck I grant you, but something very near." He was anxious to terminate the interview and return to his football pools. "Your girl friend's getting impatient," he nodded towards the door.

"I've got no girl friend," Ginger grunted. "Look," he ran his hand over his face, "can't you give me anything for it?"

"Thirty-five bob."

"Make it two quid."

"Thirty-five bob."

"All right," Ginger sighed.

109

It would seem that thirty-five shillings was all that the jeweller possessed in the world. He brought out a tin box and gave Ginger the entire contents, one pound note, one ten shilling note and five shillings.

Ginger pocketed it without a word of thanks. He felt no doubts as to the jeweller's honesty, he felt only a deep depression. It was just his luck. He mouched out of the shop.

The jeweller took the snuff box into his office where he examined it again with great care. So engrossed in his examination was he that he noticed nothing of what was taking place immediately outside his establishment. He seemed satisfied with his findings for later he locked the snuff box away in his safe.

* * * *

Ivy leaned nonchalantly against the plate glass, she was wearing a jeering smile.

It was just one damn thing after another; Ginger bore his burden bravely: "You've been following me around all day," he observed.

"But you didn't catch me at it."

"Oh yes, I did. I knew all right."

"Liar." Ivy was proud of her bit of sleuthing, it had not been easy with all the going back on his tracks he had done; it had been evident, however, that he was seeking something and Ivy had not relaxed her vigilance until she discovered what it was. She had not actually seen the transaction taking place, each time she had looked over the top of the frosted glass she had found the magnified eyes of the jeweller fixed on her, but she knew perfectly well what had been going on and she did not hesitate to tell Ginger so.

"How much did he give you for the snuff box?"

Ginger did not answer.

"Uncle Matthew would blow up," Ivy said, "it has sentimental value. It belonged to his wife. They say Queen Charlotte

110

gave it to her great-grandmother St. Chad." She laughed derisively. "Queen Charlotte my foot! Don't stand there shivering, you look as happy as a seasick cat."

And he felt it.

"You don't know your luck, Chad my boy!"

Chad! She still thought he was Chad!

"Sooner or later someone, Mildred or Uncle Matthew, is going to notice that snuff box has gone."

"I shan't be there to bother," Ginger snapped.

"Not there!" Ivy's eyebrows rose. She shifted her position. "All the worse for you. I saw you take it, you know. You hadn't been in Uncle Matthew's house ten minutes before you'd got that snuff box in your pocket. I saw you through the window, there was no making a mistake."

It was cold standing there by the jeweller's shop. It had begun to rain. Ivy brought a pencil out of her handbag and carefully wrote down the name of the jeweller, the name of the street and number of the shop in the street.

"I wonder you had the nerve," she said, snapping her handbag closed. "Is it drink, the same as your father?"

Ginger turned up his coat collar and drew the Etonian muffler closer round his neck. She took his arm. "Come on," she said, "we'll find a tea shop."

* * * *

Ivy looked admiringly at her own plump white hands, side by side on the marble top of the table.

"I've always been interested in Cousin Martin, that's your father, he's always seemed to be the only Quest who wasn't just dull and stupid. Uncle Matthew had an awful time with him, you know. After he was sent down from Oxford, Uncle Matthew tried to get him some sort of job but they used to find him drunk, lying outside in the drive or down in the cellars; often two footmen had to carry him to bed. Can you imagine it at Rivington? And yet Mildred's said more than once that she's sure Uncle Matthew loved Martin the best of his sons. Even Mildred admitted once that the other two were dull That's why he's making such a fuss of you and Marie Céleste. It's because Martin was his favourite son. Fancy! He's done nothing but think about Martin all these years and years!"

"Fuss!" Ginger could not agree that a fuss had been made of him.

"Yes, fuss, my lad. You don't realize. Nobody ever stays with Uncle Matthew, he's known as a recluse in the village. Once a year he turns up for a cricket match and it's quite an event, I can tell you. They still call him the squire, in the village, and everyone's pleased he's there, but mostly nobody ever sees him."

Ivy sipped her strong tea noisily. "You've got the run of the house, in and out of the kitchen, everywhere." She laughed, "and all the time that snuff box in your pocket! Poor old boy, I bet he'd never think it was you! He'd say some tramp or a gipsy had taken it. The front door is always left unlocked, he thinks nobody would ever come in, and, honestly, I don't think they would!"

Ivy ate her tea with apparent gusto, she was enjoying herself mightily, something had at last happened to ease the agony of her boredom.

Ginger could eat nothing. He pushed aside his cup and saucer and reflectively picked his teeth with one of his French toothpicks. He was in a mess good and proper now; it was all part of the run of bad luck through which he was going, of course, but he would have to make a snap decision as to what he was going to do. He could not return to Rivington with Ivy because he could not keep up the filmy pretence of being Chad Quest. If he stayed away, letting them know in time that he had found a job and was working he could still remain Chad Quest, part-heir to Sir Matthew's 'fortune'. But he now had exactly thirty-seven and sixpence between himself and the east wind. How was he who had never done any work in his life to 'find a job', either straight or crooked, in the apparently respectable town of Birmingham? What good purpose could be served by giving the dame Ivy the slip again? Or had he given her the slip before? Quite frankly, he told himself, he hadn't.

But he need not have bothered to think. Ivy was doing all his thinking for him.

"What did you mean—you weren't coming back home?"

"What I said."

"That you've had enough of Rivington?"

"Yeh."

"What are you going to do? Live on the proceeds of selling the snuff box?"

"Never you mind what I'm going to do."

Ivy laughed happily. "You're a bad lot, aren't you, Chad? You speak more like a Cockney than a French boy. What was the idea, shamming dumb?"

"I been a lot in London, see? More than in France, reely."

"It's a shame on poor old Uncle Matthew. I can't say he's exactly thrilled with you in the flesh, but he used to think a lot about you. He's always let Mildred read Marie Céleste's letters, he was always ever so pleased to get them. She made up all those, didn't she?"

"No, she didn't."

"Come off it, you know she did! All sorts of drip about you being such a sweet-natured boy, so kind to animals, stray cats and such like, and watching birds in the park. You weren't there at all, were you? You'd run away from home, hadn't you? What were you doing, Chad? Backing dogs at the dog tracks in London, doing tick-tack for the bookies, or what? You look that type, you know, you look the complete spiv."

Except that he ran his hand once or twice over his face Ginger might not have heard anything she said.

"What went wrong? Why did you come running back to

Mother? Eh, Chad? What went wrong? Poor old Marie Céleste! I bet it was you put her up to coming back to the old home, wasn't it?"

Ginger was getting distinctly restless. He was not used to women who thought, who indeed, had anything to think with. Marie Céleste was the first woman he had ever met with brains. But here was another, and a blonde too! Honestly, Ginger told himself, she scared the pants off him, she did!

On further thought he realized that the conclusions she had drawn might have been a great deal worse.

Ivy wiped her mouth on the back of her hand, a trick of which Mildred had never been able to break her. She always left streaks of lipstick across the back of her white hands, that and the enamel on her finger-nails which was always imperfect, chipped and vestigial in places, added to her general air of having been picked up cheaply in the July sales.

"Never mind, Chad," Ivy said comfortingly, "you've met the right person in me. I was born bad, too, I've been told so often, at school and at the training college I went to in London; everyone tells me sooner or later: 'You're born bad, Ivy'. Mildred isn't my real mother, you know. Did you think she was? Jemima, no! My mother was an absolute smasher! I—I'd be ashamed to have an old bag like Mildred for a mother."

In spite of himself Ginger felt more than a twinge of interest.

"What about your father?"

"Well—" Ivy put her head on one side rather winningly, like a pantomime child, and lisped: "I've thought a lot about my Daddy, and I guess he was born bad too."

She brought a box of cigarettes out of her handbag and handed one to Ginger.

"Mildred has been ever so worried about me. She took me to a psychologist when I was in London," she said proudly.

"I've been to a psychologist, too," Ginger said eagerly, "Several. I've been treated."

"I've been treated too," Ivy said, not to be outdone.

114

Ginger ran his hand over his face. This was his favourite subject, the only one, in fact, on which he could be counted to launch forth with a certain amount of animation but clearly to do so now would be to fraternize with the enemy. He restrained himself with a great effort.

"I'm very sensitive," Ivy went on, "I'm different to other people; I can't do with a lot of restrictions and people telling me to do this and do that. That's why I didn't get on at school. They didn't understand me. You can lead me but you can't drive me. Mildred and I have got on a lot better since I was treated. Mildred was a bit nasty about it, she said it was more like her being treated than me. But ever since then she hasn't dared to punish me like she did, otherwise these clever doctors would tell her off. If I'm thwarted, I mean if I don't get what I want when I want it, I get frustrated and when I'm frustrated it upsets my nerves, see? I get," she giggled importantly, "I get hysterical. Ooh, they used to have awful carry-ons with me in hysterics. So I've got to be allowed to go my own way, grow up in my own way was what they said." Ivy paused then heaved a gusty sigh: "Only it's so boring!"

Unwillingly Ginger was interested.

"It was boring in London, living in a hostel with a lot of other women—ghastly! As soon as you went out to try and have a bit of fun you'd get up against the police. They're a smarmy lot, I hate the police," Ivy declared broodingly. "They'd call me every name under the sun, filthy language, really. Then they'd take me back to the hostel, 'escort' me, they called it, and hand me over to the lady supervisor as nice as you please. 'We've brought the young lady back, ma'am!' Very old fashioned! Brr, I hate the police!"

"So do I," Ginger agreed, he, too, had noticed just that touch of hypocrisy about them; in court, with their hats in their hands, they looked as though butter wouldn't melt in their mouths.

"And it's just as boring at home, though I do get decent

food and a good comfortable bed. I'm longing to get away, to *be* somebody."

"Meet a rich husband," Ginger said in a burst of inventiveness.

"Exactly. But can you see me meeting a rich husband in Rivington? There's nobody. There isn't even a chance for a girl in London either. There are too many people in London, too much competition, too may blondes; a girl doesn't get a chance. Is it the same in Paris?"

"I dare say," Ginger concurred.

"I bet it isn't like that on the Riviera, that's where I want to go. I'd like to lie on the sands and go a marvellous brown so my bod is darker than my hair. They don't mind if you lie naked on the sands there, do they?"

"Oh no," Ginger said, knowing less than nothing about the Riviera.

"Well, I'd lie on the sands until some rich dago came along. An Argentino, travelling in meat." Ivy, fascinated by her own rhetoric, gazed dreamily into her cigarette smoke.

"And then what?"

"And then. Well, I'd just go on lying," Ivy gave Ginger what he would describe as 'ever such a look'.

"Maybe," she said, "I'd have better luck on the Lido. What do you think? Venice is smarter than the Riviera now, isn't it?"

"Haven't a clue," Ginger mumbled.

"Dagos always fall for girls like me," Ivy said complacently.

"How do you know?"

"Instinct," Ivy explained, "dagos like flashy cars and women men turn to look at in the street, they've always got pots of money, too; usually they're company directors—and things," she said vaguely, "big business men, sort of idea. What do you want from life, Chad?" She leaned forward so far across the table that Ginger could see well down inside the 'V' of her blouse. He looked hurriedly away in some embarrassment and alarm. He was no philosopher, he had never asked himself

116

what he wanted from life, he was an opportunist, he took what came along, he never looked further ahead than the next five minutes.

"You don't have to worry," Ivy comforted, "you'll be quite well off when Uncle Matthew dies, you and Mildred."

"So will you."

"Me? Whatever makes you think that? Mildred's got the idea that it is bad for me to have money. She gives me a pound a week pocket money and out of that I've got to have my hair done, and buy all my cigarettes and chocolates and sweets and powder and lipstick. She buys my clothes, just my bare clothes, none of the etceteras. She says she hasn't got the money and I honestly think she's pretty badly off. We don't have any maids, only an old woman or so who comes in, and she's frightfully economical with gas and coal. Coal! We never had a fire in the drawing-room once last winter, nor this winter, yet. She says she can't afford it. And look at her car! No, honestly, I think she hasn't a sausage. She will have one day, but I shan't see any of it, believe me!"

Ivy sat back so that Ginger could again look at her without feeling uncomfortable. "You're the one who'll be rich," she looked at him for a long time, thoughtfully, "when Uncle Matthew dies——"

*　　*　　*　　*

"Well, I must get cracking," Ginger said briskly; they couldn't go on sitting there much longer and he did not intend to be the one who paid for the tea.

Ivy pressed out her cigarette. "Where to?"

"To where I'm spending the night," Ginger retorted cunningly. ·

"I'm driving you back to Rivington."

Ginger shook his head. "I told you I'm not going back."

"But I've told you you are."

Ginger looked at her with exasperated dislike. "So long," he said casually.

Ivy stood up. "It isn't any good trying to get away. I shan't lose you. It was a bit of a job following you this afternoon, but I managed it and I'll manage it again. It's no good your trying to give me the slip. The girl's waiting, hadn't you better pay for the tea?"

Longingly Ginger eyed the door.

"Come on," Ivy prompted, "do behave decently, Chad; everyone's starting to look at us." And to the waitress: "The gentleman will pay." Ivy sauntered towards the door with an affected swing of the hips and stood waiting for him. Cursing, Ginger gave the waitress Marie Céleste's second half crown.

"Haven't you tipped her?" Ivy asked as he joined her.

Obediently Ginger went back to the table and slipped a threepenny piece beneath the saucer whilst Ivy watched him disdainfully.

Out in the street she took his arm. "You need me to look after you," she murmured, pressing his arm.

"No, I don't," Ginger declared, "and what's more I'm not coming back with you, get that. Honest, I'm not." If only he had an alternative scheme his protestation would have carried more conviction.

"I warn you," Ivy said firmly, "that I always get what I want, if I want it enough. I want you to come back to Uncle Matthew's cottage. I feel it, somehow, in my bones, that there's a good time coming for us two. I don't know how or what sort of good time but I do know it's coming——"

Ginger was getting impatient and irritable. He shook off her arm. "Cut it out," he snarled.

Ivy stopped dead and faced him. "You'd better be careful," she warned with eyes narrowed. "You'd better not start getting nasty. Don't forget I've got the name of that jeweller. I can go straight to Uncle Matthew and tell him where the snuff box is and who took it there. And how's that going to look? How is Uncle Matthew going to feel about his precious grandson and heir? Think that one over."

Ginger did think it over, following her along the pavement towards the car park.

"See here," he said angrily when they reached the ramshackle motor car. "You're blackmailing me, nothing short. That's what it is, blackmail. It's a criminal offence, what you're doing."

"Criminal offence!" Ivy repeated with an unpleasant laugh. "I like that! What's pinching a snuff box out of a case and taking it along to a jeweller and selling it, I should like to know? The less you say about criminal offences the better!"

She got into the car and patted the seat beside her. "Come on."

Ginger stood by the open door.

"Come on," she said impatiently, "it's no good your stopping to think, you've got to do what I want from now on. *Get in,* I tell you!"

There was nothing for it but to get in, Ginger saw that quite clearly.

Ivy was quite silent for the first ten miles. Birmingham is a confusing town even for an experienced driver; all her attention was required to get them on to the Rivington road. When they were at last rattling along the straight highway Ivy said comfortably: "You feel like killing me, don't you? Someone did try and strangle me once."

Ginger was considerably startled. He had, in fact, been telling himself what he was going to do to Ivy but so far it had not reached strangling-point.

"It was one of those M.D. boys from Rivington Court."

"A what?"

"One of the mentally defectives. I was sitting in the park, just sitting, not doing any harm to anyone. And then, as I got up to go he sprang at me. He'd been watching me from behind a big tree, see?"

119

"What happened?" Ginger asked reluctantly.

Ivy laughed; it was, indeed, more of a snigger. "He was in the sanatorium for a fortnight," she said. "I knocked him right out." She added: "With my knee."

A mile or so further along Ivy said: "So you see, it wouldn't be worth your while trying to do anything to me. I'm twice as strong as you. Besides, suppose you did manage to take me by surprise—say you'd got a cosh in your pocket and you dotted me one with it, then chucked me out of the car and drove off— you'd come to a sticky end, Chad. Much stickier than mine. You'd hang for a certainty. So you'd better not try anything on, my lad."

The wisdom of this was ineluctable. Unwillingly Ginger had to admit to himself that he 'couldn't agree more'.

*　　*　　*　　*

Mildred's Women's Institute afternoon had gone well, a friend offered to drive her home but Mildred, ever thoughtful of her uncle's welfare, asked her friend to drop her at the Lodge so that she might look in and see how they fared. Ivy would, no doubt, bring Chad back to the Lodge before returning home herself, Mildred would wait until they came back from the trip to Birmingham.

They were resting, Marie Céleste in her room, Sir Matthew in the living-room. He was looking pleased and happy. "Come in, dear Mildred."

"Wouldn't you like to go round the garden before tea, Uncle?"

It was drizzling slightly but that was no deterrent. At least twice a week in the winter months Mildred and Sir Matthew went round the garden and as the year progressed their goings round the garden became more frequent until it was a daily event and one which they both enjoyed to the full.

"Well, dear, I had a very excellent luncheon," Sir Matthew

said as they peered at the clumps of herbaceous plants beginning to grow in the border. "I mustn't forget to get some wide-
meshed wire to put over the peonies."

"I'll bring you some, I have plenty. What did she give you
to eat?"

"Oh, thank you dear. I might try putting some over those
big poppies, too. Well, it was some sort of vegetable stew,
quite delicious. And an omelette with jam sauce."

"Hallo! Here's a day-lily appearing right up against the
grass edge. I should move that, Uncle. If only she didn't look
so frail I would feel happier about her."

"A day-lily, so it is! You're right, Mildred; she has a bad
cough, too. I must get the doctor in to give her an overhaul, I
don't like that cough. Yes, I shall move that lily."

"There's going to be much too much of this *aconitum.*"

Sir Matthew peered at the plants. "Do you think so?"

"I do, indeed."

"But that's the *Anthora,* that new one I got, the yellow one,
it's so pretty."

"There's too much of it, in my opinion," Mildred repeated
firmly.

"It's nice to have the yellow flower in July," Sir Matthew
said plaintively, "there's too much blue in the border." But he
always took Mildred's advice. The aconite, or at least, some
of it, was doomed.

"Too like a weed for my liking," Mildred said, "whatever
type it is it's only monkshood, after all. Common."

"Perhaps you're right, dear," Sir Matthew said meekly.

They passed into the rose garden which gave material for
much delightful discussion. Sir Matthew was always gently
teased about his childish impatience to get his roses pruned.
Mildred was of the opinion that they should be left as long as
possible and each year the friendly argument took place.

"I'm sure you made a mistake when you pruned the
Frensham so early last year," Mildred said finally. "I had a

121

great many more flowers on mine and, as you know, I pruned them on Easter Monday."

"Now, dear Mildred, my *Frensham* were a sight last year, a sight! I can't agree that yours were any better."

Mildred smiled. "Very well, we'll get the vicar to act as referee this year."

"I shall prune the *Frensham* next week," Sir Matthew said, firmly.

"Very well, dear, and I shall leave mine for another three weeks."

"I'm not very happy about Chad," Sir Matthew said, glaring down at his *Frensham* rose plants.

"In what way, dear?"

"I think, between you and me, Mildred, he's a bit of a ne'er do well."

"I had wondered——"

"Too much of his father in him, perhaps. I may be wrong. If only one could talk to him one would get a much better idea. These French young men. Do you remember the Free French we had in the village during the war?"

"Do I not!" Mildred laughed at the recollection.

"They're so completely different from our own young men. I—er—I must confess I don't know how to take Chad."

"It's the language difficulty, I'm sure," Mildred said comfortingly.

Sir Matthew stooped and tugged out a plantain. "Perhaps in time we shall understand each other. I don't want to make the mistakes I made before, with Martin. I realize that a great deal of the trouble with Martin was my own fault. I was too intolerant, I expected too much of the boy. Old age has its compensations, Mildred, my dear. Now, what am I going to do with this bed this year? Definitely not zinnias again."

"No, they weren't a success, were they? But it was partly the weather."

"Partly! It was wholly the weather, nobody can expect zinnias to thrive in a cold east wind."

Mildred, however, had had quite a good show of zinnias. She looked at him laughingly and he smiled back at her; they understood each other perfectly.

Sir Matthew turned back to the empty flower bed. "I'll dig in the hop manure to lighten the soil. I've got an idea for this bed but I won't tell you what it is—you'll disagree. You know, I'm disappointed there is no family likeness."

"He isn't a bad-looking boy. Very French, of course."

"Martin was a fine-looking boy indeed, the best of the bunch, Mildred, as far as looks went."

"His looks didn't get him far," Mildred returned a trifle shortly.

"Chad is not a bit like him in looks, of course, he takes rather after his mother, with that crop of black hair. Bless her, Marie Céleste is the soul of loyalty. I tried to draw her out on the subject. In fact I told her how I was leaving my will. I felt it was the wise thing to do, Mildred. It concerns her very closely. I told her that Chad might expect to inherit a certain amount of money on my death and gave her the opportunity of telling me anything about Chad which I ought to know. But she said nothing. I knew she was hiding something, of course, I feel sure Chad's upbringing has not been straightforward. But I have left things as they are for the present. My own guess is that she has had rather more than teething troubles with him and she brought him over here to get him away from unsuitable companions. I dunno——"

"Something like that," Mildred agreed.

There was a large weed flourishing in the centre of the flower bed in front of which they were standing. Mildred expected him to pounce upon it with angry cries but instead he turned to her and banged his fist into the palm of his hand. "I am determined," he declared, "not to fail my grandson as I failed his father. I have spent a great many years regretting my treatment

of Martin and now, when I have so little time left I have been
granted a second chance, Mildred. This time I shall make a
success of it, I hope."

He turned back to the flower bed, saw the weed and
snatched it out of the ground. Then he forgot he was holding
it in his hand and went on: "Whatever I, personally, may think
of Chad is neither here nor there; I shall do my very best for
him. I am sure that is what your dear aunt would have wished."

"That's jolly decent of you, Uncle," Mildred said; she took
the long dangling weed from his hand and threw it on the
compost heap.

CHAPTER XII

MARIE CÉLESTE awoke suddenly, it was the bells of Saint-
Séverin which had awakened her. Were they ringing out for
Benediction? Perhaps she would go to Benediction, she would
like to hear the priest chanting high and impersonal, she would
like to smell the incense.

She swung her thin legs from under the pale silk eiderdown
and sat up. The sound of the bells ceased instantly. She must
have been dreaming. She was at Rivington; outside the window,
in the English pear tree, a blackbird was singing.

She was aware of an extraordinary feeling of well-being;
she had had a good after-luncheon nap and she felt a great
deal better than she had felt for many weeks. She opened the
window and looked out, sniffing the damp fresh air. Sir
Matthew and Mildred were walking round the garden, they
were always walking round the garden. Marie Céleste was just
a little jealous of Mildred. It was she who should be walking
round the garden with her father-in-law.

What a delightful meal they had had! It was one thing
cooking a meal for Chad—or for Ginger, but quite another to
cook a meal for a real English gentleman. And to eat it with

him. Marie Céleste had been happier than she had been for many years. How happy she and Sir Matthew were going to be! She was going to fill a gap which was badly in need of filling, there was a place for her here and she was going to take that place and fill it to the best of her ability.

Now that Ginger had gone a great load was lifted from her mind. Oh, she wouldn't lose touch with Ginger: there would be ways and means—no need to bother about that now.

Oh happy, happy day!

Marie Céleste tugged on her best black cotton stockings. It was only a matter of time before she, Marie Céleste, would be walking round the garden with Sir Matthew, taking Mildred's place. But for the present she would show her independence, she would go for a walk by herself.

> *"Allons enfants de la Patrie,*
> *Le jour de gloir-re est arrivé,"*

Marie Céleste sang.

It sounded like a cat upon which somebody had carelessly trodden but Marie Céleste smiled at herself in the looking-glass of her dressing-table, took off the large veiled hat which certainly looked ridiculous and replaced it by a white handkerchief tied, peasant-like beneath her chin. If she was going to be an English country lady she must dress accordingly.

She peered out of the front door, it wasn't raining much, just a slight drizzle. It was perfectly foolish, of course, to go out for a walk in the rain but, as everyone knew, the English were mad and if she were successfully to emulate the English she must be mad too.

Mrs. Martin Quest went back into the narrow little hall for her umbrella.

Outside she could turn to the right and go out by the small gate beside the big gates and along the road to the village which, as she knew, lay about a mile along the road. Or she could turn

125

to the left and walk up the drive towards the house. It was quite a pull up the drive, Marie Céleste remembered how great a struggle it had been to get up the drive only a few days ago. But now she felt so very much better that she decided to venture up the drive. *Enfin*—she would like to give a closer examination to Martin's old home.

So up the drive she went, uncertain of gait, unsteady of pace but happy and purposeful. The heels of her shoes were not high but neither were they low, they were designed for the streets of Paris and not for walking upon the moss-grown, neglected drive of an English chateau; her bird-like ankles looked so fragile that the next time her heel slipped and her foot went over sideways her ankle might snap. But it didn't. She tottered on.

The view from the top of the drive was not enough. Marie Céleste wanted to examine the house closely, as it was no longer drizzling she put down her umbrella and rolled it neatly, using it now as a walking stick.

It was, indeed, a very fine house. Marie Céleste had had many surprises since she came to Rivington, the house alone came up to expectations. It resembled a little the mansion which had stood on the outskirts of the village in which Marie Céleste had been born. Looking up at the imposing frontage she remembered herself as a small girl, standing with her face pressed between the iron bars of the gate, gazing at the fine chateau at the end of the drive of ilex trees. She remembered, too, how someone had come out of the lodge and shoed her away. *"Va t'en, Va t'en——."* she could hear the shrill voice as though it were yesterday.

Now, however, she could look at the big house for as long as she liked. But for this and that, small circumstances, she would be mistress of the house. The great porch, the fine oak door, the tall windows, the stained glass . . .

Marie Céleste's heart turned right over; round the side of the house there came Chad . . .

He shambled along in just the way Chad had shambled, the too-long arms swinging, the great head moving from side to side, the small eyes, the loose grinning mouth . . .

There he was, her baby, her boy, a poor thing but her own, her very own.

Marie Céleste ran to him and with small whimpers ran her hands over him. He was warm, he was alive, standing on tiptoe she put her thin arms up and round his neck.

"Hi, there—" there was the sound of running footsteps. It was just like the 'va t'en' of olden times.

"Oh, it's you, is it?" the attendant said. "You're crackers, ain't you, old girl. Come on now, let go of that boy."

Marie Céleste stepped back. It was not Chad, she could see clearly now that it was not Chad. But it was very very like him.

"I shouldn't hang around here, if I was you," the attendant said kindly. "No one's allowed in the grounds, you know. These boys are not to be relied on; you never know when one of them mightn't, well, I mean, you never know."

"What boys?"

"The boys we've got here. They're not a bad lot, mind, don't get me wrong. But just every now and again we get one goes a bit—well——"

As a fearful comprehension began to break over Marie Céleste, she shivered. "Are all the boys—like this one?"

"Yes, they're all M.D.," the attendant said cheerfully. "Nuts. This is the County Council School for Mentally Deficient Boys. Didn't you know, dear? Fine place, ain't it?" But he did not look at the house; he looked at Marie Céleste, he could not look away, though somehow he felt he ought to do so.

Later he said to his colleague: "You know that old girl who created the other day in the porch, name of Quest or something? Well, she was up here again today carrying on like she'd found her long lost son. Gave me quite a turn. But I've never seen such eyes in me life."

The other attendant laughed suggestively. But the first

127

was not amused. "No, honest," he said, "talk about orbs, I've never seen anythink to touch them, I haven't, not on a fillum star, I haven't."

So he could not look away from Marie Céleste and the spell was only broken when she turned and began to walk away from him. Stagger is perhaps the better word.

The other day, he remembered, she had dropped her reticule and her cotton gloves, this time it was her umbrella, it lay unnoticed upon the gravel sweep. He picked it up and hurried after her. "Hey," he said, "you've dropped something."

But she took no notice, she seemed in a hurry. He hooked the umbrella on her arm: "There you are, ma'am," he said but still she took no notice.

The attendant took the arm of the idiot boy. "Come on, lad," he said, "you must get back to your tea. It isn't often you get kissed and hugged by a lady, don't you go and get above yourself now!"

She was sobbing a little as she hurried away and when she reached the turn in the drive she had no more breath left. She sank down against the bank where the rhododendrons grew.

A home for idiot boys! Of all the shocks that Marie Céleste had sustained this was by far the greatest. It was, perhaps, the significance of the whole thing which was so shocking. Chad would have been perfectly happy here at Rivington. He would have been one of many, attended by kind men who were trained to attend idiot boys. Dear Chad, there had been nothing repulsive or harmful about him, he was humble and gentle and grateful. His only fault was that he was always very very hungry. Here, amongst all the other boys of his kind, he would have been one of the best, they would all have liked him and admired the cleverness of his wood-carving. He could have walked in the park and no one would have been unkind to him, shouted after him or thrown gravel into his face. He would have tossed pebbles into the lake and laughed to see the pretty rings they made on the water and no angry park-keeper would have chased him away. (*Va t'en, va t'en!*)

And what was more he would have been in his own park, beside his own lake, treading the turf which his ancestors had trodden. He would have been *at home.*

Maire Céleste had no breath left for sobbing, soundlessly the tears gushed out. She coughed a little and the blood gushed out too. The blood poured from her mouth, just as it had done before, warm and terrifying. She lay against the bank and let the life-blood pour from her.

It was going dark.

And there were the bells again.

Marie Céleste needed her rosary and it was beneath her pillow, miles and miles away, or perhaps it was only a few yards.

Swaying from side to side she went on down the slope of the drive.

She opened the front door of the cottage. There was yet the staircase to ascend, she could just see it through the darkness. She crawled up the stairs and there she was in her pretty bedroom in which she thought she was going to be so happy.

The rosary was beneath her pillow and there was something else there too. Marie Céleste pressed her small possession into the palm of her hand. Then she knelt down beside the bed.

"Our Father . . ."

"Is that you, Marie Céleste?" Mildred called. "We're making tea."

"Holy Mary . . ."

"Come and have some tea, dear. Or would you rather I brought your tea up to you?" Mildred called.

" . . . *pray for us sinners now and in the hour of our death . . ."*

Marie Céleste slipped sideways on to the white bearskin rug beside her bed.

And then she died.

CHAPTER XIII

HER eyes were open but they now had no more light in them than lozenges of black broadcloth; she had torn off the white handkerchief that she had worn peasant-style round her head and used it to assuage the blood; it lay beside her now on the floor.

It was Mildred who found her. She called Sir Matthew and together they lifted her on to the bed.

Mildred closed the eyes, whimpering: "Poor dear, poor dear, I thought from the first that she was ill. Look, Uncle, she has had a hæmorrhage. That cough of hers! Oh, poor dear. Here is her rosary——"

And here, too, was something else. It fell from her hand as they lifted her on to the bed.

"Look what she was holding in her hand."

It was the little wooden donkey which Chad had carved.

"It is a toy of some sort," Sir Matthew examined it.

"Well, I never!" Mildred exclaimed.

Sir Matthew put it in his pocket. "We must get the doctor at once. This is a great shock, Mildred, she seemed so lively at luncheon, busy all the morning in the kitchen——"

"But she was very ill, you could see that——"

The doctor diagnosed death following hæmorrhage from pulmonary tuberculosis. He did not sign a death certificate but hurried away to inform the coroner, saying that a post mortem might be necessary but that he would try to avoid having one if possible.

"This is going to be a dreadful shock for Chad," Sir Matthew said, "how are we going to tell him, Mildred?"

"Leave it to me," Mildred said.

"He will be very upset, poor boy."
"I wonder . . . ?"

*　　*　　*　　*

In fancy both strangled and brained with a tyre lever, in fact very jauntily conscious that she had the upper hand, Ivy brought Ginger back 'home'.

His mind having been given wholly to the consideration of Ivy's sudden demise, Ginger had not been paying attention to more important matters, viz, what he was going to say to Marie Céleste, how he was going to explain his return to her. It was possible that during luncheon she had prepared Sir Matthew for his non-return. She had told Ginger that she would let Sir Matthew know that he was restless and anxious to find a job so perhaps she had, in her impetuous way, already told the general that Ginger would not return from Birmingham.

What was he now going to say? How was he going to convince Marie Céleste that his return was inevitable without telling her the miserable truth?

He sat in the car, biting his nails.

"Go on, get out," Ivy said.

Mildred called from a window. "Ivy, I want you a minute."

Ivy could see Ginger's face dimly in the light from the dashboard; she looked at him for a moment, then she turned the ignition key in the lock, put it in her handbag and got out.

"Hallo, Mildred," Ginger heard her say, "what is it?"

The front door shut.

So she didn't trust him for a moment.

Ginger thought of a string of corrosive names for Ivy; such thought needed less effort than concerted planning and had an almost soothing effect.

The front door opened.

Ginger heard: "I'll tell him."

"But why you? *Ivy,* come back!"

Ivy came running round the corner of the cottage and out

into the road. She opened the door of the car. "Something awful's happened," she hissed: "your mother has died."

Ginger turned his face to hers, she could see clearly even in the dim light, that it wore a look of complete non-comprehension.

"Pardon?"

"Your mother—she's dead!"

Still Ginger did not understand.

"Get out," Ivy said firmly. She took his arm and pulled him out of the car.

Mildred was waiting in the hall, her lips were moving, she was practising her French. Ivy propelled Ginger up the steps and inside the narrow brightly lit hall; he stood blinking from the light, trying to pick up the threads of the complicated and insecure existence which he had, only this morning, left for good. He was French, he must remember, he was Chad Quest—and then, suddenly, the awful implication of what Ivy had been saying to him broke over him. "Crikey!" he exclaimed, his expressions were ever inadequate. He pushed past Mildred who was mouthing: *"Votre mère est mort, la pauvre femme——"* and rushed up the stairs to Marie Céleste's room.

Her spirit had now been gone long enough for all traces of its troubles to have left Marie Céleste's face. Ginger looked down at her face, it was smooth and young and almost smiling.

Wherever Marie Céleste might be she was not there and she had gone without him. Ginger felt an unbearable loneliness; he flung his arm across the slight form, buried his face in her side and burst into passionate weeping.

It may be that his tears were for himself, but, whatever may have inspired them, it was the first genuine full-blooded emotion he had ever felt and as such is worthy of record.

Mildred tiptoed up the stairs after him and looked into the room. Quietly she shut the door and came down to Ivy and Sir Matthew standing in the hall. Ivy had lighted a cigarette and was leaning against the banisters looking, to put it mildly, cryptic. Her look, in fact, was so great a change from her habitual expression of boredom that Mildred shot her a few sharp glances. She told herself that to have allowed Ivy to drive Chad into town had been as unwise as she had realized it to be at the time; she knew, also, that Ivy would have gone whether she had given her consent or not and for form's sake she liked to retain some fragments of authority.

"Well?"

"Poor boy. He's very upset."

"What are we going to do? Are we to announce the death in *The Times,* Mildred?"

"That would be absurd. To whom would it be of any interest?"

"She was Martin's wife."

"My poor Uncle. You naturally want to do the right thing, but it would be quite absurd to announce her death. I suppose people who know us *do* know of her existence but, surely, it is of little interest? The people who knew Martin as a child and a boy are either dead or too old to care. It's all very ancient history."

"You are never too old to care, Mildred," her uncle said suddenly. "Well, she shall have a good resting place."

"Not in the family vault!"

"Certainly. She was Martin's wife, must I repeat it? And a very, very nice woman."

Nice. Mildred considered the adjective, it was not one that she, personally, would have used. She was not sure, however, what adjective she would have used with reference to Marie Célèste other than 'poor'.

"Very well, dear," Mildred concurred meekly, leaving 'after all, it's *your* family vault' unsaid.

"What are you going to do about Chad?" Ivy put in.

They both turned to her and there was a moment's silence.

"Do about him?" the general repeated vaguely.

133

Ivy watched the smoke rising from her cigarette, she was enjoying herself immensely; it was pleasant to be in possession of information they did not have, it gave her a feeling of extreme satisfaction.

"You'll keep him here with you, won't you, Uncle?"

As a rule Sir Matthew endeavoured to ignore the existence of Ivy, more often than not without success; he had got over the period of wincing whenever he caught sight of her, now he simply put up with her so long as she did not take up Mildred's time, the time, that is, that Mildred must devote to him. As Ivy grew older she took up less and less of Mildred's time and it was for this reason that she was tolerated.

"I can't say. Chad must do as he pleases; he is, after all, adult."

"But there's the language difficulty, you can't talk things over with him, can you?"

Sir Matthew stirred uneasily.

"I can explain things to him," Mildred said.

"What things?"

"I mean—I can cope with him," she corrected herself.

"But you must have some sort of plan," Ivy declared.

Plan. Sir Matthew glared at her. He didn't like plans—or planners.

"What has Chad been doing in town today?" Mildred asked sharply. "I understood there was something about a job in the air."

"He went after a job, but he didn't get it."

"Did he indeed," Sir Matthew growled, "what sort of job?"

"I haven't a clue," Ivy said airily, "I only know he didn't get it."

"That's funny," Mildred said sharply, "how did he hear about the job? Has he any friends in England? It's all very mysterious."

"I'm only too pleased to hear the boy wanted to find work, it seems a good sign," the general said.

134

Ivy was smiling rather unpleasantly, she made her elders feel slightly uncomfortable.

"Well, Ivy," Mildred asked, "what plan have you got for Chad?"

"I can't understand why you and Uncle Matthew don't see it. It seems obvious to me. Uncle Matthew's got no one to look after him; Mrs. Angel is *not* here much more often than she *is* here. I should make Chad stay and do the cooking. He's a French boy, after all, and all Frenchmen are good cooks. From what you've told us, he's tossed up some quite good meals for you."

"That's no job for a man," Sir Matthew snapped, but was instantly aware that he had spoken those words before, with reference to artists, it was a very long time ago but those exact words. "Housework! Dear me, no!"

"Cooking."

"Ridiculous idea," Mildred declared, "a young man like that wouldn't be satisfied here at Rivington employed as cook to his grandfather. You're a silly girl, Ivy."

She knew, of course, why Ivy was taking up this line, she wanted to have Chad about the place. All the young men in the district now gave Ivy a very wide berth; she had a very dull time; consequently she wasn't going to let Chad go without some small struggle. But Mildred was uneasy. She didn't like the look of Ivy at all.

"Ivy," she snapped, "did you have your hair done this afternoon?"

In the ordinary way Ivy would have thought up a ready answer to that one; as things were, Ivy's mind had been pretty well occupied.

"As a matter of fact—I didn't."

"Obviously not. What were you doing?"

"As a matter of fact—they couldn't take me." Inspired suddenly she said: "I was learning French."

"From Chad?"

135

From Chad! What an idea! Ivy laughed, or rather she began to laugh but remembered that Marie Céleste lay dead upstairs and stopped.

"No, not from Chad. I went to the public library and looked up a French conversation book. I learned quite a lot."

No one believed her, of course, but Ivy was complacent, she felt she had not done at all badly.

*   *   *   *

No conscious effort that Ginger could have made would have influenced Sir Matthew and Mildred in the least, but his evident distress at the death of Marie Céleste impressed them favourably.

"He seems to have been very fond of his poor mother," Mildred observed, "he looks quite shattered. Dr. Sands is coming back to talk to him about Marie Céleste's state of health. I hope it won't upset him even more."

"How can he talk to Chad about her state of health," Ivy asked. "Can he talk French?"

"I expect so. Most young people can nowadays," Mildred said, meaningly. "Chad will have to give him all the help he can, we must try to avoid a post mortem examination if possible."

"Why?"

"Don't be silly, Ivy. Post mortems in the family are always unpleasant. It means a coroner and possibly an inquest and all that sort of thing. Dear me, what an upset this all is."

Ivy lost no time in conveying the information to Ginger.

"Dr. Sands wants to talk to you about your mother's state of health," she said when they were alone in the sitting-room.

"Whatever for?"

"You can tell him if she's been ill before, and how long she's been ill and that sort of thing."

"Well, he can't talk to me," Ginger snapped.

"No, he can't can he?" Ivy reflected maliciously. "As soon as you opened your mouth he'd know there was something badly wrong somewhere. What are you going to do?"

"Tell him to go to hell."

"That'll be a lot of help!"

Ginger said nothing, he always found it easier to keep quiet than to talk. Ivy, however, was as voluble as ever. "Aren't they fussy? You've got to have a form filled in when somebody dies saying what they died of. Dr. Sands says he won't fill it in till he's sure. So he's bringing another doctor along to examine her, the body I mean, and they're going to ask you all about how she was before she came here."

Ginger nervously ran his hand all over his face. "What happens if he doesn't sign the form?"

"It's got to be signed, otherwise she can't get buried."

"But suppose they don't find out what she's died of?"

"Haven't you ever heard of post mortems? Cutting up dead people to discover what they've died of? That's what they do."

Ginger looked horrified. "That's only when someone's been murdered, or something."

"Don't you believe it! If they don't decide any other way what she died of they'll be cutting up your—her—to find out."

"Cutting up——" Ginger felt the twinge of altruistic feeling that he had felt once or twice before.

"Yes," Ivy said pleasurably, "horrid, isn't it?"

"They're not so fussy in France," Ginger declared, "you can die sudden there without they get busy with their questions and their knives."

"Oh, can you?" Ivy said with great interest.

"Yeh," Ginger grunted in an attempt to terminate the conversation, "you can."

"Well," was Ivy's comment, "this isn't France, it's England and we're a lot more fussy here and quite right too. You never know."

Know what? Ginger looked at Ivy with narrowed eyes. She was asking for it, was that girl, simply asking for it.

"Yes, you never know," Ivy repeated comfortably.

"Look," Ginger said. "I can't talk to those doctors."

"They'll probably be able to talk French to you," Ivy said, "Mum says they will, anyway."

Ginger winced. And then he thought.

"Look," he said. "I don't want to talk to the doctors about Marie Céleste."

"Marie Céleste? Do you mean your mother?"

"Of course. I don't want to talk to them about her. I'm too upset. It's my nerves. Look, you'll have to talk to them for me. You can tell them she's been ill for months, see? She's had this blood from her mouth twice before. The doctor in Paris said it was consumption and that it had gone too far. She never took no care of herself, see? She should of gone away to a sanitorium, see? But she didn't."

"Why?"

"Why?" Ginger repeated irritably. "I dunno why. Last time she was so bad they fetched the priest and he said prayers and the like. She was as good as gone. But it didn't seem she was ready to die, no one was more surprised than me when she got better. You should of seen her, lying there half dead one day and the next day up and about," Ginger drew in his breath with a long hiss: "She was a marvel, and no mistake, a bloomin' marvel."

Ivy said: "You want me to tell them all this?"

"Well——" Ginger gesticulated feebly.

But Ivy liked to prolong the agony. "I don't see why you can't tell him all that yourself."

"Come off it," Ginger said, "you've just said yourself that as soon as I opened my mouth they'd guess there was something wrong."

Ivy examined her finger-nails. "Well, there is a lot wrong, isn't there?"

Ginger grabbed hold of her wrist.

"Ow, leave go, you're hurting me."

"Hurting you! It'd take a lot to hurt you. Listen to me, you'll talk to those doctors for me and tell them all I've told you, or else——"

Ivy squirmed with delight. This was a great improvement on the indifference which hitherto he had shown.

"You wait and see!" Ginger had seen a Japanese murder film in Paris and had been delighted by the villainous expression on the face of the bad man of the piece. He assumed now what he thought a good imitation of the expression on the face of the Japanese murderer going into action. Ivy roared with laughter.

"You're barmy."

Again Ginger rubbed his hand all over his face. "It's you that's driving me nuts."

Ivy walked across the room from the chimney piece in front of which she had been standing to the little marquetry table with the glass top. She stared down at it. "I can't think why the disappearance of the box hasn't been noticed. It goes to show what a lot Uncle thinks about his possessions."

"What are you doing?"

Ivy had raised the lid and her hand was inside the table-top. "Don't worry. I'm not being as stupid as you were. I'm only moving the other things a bit so that the gap the snuff box has left isn't so noticeable." When she had finished arranging the objects to her satisfaction she put down the lid and came over to Ginger: "You don't seem to realize what a tricky position you're in. You can't threaten me. You've got the whole position the wrong way round. It's for me to say: 'You'll do what I tell you—or *else*—' not you. See, my lad?"

She allowed a small pause for effect and went on: "Just so's you've got that quite clear."

Ginger grunted.

"I can quite understand you don't want the doctors nosing

139

about your private affairs. I'll fix it so's you're left in peace."

"How?"

"I don't know how, but somehow. Leave it to me."

Ginger regarded her with dislike and suspicion.

"I'll fix it somehow. But remember, I don't do anything for nothing."

"What do you want?"

Ivy fidgeted with the ornaments on the chimney piece. "I don't say I want anything. I'm just reminding you——"

*   *   *   *

As it turned out the amount of help Ivy gave Ginger in the affair was negligible.

Marie Céleste's firm belief that *'les choses s'arrangeront'* was justified in this instance by herself. During the meal she had prepared and eaten with Sir Matthew, she had told him that she had been very ill; she had, in fact, given him a short history of her illness which he passed on to the two doctors who found that Marie Céleste's condition was that of advanced pulmonary tuberculosis and signed the death certificate to that effect.

During the doctors' visit Ginger remained in his room and though Ivy was hovering about in the hall and on the stairs she was given no opportunity to intervene.

Afterwards Sir Matthew said irritably to Mildred: "I wish you could find something for that girl to do."

"Give her a chance," Mildred said defensively, "it's not easy to find work in a place like this."

"I don't mean here. Why can't she go up to London and go after jobs until she gets one?"

Mildred's mouth tightened. He knew perfectly well why; all this had been said before.

Mildred had always defended Ivy; at first she had done so out of genuine affection for the child but latterly she had been defending her own misjudgement in adopting Ivy at all. She clung pathetically to the belief that plenty of affection, a good home, good food and persistent kindness would, ultimately, defeat the devil in Ivy. She had always passionately upheld the theory that it was environment that counted and, though her belief in it had become a little frail, she persisted.

"I am not convinced that London is the place for Ivy. I am watching the advertisements in *The Lady;* I feel sure that something in the country, a nice suitable job as secretary-companion to some titled lady, will turn up soon."

Sir Matthew made a sound that was not quite a snort and a little more than a sniff. "She'll never settle down in the country, anyone could see that." He did not say much more because he knew that Mildred was acutely sensitive where Ivy was concerned; he added, simply: "I shouldn't stick at a titled lady, either," and left Mildred to form her own conclusions as to his meaning.

CHAPTER XIV

FUNERALS. Ginger, looking out of the window of the hired car, thought of the rows and rows of graves in the Cimetière d'Ivry and of one new grave in particular. He wondered how long it took to prepare a head-stone and whether the head-stone bearing the name *Matthew St. Chad Quest* had been erected above the grave. He was not given to reflection of any sort but Marie Céleste's death had shocked him out of his normal and every now and again great waves of self-pity broke over him.

A Roman Catholic priest had been procured for the obsequies and the hag-ridden little body of Marie Céleste now lay, in a fine coffin, beside the ancestors of her husband who had himself received a pauper's burial. It lay in the musty-smelling vault amongst the silent spiders. Outside the winter

141

winds would shriek round the little old church, snow would silt up against the graves, daffodils would press up into the spring sunshine, bees would hum over the wild thyme and the scabious, the leaves would gently fall from the trees in the autumn mists but inside the vault nothing visible would change, not even in the air.

Somewhere, however, Marie Céleste's spirit was ranging around, an entity of which the properties, whether of love and compassion or of furious impatience, were indestructible.

The mourners were Sir Matthew, Mildred and Ginger; Ivy had been excluded. The local undertaker had supplied an ancient but splendid Rolls-Royce for their conveyance; it was equipped with a black bear-skin rug, silver trumpet-shaped vases, ladies' companion, inset ash-trays and movable arm rests; it smelled a little like the vault where they had left Marie Céleste's coffin. It had once belonged to a dowager countess who, whilst travelling, had been able to take furtive peeps at her toque in the strip of looking-glass in the centre of the partition between the driver and passengers. Ginger, sitting in one of the two central seats, felt the urge to bring out his comb and run it through his hair, but, remembering Marie Céleste, he resisted, contenting himself with a glance in the looking-glass. What he saw caused his attention to congeal; terror poured all over him like ice-cold water.

His hair was growing.

On either side of his parting was a small line of new hair; it was as distinctive as a glimpse of a fox in the thicket. At present there was not more than a millimetre of fox-coloured hair but it was there all right, and as surely as night follows day the millimetre would become a centimetre and the centimetre an inch.

Ginger closed his eyes and thought Marie Céleste's least-favourite oath: . . . no peace for the wicked, no time to think what he was going to do next, no time to make careful plans!

He had known, of course, that his hair would grow and that

in time the rich black would give way to the natural auburn, but he had not known how things were going to turn out; Marie Céleste's death, in spite of the overhanging threat, had been the last thing he had expected; he wasn't prepared to carry out their combined plans on his own. He felt lost, bewildered and deserted. And now, on top of everything—his hair, precipitating action which he was not ready to take. He must get to hell out of here before his hair grew much more, he told himself. What with that and the language difficulty the whole thing had got beyond him now that Marie Céleste was no longer there; with her anything was possible, without her—nothing was. With her he felt a certain pride, a slight confidence in himself as the rightful heir to the Quest so-called fortunes; without her he knew himself to be a shuddering, cringing impostor.

"I wonder how old she was," Sir Matthew said, "I should like to know in order that the wording on the stone may be uniform with all the rest."

"I think it's a mistake to put ages on grave-stones," Mildred said. "I hope you won't put my age on mine, Uncle."

"Upon my word, Mildred; how foolish! All the Quest women have their ages on their graves."

"What possible interest can it be to anyone? Anyway, I'm not a Quest woman."

Sir Matthew put his hand affectionately on her knee. "My dear," he said, "I sincerely hope that when the time comes to decide whether or not your age shall be recorded on your grave-stone, I shall not be there to give an opinion."

Mildred leaned forward and tapped Ginger on the shoulder; deep in his unhappy thoughts he started violently. *"Quelle âge avait'elle, votre mère?"* Mildred enunciated carefully.

After the time he had spent in Paris Ginger couldn't help understanding a little French, even Mildred's; he shrugged his shoulders and grunted something like *"sais pas."*

Mildred turned back to Sir Matthew. "He doesn't know."

"She was a good deal younger than Martin," Sir Matthew

143

mused, "she looked on the old side, but on the whole there was an extraordinary youthfulness about her."

"You can't tell with French women," Mildred said.

"I'll have to leave out her age," Sir Matthew decided, "and simply have the date of her death. 'Marie Céleste, beloved wife of Martin Quest, died so-and-so'."

"You couldn't do more," Mildred declared.

"Not now," Sir Matthew sighed, "I could have done more, but not now."

"You're coming back to me for tea," Mildred told him, "I hope Ivy has made up the fire in the study, it's turning cold again, and I hope she has remembered to put the scones in the oven; we all need a little warmth and comfort."

*   *   *   *

Mildred and Ivy were overhoused; the house was large and shabby and untidy; it was also draughty and cold. After the death of Lady Quest it had been suggested that Sir Matthew leave the cottage and live with his niece but the idea had been rejected for three reasons. The first because the house was undoubtedly uncomfortable, the second because it obviously could not comfortably contain both Sir Matthew and Ivy and the third reason was the gardens. Mildred was devoted to her garden and with the help of two jobbing gardeners she had made it very delightful indeed; she could not bear the idea of allowing Sir Matthew to share her garden, nor would Sir Matthew even contemplate the idea of leaving his own. So they compromised, each keeping their own establishment and Mildred visiting her uncle daily.

Mildred's house was called The Rookery; the rooks had left long since and the elms in which they had built had been cut down but the house still retained its name because Mildred could not think of another.

The hired Rolls-Royce turned in through the gates of The

Rookery, crunched round the gravel sweep and stopped at the front door.

Ivy opened the door and bounced out of the house; her face was not suitably arranged for greeting a party of people returning from the funeral of a near relative. She appeared to be considerably elated about something.

Contrary to Mildred's expectations a good fire was burning in the study and the tea table was laid; they crouched round it, holding their hands out to the blaze, their faces softened in the light of the leaping flames. The chilly vault, so silent and so dark, seemed a very long way off.

* * * *

"I don't know whether to tell you now or wait till Uncle Matthew's gone," Ivy said when she could no longer contain herself. "But the offer of a job's arrived."

"Oh splendid!" Mildred exclaimed with enthusiasm. "That's topping. I'm so very pleased, Ivy dear."

"Um. I can't start straight away. I mean, that is, if I get it."

"It isn't all fixed up then?"

"Not exactly. I've got to go for an interview but I don't think——"

Mildred exclaimed impatiently: "I thought from the way you spoke that the whole thing was arranged."

"I wouldn't fix up anything definitely without your consent, Mildred," Ivy said sweetly.

Mildred froze with apprehension; when Ivy was in this mood the worst was imminent.

"Where are you to go for the interview?"

"London."

Heavy silence.

"London, dear?"

"Yes," Ivy groaned. "I wish I'd waited till Uncle Matthew's

145

gone. It's going to be two against one. It's going to be just like it was last time."

"It's not another modelling job, is it?" Mildred asked sharply.

"No," Ivy compressed her lips. The modelling incident caused her pain even to contemplate.

"I want Uncle Matthew here," Mildred said firmly, "I need some support when you start talking about the job you want, Ivy. You've had a perfectly good secretarial training, I can't think why you don't really want to take that sort of job."

"There's more money, more opportunities in the sort of job I'm looking for," Ivy said.

"You'd better tell me the worst," Mildred sighed.

"You won't like it——" Ivy told her.

Ginger crumbled his warm scone; he was not following the conversation nor did his eyes turn from one to the other, but something of what was happening penetrated his already overburdened mind.

"I answered an advertisement. Oh damn!" Ivy exclaimed, "I wish I didn't have to tell you all this."

"How can you expect me to give you your fare to London and back if I don't know what it is all about?" Mildred asked.

"That's just it," Ivy said angrily. Then she added: "I hope I won't need the fare back."

"Hadn't you better see the letter she's had?" Sir Matthew suggested gently. He was infinitely sorry for Mildred; he sensed that she was anxious as he to allow Ivy to leave home but equally determined to do the right thing and not allow Ivy to go where she pleased and to get herself into any and every sort of trouble.

"Here's the letter," Ivy said, "they're Jews, that's enough to make you say I can't go."

"That's not quite fair," Mildred said, "I did object to the letter you had from the man who wanted you to go as model to his wholesale firm, but this seems a pleasant enough

146

letter, Ivy. It simply says they will be pleased to see you for an interview next Thursday. I don't know the address but the writing paper is of quite good quality."

Tensely, Ivy explained. "You weren't supposed to reply by letter but I had to and I sent a photograph. They must have liked the look of me."

"Let's get down to facts," the general said testily. "What is this job?"

From beneath the cushion of a chair, the time-worn place to keep literature of the kind Ivy read, by girls of Ivy's ilk, she brought out a weekly stage paper. In a column of small type advertisements one was heavily scored in pencil. Sir Matthew slowly sought his glasses case and put on his glasses. "Now, let me see it."

Ivy handed it to him, mutely pointing to the advertisement.

Sir Matthew read it aloud, he started with the enthusiasm of a town crier but tailed off apologetically:

WANTED, 3 girls for Semi-draped and Posing; one girl strong in body and arms to hold 11 lbs in weight. Auditions, Thursday, April 15th, 2.0 p.m.—501B Charlotte Street, W.1. (3rd. floor) Auditions in bathing costume. Blubberstein.

Ginger looked up from his plate of crumbs; he glanced from Sir Matthew to Ivy and from Ivy to Mildred, then he put his hand up to his mouth to hide something that was very like a smile.

"I'd be the one holding the weight, see?" Ivy pointed out.

Sir Matthew made a very general-like noise, clearing his throat with an important rumble, like the sound of distant guns.

Mildred, unable to believe what she had heard, snatched the paper from Sir Matthew and read the advertisement herself.

"Who is this Mr. Blubberstein?"

Silence. Evidently no one was prepared to vouch for them as the Gloucestershire Blubbersteins.

147

"It might be a Mrs. Blubberstein," the general murmured helpfully.

Mildred again scrutinized the advertisement. "It doesn't say what object weighing eleven pounds you might have to hold, Ivy."

No one could accuse Mildred of unfairness; she was always scrupulously fair and she demonstrated the truth of this by giving her careful attention to Ivy's project.

"Eleven pounds isn't a great deal," Sir Matthew pointed out, "it could hardly be one of the other two semi-draped girls she would have to hold up, ha ha!" But it was not the moment for laughter; Sir Matthew instantly tried to make up for his lapse by serious application to the subject at issue.

"A vase, perhaps," Ivy suggested.

"A vase," Mildred exclaimed in horror.

"Grecian, sort of thing."

"Quite harmless," the general interposed.

"Well, well," Mildred exclaimed bitterly, "it is a little hard that one should make sacrifices to send one's daughter to the best girl's school in England in order that she may follow the career of standing on a stage, semi-draped, holding a *vase*."

"Well, what would you like me to hold?" Ivy exclaimed impatiently.

The general again cleared his throat; he was in a very tricky situation indeed. He, personally, felt that for Ivy to stand upon a stage, semi-draped, holding a vase or anything else, would be eminently suitable and a good time had by all, particularly by himself and Mildred who would get on very nicely indeed without Ivy's continual demands upon Mildred's attention. But on the other hand he clearly saw Mildred's point of view.

"Don't be impertinent to your mother, please Ivy," he said, "she is doing her best to help and advise you in this matter."

Ivy looked sulky.

Mildred said: "I intended to put an advertisement in *The*

148

Lady to help you find a pleasant post in the country——"

"But I don't want a post in the country——"

Sir Matthew interrupted sternly: "What you want, my dear, is not relevant. Please remember you are still a minor, you can't do just as you please until you are twenty-one. You are an infant in the eyes of the law; your mother is responsible for you and you have already shown that you are incapable of looking after yourself in London. Naturally she is anxious that there should not be a repetition of past occurrences."

Ivy gave a very gusty and elaborate sigh. "I knew this would happen." She looked resentfully at Mildred. "You know what that last doctor in Harley Street told you?" She turned to Sir Matthew: "He said it was definitely bad for me to be frustrated, he warned her——"

"I forbid you to talk like that!" the general said sternly, angry at last, "if you had had a few good whippings when you were a child, things might have been very different!"

"There you go," Ivy said, "it's shockingly out of date to talk like that. You think I'm afraid of you, but I'm not."

"I should let her go to London, Mildred," Sir Matthew said, "perhaps Mr. Blubberstein will be able to put the fear of God into her."

Mildred's eyes were closed, her face looked immeasurably tired.

"—or even good wholesome fear of Mr. Blubberstein," he added as an afterthought.

Perhaps the continued use of the inept surname decided her but whatever it was Mildred seemed suddenly to make up her mind.

"I can't possibly allow you to go, Ivy. I should never forgive myself, never."

"If what?"

"If—if I were to allow you to get mixed up with people like that."

Ivy held her head and moaned: "People like what?"

149

"Don't argue, Ivy. Uncle, please support me in this matter."

The general drummed his fingers on the arm of his chair. He was plainly disappointed. "Your mother is right, Ivy. Heaven knows, one tries to be broad-minded these days and up to a point one succeeds, but upon my word broad-mindedness seems to me to have been carried so far that it has no bounds at all and becomes a sort of marginless swamp. Sloppy-minded, that's what we are all asked to be and I dare say I have become as sloppy-minded as the rest. I don't see why you should not fare as well, semi-draped, under the guidance of Mr. Blubberstein as you would anywhere else but I respect your dear mother's feelings in the matter. She really has your good at heart, you know, Ivy."

In the nick of time Ivy caught back a very rude word indeed.

*　　*　　*　　*

Funeral or no funeral, a visit to The Rookery without a walk round the garden was unthinkable. Mildred and the general went out in to the garden though the light was failing and there was a cold wind; 'the young people' were left to clear away the tea things and wash up.

"You see," Ivy said, when the elders were out of earshot. "It's damn well hopeless." She almost hurled the tea cups on to the tray. "What a silly fool of a woman, she hasn't a clue, she just hasn't the slightest clue. She's so stupid that I could kill her, honestly, there are times when I could kill her! Stupid, stupid, *stupid*! How I hate stupid people!"

Ginger said nothing; he was content, for the moment, to have attention deflected from himself; meekly he followed Ivy into the kitchen and helped with the washing-up whilst she raved on, banging the china down on the draining-board as though she were trying to break it. At last he said: "Well, if you feel like that about it why don't you go?"

Ivy turned on him like an angry cat. "Go, how the hell can I?"

"Can't see why not."

"You're almost as stupid as her. You can't do anything, not anything, without money. It's the only thing that makes life worth living."

Ginger agreed there.

Ivy went on: "Why can't everybody have their share of money? It's not fair the way some people are born with money and others aren't. They're always making a fuss about the increase in crime, well, let them give a fair share of money to everyone, I say, and then there wouldn't be any crime."

"You're not a Tory, are you?" Ginger observed.

"Tory? Of course I'm not, I'm a blooming anarchist, I believe in down with everybody—except me." Her outburst having made her feel a great deal better, Ivy's ill-humour began to recede, she even giggled a little. But Ginger did not see anything to laugh at; he had his burning anti-Tory light in his eyes and if it had not been that he was afraid Mildred and Sir Matthew might overhear him he would have launched into his usual tirade about Tories and snakes and so on. He contented himself with the simple understatement that he was not a Tory either.

Ivy eyed him speculatively. "Have you any money at all, Chad?"

"Not a sausage."

"What about the money you got for the—you know what?"

"You know how much I got for that."

"You shouldn't have accepted that jeweller's offer. I'm sure it was worth more. You didn't bargain with him at all. I could have kicked you for accepting. I should have, in fact, if I hadn't been so intrigued."

Intrigued! What language the girl used; Ginger couldn't make head or tail of her.

"That's all the money you've got, is it?"

Ginger said nothing, he resented her possessive attitude towards him. Ivy dried her hands on the roller towel, she made

a lengthy process of it, pushing down the cuticles of her finger-
nails and stopping for frequent examination of them.

"I want fifty pounds to do the thing properly," she said
"that would pay my fare up to London, buy me a new rig-out
put me up at a decent hotel, stand some taxi fares and leave
me with some over so there was nothing to worry about. If
you're going after a job like that you want to look someone
I'm absolutely certain I could get that job if I go the right way
about it, and once I got the job I'd be independent of Mildred
and Uncle Matthew and everyone. And it would lead to things
Don't imagine I want to stand holding a blooming vase up for
the rest of my life, but I'm keen on what it would *lead to,* see?"

She looked up from her hand-drying. "You've got to get
that money for me."

"How?"

"Somehow," Ivy said, compressing her mouth. "You know
how it's done."

Ginger said nothing. He lit a cigarette and pulled nervously
at it.

"Look what I've done for you," Ivy said. "I don't know
where you'd have been if it hadn't been for me."

"I don't see's you've done much," Ginger said sulkily.

"Don't you, indeed? You didn't have much trouble from
the doctors, did you? If it hadn't been for me you'd have had
to see them both and tell them all about your mother's illness,
like I told you. As it was I fixed that for you. You'd have looked
pretty ridiculous if I hadn't. What would they have thought?
Sir Matthew Quest's grandson, supposed to have spent all his
life in France, turning up with a Cockney accent you could
cut with a knife. Honestly, if it hadn't been for me I don't know
where you'd be, certainly not tucked in cosily at Rivington
Lodge! So you owe me something, see?"

"I don't owe you nothing."

"Are you stupid, too? What about the snuff box?"

"What about it?"

"I've only got to go to Uncle Matthew and tell him it's gone——"

"So what? He doesn't like you, anyone can see that."

"You *are* stupid. You know perfectly well I've got the name and address of that jeweller, I've only got to tell Uncle Matthew where his precious snuff box is——"

So that was how the position was, was it? Ginger rubbed his hand over his face nervously.

"Look," Ivy went on, "since I got this letter from this man Blubberstein this afternoon, things have changed for me. I only want to get out of here. I only want to have the money and beat it. It's no life for me here, I hate it and I hate Mildred, she's so stupid. I don't think much of you, either. Now I've had that letter I don't give a damn what happens to you. I know you're a thoroughly bad egg and I guess your mother brought you over here as a last resort to save you from something or other, I don't care what, *except*—" Ivy paused and there was a wickedness in her deliberation which caused Ginger to shiver, "—except that I shall tell Uncle Matthew *and* the police everything I do know about you, *unless*—" she paused again, "—unless you produce some money for me pretty damn quick. Now you've got it in black and white."

Black and white! Ginger slouched round the kitchen table, cigarette hanging from his lip. Black and white. Black and auburn! He took his comb out of his pocket and stood in front of a small looking-glass combing his hair, peering nervously at himself.

"Look," he said at last, running his tongue over his dry lips. "I don't want to stay here any more than you do, it's no place for me. I—I'd go back to Paris if I had the money, that's what I'd do."

He felt a sense of relief, he had never thought of returning to Paris until the words were out of his mouth, but once he had spoken them he realized that that was what he wanted to do, the only thing, in fact, that he could do. He would go back to

153

the flat in the Rue des Mauvais Garçons; it was so short a time since they had left it that it would still be in Marie Céleste's name; the Duflos would keep it faithfully in readiness for her return so long as they believed that she would return. Going back to the Rue des Mauvais Garçons would be like getting back a little of Marie Céleste.

"And what's more," Ginger went on, his brain working furiously, "if you start any of your funny stuff you'll mess up everything between me and the old man."

"That's what I intend to do, ass!"

"Worse than you think. He's made a will, see?" Ginger lowered his voice to a mere hiss, "He's left all he's got between me and your foster-mother, see? If you start monkeying about you'll dish up all that."

"I see—e—e—" Ivy returned, she was whispering too now, and she drew out the E of see so that Ginger gritted his teeth with irritation.

"I want to get out of this dump a lot more than you but it's got to be decent, see? If the old man takes a dislike to me, I've had it. So I've got to act decent."

If Ivy said 'I see—e—e—' again he would hit her.

She did.

But he didn't hit her, he hadn't the nerve.

CHAPTER XV

BITING his nails helped his brain to work; Ginger bit and bit but no amount of biting solved his problem.

The general at once settled comfortably into a master and servant relationship with Ginger; he found a normality about himself and Ginger alone at the little lodge that he had not found when Marie Céleste was there, making the party three. Ginger did the cooking because if he had not done so there would have been no meals prepared; Sir Matthew gardened morning and afternoon and read *The Times* in the evening. No doubt he reminded himself from time to time that 'Chad' was his grandson and not his servant but the fact that he could not converse with him seemed automatically to put him into the batman range and often Sir Matthew had to stop himself on the very edge of telling his 'grandson' to stand up properly, not to slouch about and to address him as 'Sir'.

There was no variety about the food, Ginger cooked only what he had watched Marie Céleste cook and made no experiments of his own. He made black coffee and omelettes and cheese *soufflés* and vegetables *à la creme* and fried potatoes and an occasional pot roast of the fragment of meat which the butcher sent. He ate his meals alone in the kitchen and the general, after consideration, allowed him to do so, for he liked to study horticultural catalogues at meal times, and, what was probably more important, he did not like Ginger's table manners.

The general telephoned his order for provisions so Ginger had no shopping to do; he had, in fact, literally nothing to do between meals but bite his nails. When he had bitten them right down to the quick he started on the skin round his nails and when he had bitten that until his fingers were painful he combed his hair, peering fearfully at the dread line that was his dead-line.

Once, just once, he crept into Marie Céleste's room and buried his face deeply into her old fur coat but afterwards he tried hard to forget that he had done so.

For twenty-four hours after Marie Céleste's funeral, Ivy had left him alone but in the early evening of the following day she turned up. Sir Matthew was mixing weed-killer in the yard outside the kitchen, making a wholesome clatter with watering cans.

"Well," she said, "have you thought anything up?"

Ginger, a cigarette hanging from his lips, was scraping

155

carrots, his white hands and his long thin fingers looking like incongruous visitors to the sink. He shook his head.

"Then you may be pleased to hear that I have thought of something."

Ginger shrugged his shoulders apathetically.

Ivy looked out of the window at the bent back of the general, stooping over his task. "I can't tell you here, you'd better come outside; we'll go for a walk."

Very deliberately, almost insolently, Ginger finished scraping the carrots and put them in a pan on the gas stove.

"—!" Ivy swore unhelpfully, "what a fool you look!"

Ginger swung round on her but she stepped back quickly to avoid the blow which might, but did not, ensue.

They went out of the front door and turned left up the drive, the way Marie Céleste had started joyfully on her last walk. The drive, it may be remembered, sloped up between the high trees and the rhododendron bushes until it came out into the open and fell away down another gentle slope to the great house which lay in a sheltered hollow of the park. At the point where the drive came out into the open park the grass was dry and springy; it was a pleasant place to sit and look down at the house and at the stables. It was, in fact, a point of vantage.

They sat down within a few yards of the spot where Marie Céleste had lain, bleeding to death.

"Now look," Ivy said, "I'm sure you know a damn sight more about house-breaking than I do so I needn't go into details but I'll tell you where there's plenty of stuff you can lay your hands on."

Ginger looked at her with extreme dislike, her amateurish gangster-language fell uneasily upon his ears. "Stuff?"

"Stuff, or whatever you call it. Jewels, if you like. There's an old woman who lives in a great big house over there, about a mile away. You should see her when she goes out, she's always covered with pearls and diamonds and what-have-you.

156

She's got some servants, but no husband or relations living with her. I guess it wouldn't be difficult to get hold of some of the jewels. She's often had burglars, as a matter of fact, but she seems to have plenty of jewellery left. They say that at the Hunt Ball, at Christmas time, she looked like a Christmas tree, absolutely covered with sparklers. She's simply asking to have some of it taken off her; no one's any right to all that, least of all a hag like Mrs. Bellamy."

"You'd best go and help yourself," Ginger suggested sulkily.

"Not me, my dear boy, you."

"Certainly not me," declared Ginger with finality.

"But why not?"

Why not? Because Ginger was not that sort of thief, he was a sneak thief, a small-time pick-pocket, he had neither the brains nor the courage to organize himself into committing a full-blown house robbery. He had often assisted in small ways but he had never actually broken into and entered a house, he had not the nerve.

The jobs he had taken on had always been ones from which he could extricate himself rapidly if anything untoward were to happen.

"Why not? Because I couldn't get rid of it."

"You didn't have any difficulty in getting rid of the snuff box!"

Didn't he, indeed.

He said: "Look, you've got to know a regular fence before you try that sort of game."

"I bet you know plenty of fences."

"I do, but not in this part of the world. There's many a good reliable fence knows me in London. But in Birmingham—gawstrewf, what a hole!"

"I've thought it all out," Ivy said, "I'd help you. Mildred knows Mrs. Bellamy quite well, I could call there just to talk with the old woman. I've never done it before but it wouldn't surprise her too much if I did. I could have a good look round

157

and maybe I might succeed in leaving a window unlatched, or something, I don't quite know what but it would depend on the opportunity."

"Don't go on harping," Ginger told her. "It's out, see? Out."

"What? Just because of getting rid of the stuff?"

"Yeh. You've got to get rid of it quick. It's no good hanging on to it. None of the big boys keep it more than a few hours. It's hot, see? An' the sooner you get rid of hot stuff the better."

"What a pity," Ivy said, "what a stinking pity!"

"Pity's the word. It'd be a pity if I got myself landed with a lot of hot stuff I couldn't get rid of."

Ivy was by no means without brains, now that it had been explained to her she saw the point clearly. She pulled a blade of grass and put the end of it in her mouth, chewing it reflectively. There was a long pause. They both stared at the great block of Rivington Court. It was a beautiful mellow evening, the sun was going down behind the trees and the house lay in the sunless hollow as irritable and frustrated as Ginger himself.

"It's a hell of a house," Ivy said, "I don't wonder your father left it and never wanted to come back."

His father? Oh, yes. Martin Quest.

"I never liked it," Ivy went on. "It gives me the willies. Uncle Matthew and his wife lived there all during the war, you know. I used to have to go there a lot when I was home from school. How I hated it. For a long time there were crowds of children there, kids from the streets of Birmingham, evacuees. But I wasn't allowed to play with them. I used to go up to the attics and ride on the old rocking horse your father and his brothers used to play with and then I got ticked off for making myself dusty. You never saw anything like those attics. Dust! They were filthy! They were all cleared out at the sale they had and now they've been modernized with hand basins and electric light and used by the attendants. Oh my hat, I've got an idea!" She turned to Ginger. "I knew I'd get an idea. It's the secretary. She's a hell of a woman, never stops talking."

"What secretary?"

"The secretary of the institution, of course. The woman who runs the office which is the old library. There, do you see, there?"

She pointed to one of the many off-shoots from the rest of the house. It was connected to the main house by a Gothic isthmus; it might have been a billiard room or a ballroom.

"That's the library, now the offices. She works there and there is another room down below where they keep all the records and where the secretary's two typists work. She lives in." Ivy's eyes narrowed, her mind was bounding ahead of her, she could scarcely keep up with it.

"Listen, Chad, listen." It all came out as automatically as a lesson learned by heart. "Her name's Miss Brock, or something, I can't remember, but it doesn't matter. Every week on a Friday morning she goes off to Birmingham on the bus and everyone knows exactly what she's going for because she tells everyone, whether she knows them or not. She never stops talking, see? You've never met such a damn fool, she takes a case with her and says she's going to get money out of the bank and all the way back she chatters about it, hoping that no one will 'do her in'. I don't know how much it is, she's never said how much it is, as far as I know, but the way she goes on it might be millions! Actually," Ivy put her head on one side thoughtfully, "actually I don't suppose it's more than about fifty pounds. She pays the gardeners and the cleaning women and the kitchen hands." Ivy did a little mental calculation; "Yes, I reckon it would be round fifty pounds. Then when she gets back she puts it all in little envelopes and hands it out to the staff."

"How do you know all this?"

Ivy grimaced. "How do you think? I had to work there for a month. Mildred made me. Ugh, how I hated it. They advertised for a shorthand typist and Mildred said it was just the thing for me. She was wrong. Miss Brock, or whatever her name is, had Mildred up to her office after a month and told her what she thought of me." Ivy sniggered, "So I don't owe her anything. She's a perfect beast."

"Fifty pounds," Ginger mused.

"Just what I reckon I need."

"You'd get half of it."

"How damn mean of you."

"I need money more than you, as a matter of fact," Ginger stated simply.

"You don't. You're sitting quite pretty, scraping carrots and generally being the good little grandson. I've got to have the money, otherwise I'll go raving mad and do something really— *something*!"

"You don't need fifty pounds," Ginger pointed out, "all you've got to do is to go up to London and get the job you want."

"And you don't need fifty pounds to get you to Paris," Ivy retorted, she threw away the chewed bit of grass and said: "Here we are, squabbling about the fifty pounds when we haven't got it."

"Nor anything like it."

"It might be more than fifty pounds, it might be less."

"We'd best agree to halve it whatever it is."

Ivy leaned back, her hands behind her, pressed palm downwards into the grass; she was in what she felt rightly to be a seductive attitude. "You'll do it, won't you? I knew you would." She sighed voluptuously. "What a pity you're made the way you are. We'd have made a marvellous couple, you and I."

"In what way?" Ginger asked nervously, edging away from Ivy. Given time, time to get Marie Céleste out of his system, Ginger might well find Ivy to his taste. But he did not want to.

"You know what way," Ivy said modestly.

Ginger looked at her and quickly looked away.

"Well, what have I got to do with the secretary person?"

Ivy followed her immediate train of thought. "You could make love to her, I bet she'd be only too pleased. That's why she's always talking about being attacked by a man. She'd be thrilled!"

"Of all the damn silly ideas," Ginger said scornfully, "you mean kiss her and such?"

"Um."

"What then? Is she going to give me the money as a tip?" There was no trace of humour in the remark, Ginger glared angrily at Ivy.

"Oh, you've no imagination!" Ivy exclaimed impatiently. "I can see you'd make a hopeless mess of that kind of thing. Well then, if you can't do it *nicely* you'll have to do it some other way."

"What way?"

"Follow her from the bus, at a distance, and where the path goes through the coppice come up behind her and—and—er——"

"And what?"

"Dot her one."

"You mean—hit her on the head?"

"Yes, cosh her."

"Gawd blot me out! What a female! Bloodthirsty, that's you. Do you want me strung up? That would be murder, that would."

"Not necessarily. You needn't hit her hard."

"Just tap her on the loaf, then," Ginger sneered, "and have her turn round and face me!" He whistled through his teeth. "I'd have to finish her off so's she wouldn't know me in an identity parade. Nope, I'm not getting meself strung up for murder, ta a lot!"

"There's no need for that!" Ivy said patiently, "I tell you the thing would be perfectly easy. I'll give you the time of the bus she'll arrive on, you follow her until the path goes into the shrubbery——"

"That's the tradesman's entrance where all the vans go up," Ginger said, remembering the lorry driver who had given them a lift.

"No, not that. This I'm talking about is just a pathway, over the stile and into a bit of woodland and then it comes out into the open, over there, see? It's not much used except in the evening when the attendants go down to the village for a drink. In fact," Ivy said thoughtfully, "there'd be no need to touch her. You could nip up behind, snatch her bag, dive into the undergrowth and hide. She'd probably scream her head off but that wouldn't do you any harm."

"She'd see me; if she saw me it'd be all over. I'm not going to risk the old man finding out—about me. He's not likely to leave his money to a bag-snatcher even if he is his grandson, anyone could see that."

Ivy sighed with exasperation. "You'd have nipped off amongst the bushes before she'd any idea what had happened. Then you could run for it before they started a search. Honestly, Chad, it's worth doing. You'd have a case of lovely, lovely money. Nice clean notes straight from the bank."

"New notes?"

"Straight from the bank," Ivy crooned dreamily.

"Fresh new notes they've got the number of," Ginger said sarcastically. "Brand new notes! A lot of good they'd be to us! Nope, there's nothing doing there! You'll have to think up something else, my girl!"

*   *   *   *

Ivy lost her temper suddenly. "What a twerp you are! You're far too choosey for a person in your position. I've told you over and over again, I can't put it clearer, what your position is. I've warned you! You don't seem to get hold of it.

162

Well, now there's a time limit. I mean to go to London after that job on Thursday and I can't go without money and by money I don't mean just two quid for my fare, leaving me a couple of bob for lunch at Lyons Corner House. I mean real money because this time, though they won't know it, I'm going away for good; if I don't get off with Blubberstein there'll be somebody else, the opportunity is far too good to miss. You've got to get money for me, Chad. You can, all right, don't go on pretending to be a softy and shuddering at the idea of being 'strung up'. You're tough and so am I. And I mean it, this time. You'll get me the money, or some money in time for me to go on Thursday—*or else* ——"

CHAPTER XVI

EVERY now and then Mildred had an idea and because her flow of ideas was not frequent she treated them with respect. Other people, too, treated them with respect because they generally concerned the well-being of others and one knew from experience that Mildred pressed on to the fulfilment of her idea, sweeping aside all difficulties with cheerful abandon.

This time her idea concerned Chad. His mother's death had upset him considerably, anyone could see that, it was written plainly on his face; the boy looked ill.

He was serving a useful purpose at Rivington Lodge cooking for his grandfather whilst Mrs. Angel was away but it wasn't by any means a full-time job and a young man like that, Mildred knew, was only happy when fully and usefully occupied. If she were only able to talk things over with him she might be able to discover what sort of work he fancied. However, that difficulty was easily overcome. Mildred had a friend with whom she had been at school who had been fortunate enough to be sent to a finishing school in Brussels. She could speak French fluently. She lived in a small town a few miles from Rivington. Mildred would arrange to take Chad over there to tea and Mildred's friend would have a long chat with him and find out what his inclinations were.

When Ginger arrived back from his walk with Ivy, Mildred's car was outside and Mildred was regaling Sir Matthew with the glad tidings of her idea. Sir Matthew, having attended to the weeds on the paths to his satisfaction, was now dealing with certain plants in the border. He listened to Mildred but did not cease to work, passionate gardeners are always a little detached.

"—don't you agree with me, Uncle?"

"Splendid idea, dear Mildred. Just the thing."

"The boy is obviously willing and anxious to please us," Mildred went on, "but it's no life for him here at the Lodge all day long."

"I quite agree."

"If he were to have even a part-time job."

"What sort of thing were you thinking of? There isn't much hereabouts for a young man."

"Why not agricultural work?"

The general considered. Great as was his respect for Mildred's ideas he could not see Chad working as an agricultural labourer.

"Well—anyway——" Mildred said cheerfully. "I'll leave it to Dorothy. She'll be able to ferret out something. He'll have to have English lessons before he could do any sort of office work. If he were to do a little part-time agricultural work and at the same time learn English, in a correspondence course perhaps, his time would be nicely filled."

Sir Matthew grunted; this was by no means the most difficult to envisage amongst the ideas that Mildred had had in her time.

"Good for Dorothy!" he said encouragingly.

"I say, Uncle old thing, aren't you being a bit drastic with that aconite? Have you taken a dislike to it, or what?"

Sir Matthew was forking out pale-coloured roots, shaking them free of soil and laying them on the grass. "I'm re-planting some of these over at the end of the border. The colour is too unevenly distributed, too much yellow at this end. But there's far too much of this aconite, help yourself, Mildred, help yourself."

"I'm not too keen," Mildred said, but no gardener can resist gifts of plants; she picked up one root and held it in her hand. "Then you think I should fix up a meeting between Chad and Dorothy?"

"By all means, it's a very good idea indeed."

Ivy came out into the garden.

"Hallo, dear," Mildred said, "I've had such a splendid idea about Chad."

"What is it?"

Mildred told her.

Ivy sniffed. "You're always trying to get people jobs."

"People? Only you—and now Chad. Young people, dear.'

"Why don't you pay attention to the sort of jobs people want, not the sort of jobs you think they should have?"

"Ivy! Don't speak to your mother like that."

"Well, it's true, Uncle. I want to go after this job in London more than anything I've ever wanted. And I'm not allowed to. Now that you've forbidden me to do that you're starting on Chad. You'll never get him working for a farmer. He isn't the type."

"I didn't ask your opinion, Ivy. I told you my idea thinking you might be pleased."

"Why on earth should I?" Ivy sloped away, deliberately slowly.

Mildred tck tck-d with her tongue against her teeth.

"She's gone straight to tell Chad," Sir Matthew said, looking after her as he leaned on his spade.

"Tell him? How can she tell him?"

"I've an idea Chad understands more English than we give

165

him credit for. I think he's too shy of speaking a word, but I know he understands what we're talking about. I'm sure of it."

Once out of sight of her elders, Ivy leaped into the house. Ginger had lighted the gas under the saucepan of carrots and was now raising the lid to look at them. As Ivy bounded into the kitchen he shied; he was tired of Ivy, he had had more than enough of her. She was getting on his nerves.

"Do you know what?" she whispered joyfully.

"Mildred is taking you over to see her old school friend Dorothy. She can speak fluent French and she's going to get Dorothy to have a heart-to-heart talk with you about what *you're going to do.*"

Ginger, lid in hand, stared at her uncomprehendingly.

"I mean what job you're going to take up! Job, idiot! *Job,* ever heard of it?"

Ginger opened his mouth to say something. It stayed open. Mildred's step was heard in the yard outside. She appeared at the kitchen door.

"Ah Chad! *Vous êtes lar! J'ai une idée——*"

She went on with what might have been Exercise Number Eight from 'French Without Tears'. But Ginger took no notice of what she was saying.

He was looking at what she held in her hand.

*   *   *   *

"Mon idée aye——" Mildred droned on, but Ginger was, momentarily, no longer there.

He was standing with his coat collar up, waiting outside the little old post office, there had been a chilly breeze but it was sheltered now in the small garden. He was watching Marie Céleste. She was on her knees, scrambling in the earth, she was digging away with a small trowel and running the earth through her fingers, not caring how dirty they were becoming. One, two, three, four, five, six; she examined each carefully before she put them in her basket and covered them with the primrose plants. Then she had stood up. The cold wind had caused her nose to run slightly, she had rubbed the drop from it with the back of her grubby hand and then she had wiped the soil from her hands upon her skirt. There was an awful implication in what she did and Ginger was irresistibly attracted by her every action. The scene was engraved upon his memory far more vividly than were his present surroundings.

* * * *

She had said they grew into a blue flower.

Sir Matthew had told Mildred that they were yellow, a special type of aconite.

The root which Mildred held in her hand was sprouting, for the year was more advanced.

But Ginger knew one thing with absolute certainty. In the whole of his curious short life Ginger had never been certain of anything but he knew now without the slightest shadow of doubt that the root Mildred held in her hand was of the same species as that which Marie Céleste had dug up that day in the *villégiatures* outside Paris, the root, the direction, disintegration and final digesting of which Ginger knew every minute detail.

Yes, he knew all about it, everything except the name.

* * * *

The store cupboard was immediately outside the kitchen door in a short dark corridor. Ginger opened the cupboard and peered inside. It was too dark for him to see the labels on the jars, tins and bottles so he switched on the light in the passage. Again he peered, shifting the jars about. He had seen it somewhere. There was jam and ginger, pepper and mustard, salt and cloves, pickling spices and vinegar, coffee and ground rice, mustard pickles and—yes—a jar of grated horseradish.

167

Horseradish, that was it. He had not been able to remember the name but now suddenly it came back to him. *Raifort* or horseradish! Marie Céleste had evidently been right, English people liked horseradish sauce with beef; there was the jar partly used and another unopened.

Ginger took both the jars out of the store cupboard. He carried them into the kitchen and put them on the dresser.

* * * *

Though it was nearly midnight Ginger was not asleep. He had heard the general come up to bed some time ago. A nightingale was throbbing in a nearby tree like some lovely harp. Beyond wondering why that blooming bird was making all that racket at that time of night, Ginger took no notice; he lay in an agony of restlessness. He heard the broken twigs rattling against his window the first time she threw them but he did not get up, he had no doubt at all that it was Ivy and he had had more than enough of Ivy for the present.

The ubiquitous, the omnipresent, the altogether clinging Ivy stood outside and frowned up at his window. One of the two casements was open, Ginger was not prone to fresh air during the night but tonight the weather was warm.

"Bother!" Ivy exclaimed, the mild exclamation falling grotesquely from her lips. Four times she threw a handful of gentle twigs but at her fifth attempt to get Ginger up the missile was half a brick. The first time it hit the wall below the sill and fell into the flower bed beneath from which Ivy retrieved it. At the second throw it fell on to the floor of Ginger's bedroom with a considerable bang. Ginger leaped to the window and hissed: "Do that again and I'll strangle you. Do you want to wake—everybody?"

"I will do it again if you don't come down," Ivy whispered back.

It was not a dark night; though there was no moon, some

of its light had diffused through the curtain of cloud which covered it. Ivy stood just below the window which was not far from the ground. Ginger held the half brick in his hand. There was no more than, perhaps, three yards between himself and Ivy, he could easily have hurled the half brick straight into her upturned face if something in his nature had not prevented him from doing so. It was not caution or prudence which held him back but that curious streak of gentleness, that reluctance to be cruel that had annoyed him by its appearance in the past, as, for instance, upon the occasion of his meeting with Chad in the Luxembourg Gardens when a child had thrown a handful of gravel into the idiot's face.

Ivy, blandly aware of the danger in which she stood, said: "You'd better come down and talk. There's something you've got to hear. Go down and unbolt the back door."

There was nothing for it but to do as she requested. Ginger pulled his trousers on over his shirt. In spite of Marie Céleste's instructions he could never remember to put on pyjamas when he went to bed.

"You've got to do something," Ivy said, as soon as he let her in by the back door. "You've got to do something quick, or you've had it. Now she's got that Dorothy person coming over to lunch tomorrow and you're to come too, and Dorothy is going to have a nice long talk to you in French, ha! ha! and find out what you're keen to do and then you're going to be found some sort of job."

"What the hell have you wakened me up in the middle of the night to tell me that for? I knew about Dorothy, you told me yourself."

"I didn't tell you when this meeting was to be. I didn't know myself but I heard Mildred fixing it all up on the phone this evening." Ivy changed down, as it were, into a lower gear. "If I were you I'd get away from here. I wouldn't let that woman Mildred mess up your life, Chad, honestly I wouldn't. Look what she's done to me. She thinks she's saving me from

169

a fate 'worse than death' but if she only knew it, it's the life she's planning for me that's 'worse than death'. And it'll be the same with you if you stay and let her organize you like she's organized me." She came very close to Ginger. "Let's both run away, let's both get out of here together. They won't miss us, really. There'll be a hell of a hoo-hah to begin with, but they'll be pleased we've gone, really. They only want each other's company, she and the old man, and their blooming gardens and a peaceful life. We're juvenile delinquents, you and me, it's hopeless our trying to mix our lives up with theirs." Ivy sighed voluptuously. "Thank God I've met you, Chad, we were meant for each other, you and me. We speak the same language."

The hell we do, Ginger thought. Ivy pressed her warm softness against Ginger; he was as unresponsive as a lamp post but he felt a fluttering of alarm, he didn't know how long he might remain unresponsive. There was something very seductive about Ivy at this time of night, in the semi-darkness. He hadn't any nails left to bite, his comb was in his jacket pocket upstairs, there was no gesture he could use to give himself moral courage. He ran his hand nervously all over his face, a sign that he was cracking.

A sort of animal warmth emanated from Ivy, her soft breasts were pressed against him, her hair was tickling his chin.

"Cor!" Ginger exclaimed, "Gimme a cigarette!"

"What a shame you don't love me, Chad," Ivy crooned, putting her white arms round Ginger's neck.

There are limits, no doubt, even to the endurance of a lamp post. Ginger didn't exactly stoop to kiss her, her mouth was right there.

In the dark, they say, all cats are grey. But even Ginger knew that it was not so. Ivy wasn't bad, not at all bad, but to kiss Ivy after kissing Marie Céleste was a dreadful anti-climax. It was like drinking grenadine after Chateau Yquem, though Ginger did not, in fact, use the analogy. He pushed her away

peevishly and somewhere, perhaps, that which was left of Marie
Céleste laughed a little . . .

Ivy, still in the kindergarten of love, was not displeased.
"You see? We were meant for each other, you and me, like I
said."

"Fer Gawd's sake gimme a cigarette," Ginger repeated.
Ivy had not any cigarettes, nor had he.

"What are you going to do, Chad?" Ivy asked.

There was a long pause. Then Ivy appeared to change the
subject: "Do you know that if Uncle Matthew was a baronet
instead of a knight, when he dies you'd be Sir Chad Quest."

"Fat lot of good that would do me."

"Sir Chad Quest——" Ivy murmured dreamily.

"Yeh. But he ain't a baronet."

"You're the last of a long line," Ivy went on. "And haven't
I heard about the Quests ever since I can remember! You're
something, you are. A Quest. You oughtn't to fool around,
Chad. Don't you realize? You're the last of them all. And yet
you're just a common gutter-snipe, aren't you?"

Gutter-snipe! What a horrible expression!

"Just because you're a Quest they won't see it. Isn't it
pathetic! And as for me, I came from an orphanage, even
though I am an adopted daughter of a niece by marriage of
the Quests, they never forget that and they've never let me
forget it. It's different for you. You're one of the lucky ones.
Born a Quest! What more could anyone want?"

Ginger experienced a sudden burst of intelligence. For once
he had listened intently to what Ivy was saying.

Outside the nightingale was pouring out its notes which
flowed over the night like chilled hock over a parched throat.
It was the time for confidences.

"What more do I want?" Ginger repeated. "I want money
and so do you, Ivy. You'll get it all right."

"Me. How?"

"Blubberstein, or whatever his name is. You're going to

171

get lots of money what with your shape and your—your——"

"And you?"

"I've told you. I'm getting half the general's money. Half of it! It comes to quite a lot."

"But he isn't dead," Ivy said, "and you can't get any money until he is dead. What are you going to do till then? Are you going to slouch around the place making omelettes and scraping carrots until he dies?" Ivy paused. "And you're not going to be able to keep it up. You haven't been here as long as three weeks yet. You may have to be here years!"

"I can cope with the general all right," Ginger said, "but it's Mildred——"

"Pooh, Mildred! I've told you she's so stupid, awfully stupid."

*   *   *   *

Mildred stopped the car some fifty yards down the road. The silence which occurred when she switched off the engine was quite dramatic. The nightingale, which had paused for breath, started another stanza.

Mildred listened, sitting quite still. How tired she was, how hateful it was to have to get out of bed in the middle of the night, wakened by some small sound, to see if Ivy were sleeping in her room. But Mildred had the courage of her convictions, she was sure that in time the good that she knew was in Ivy would prevail; only she was getting a little tired of it all, she was too old to career about the countryside at this time of night, improperly dressed in pursuit of an erring child.

The nightingale's notes were true, pure, clean—Mildred hated her own instinct which had led her here to look for Ivy. She very much hoped that her instinct would prove to be faulty and that there would be no sign of Ivy near Rivington Lodge. She had taken the precaution, nevertheless, of stopping the car some distance away so that the sound of it would not herald her arrival.

Slowly, a little reluctantly, Mildred got out of the car. It was mean of her to come here to find Ivy, it was mean of her to suspect the worst. Perhaps Ivy had got up and left her room to sit out on a windy hillock and dream girlish dreams, as Mildred herself had done when young. But in spite of this premise, Mildred was glad she wore her crêpe-soled shoes as she approached the cottage orné.

Sneakers, she thought, here I am creeping about in sneakers in the hope of finding Ivy—anyway, finding Ivy.

She tried not to feel a sense of relief that no light was shining and the cottage was in complete darkness. That didn't prove anything, of course, it could, in fact, indicate The Worst. Mildred, hating herself, walked round the side of the cottage to the back and looked up at Ginger's bedroom window.

Then she noticed that the kitchen door was not closed. It was unlike Sir Matthew to retire without locking up.

There was a low murmur of voices.

Beating back her honourable instincts Mildred stepped closer and even as she strained every nerve to hear what was being said her mind was more occupied with her own defection than by what she heard. She could not, in fact, hear what Chad was saying, he mumbled, running his words into each other. But Ivy raised her voice slightly and at last Mildred forgot that she was a Ladies' College girl acting dishonourably.

"—You oughtn't to fool around, Chad. Don't you realize you're the last of them all? And yet you're just a common gutter-snipe, aren't you? Just because you're a Quest they won't see it. Isn't it pathetic! And as for me, I came from an orphanage, even though I am an adopted niece by marriage of the Quests; they never forget that and they've never let me forget it. It's different for you. You're one of the lucky ones. Born a Quest! What more could anyone want?"

Mildred could not hear what Ginger said but she heard Ivy again: "But he isn't dead and you can't get any money until he is dead. What are you going to do till then? Are you

173

going to slouch around the place making omelettes and scraping carrots until he dies?"

And then: "Pooh, Mildred! I've told you she's so stupid, awfully stupid."

Mildred did not want to hear any more, what she had already heard had beaten her to the ground, like great hammer blows. She crawled away.

The nightingale was quite silent now, perhaps he, too, had heard what had been said and had been shocked into silence. There was not a sound in the night as Mildred went back to her car. Then, just as she got into the car a single ugly noise was dropped into the stillness. It was a night-jar. It shouted: *"Stupid!"*

"What was that?" Ginger hissed.

"What?"

"I thought I heard somebody around."

"Maybe Uncle Matthew has heard us."

Ginger was fussed now, Ivy was going to mess up everything with her foolish midnight visit.

"—I hope he hasn't," Ginger swore. "You'd better get cracking. It'll be all up with me if we're found together at this time of night."

"It won't be Uncle Matthew," Ivy said with one of her sudden flashes of perspicacity, "he'd do anything rather than have a scene. He loathes me and even though he respects you as a Quest anyone can see he doesn't like you much. So I don't suppose he gives a damn what we're up to."

"He might think we're housebreakers."

"Housebreakers here in Rivington! Not very likely. Anyway, I don't think he'd care much if we were; he's not so very keen on his property; he hasn't noticed that snuff box has gone yet."

"Mildred may notice you've gone, what then?"

"Not she. She's fast asleep dreaming about the zinnia plants she ordered. Do stop nagging, Chad, it's decent of me to take

174

the trouble to get out of bed and come over to give you the
low-down on what's going on. If you're not going to bolt, what
are you going to do?"

"Well, talk about stupid," Ginger said, "it's you that's
stupid with your talk about going away together. That'd finish
me off with the old man once and for all, you can see that much,
surely?"

"What are you going to do, then?"

"Stop keeping on asking me what I'm going to do! Mind
your own business, see? And leave me to mind mine."

"Oh," Ivy was hurt, "after all I've done for you!"

"I didn't ask you to do anything for me."

"All right," Ivy said briskly, "all right," and there was a
great deal of sinister implication in the way she said the two
words. "We'll see you at lunch tomorrow, then. Today, that is.
Mildred and me and you—*and Dorothy*! Ta ta, Chad!"

CHAPTER XVII

DOROTHY! Wasn't life quite complicated enough without the
additional worry of *Dorothy*? Ginger went back to bed but not
to sleep. He lay awake and watched the darkness melt gradually,
like ice cream melts, into daylight and when it was full daylight
he got out of bed, dressed and went out into the garden. He
walked slowly up and down the border. He'd recognize that
root anywhere but would he recognize the shoot? How could
he tell in what part of the border the plant grew? He might dig
up half the plants in the border before hitting on the right one.
If he'd only been able to take a better look at the one Mildred
had taken away with her he might have recognized the green
shoots when he saw them agin. Marie Céleste had known which
plants grew where in that small post-office garden. She had
seen the flower growing in the summer so that, in the early

spring, when nothing was showing above the soil, she had known unerringly, where to find the root.

Up and down, up and down Ginger walked. He didn't know what he was going to do with the root but he was fascinated by it; he had to find it.

The border was in excellent fettle, there were no weeds, the plants grew decorously; some of them, like the hairy poppy plant, covered with coarse wire netting to keep them from becoming untidy. Later on the border's behaviour would be less well regulated as the year advanced, but at the moment everything was under control; the soil had been lightly turned so recently that there was not even any sign of the place from which the general had removed the roots the previous day.

Sir Matthew, watching out of his bedroom window, was delighted to see his grandson in the garden, looking at the flower beds. He had not so far shown the slightest interest in the garden. Perhaps Mildred was right, perhaps, in spite of appearances to the contrary, Chad would be interested in work of some sort on the land. He watched him turn away from the flower beds and go to the vegetable garden. He was a long time in the vegetable garden. The general had done his shaving, carefully, as he always did, with the cut-throat razor he had used for well over half a century, before he saw Chad come out of the vegetable garden and walk slowly back towards the house. Was the boy looking for something?

Yes, he was looking for something. And that which he was seeking he found. The compost heap was the last place Ginger would have expected to find the roots, but there they were; with the exception of the one Mildred had taken, all the tubers which the general did not want he had thrown on to the compost heap.

Unobserved now, because the compost heap was out of sight of the windows of the cottage, Ginger picked out five of the tubers and took them into the house. He scrubbed them under the cold tap as he had seen Marie Céleste do. Then he dried them. Then he found an old carrier-bag into which he put the clean dry roots. Then he hung the carrier on a hook behind the door of the small larder.

He had to keep to the pattern.

*   *   *   *

After breakfast the general came into the kitchen for a look round. He did this every day at the same time and immediately afterwards he went to the telephone in the hall and rang up the village stores, ordering provisions which he thought would be required. He saw the jars of horseradish at once.

"Hallo," he said, picking one up and looking at it. "Mrs. Angel's very keen on horseradish sauce." He didn't seem to expect Chad to understand but he kept up a pleasant running commentary whilst he was in the kitchen, possibly to gloss over the awkwardness of the situation and to make Chad feel more at his ease. "It's meat day today, too, isn't it? Um." He turned to Chad and said, in the loud, clear tones he used when addressing him: "Do you know how to make a sauce of this?"

Ginger nodded, his eyes sliding away first to right and then to left.

"Let's have it tonight then; we've had such shocking bad meat lately, a good dollup of this strong stuff disguises the taste. Ha ha, what?"

The meat would be delivered at the door; in the meantime Ginger would prepare the vegetables. He found an old black iron saucepan in which the meat would be cooked and then he prepared the vegetables exactly in the way he had watched Marie Céleste prepare an identical meal. As he performed all his actions his mind was as near a blank as it is possible for a conscious mind to be. He did not ask himself what he was doing he simply continued to follow the pattern. When his mind was not blank it was not active but passive; he was, as it were, watching a flat still picture or series of pictures, like lantern

177

slides thrown upon the screen and the pictures were always scenes from the living-room in the Rue des Mauvais Garçons. So vivid were these pictures that Ginger lost all sense of the present; it was his defence mechanism dealing with a situation which was beyond him.

When the vegetables were prepared and ready for the addition of the meat Ginger emptied the contents of the partly used jar of horseradish into a basin and stirred in salt, mustard and vinegar. Dreamily he stirred . . .

*　　*　　*　　*

Mildred crept back to her bed. The bed clothes were tossed aside as she had left them an hour ago, the lower part of the bed was still in the form of the small cave where her body had lain but everything seemed unfamiliar, it was as though she were creeping into the bed of a stranger. She lay quite still with her eyes wide open staring up into the darkness.

After a while Ivy returned, Mildred heard the stairs creak as she came up them. Mildred, who had resolutely kept her mind free from 'nasty thoughts' where Ivy was concerned had now not the slightest doubt whatsoever that Ivy was a 'Fallen Woman'. But what upset her a great deal more was that Ivy had no affection at all for her; it was suddenly painfully evident that after all these years together Mildred meant nothing at all to Ivy. And it was the thought that she had failed so utterly to be a mother to little Ivy that caused her scalding tears to pour down her face and on to her pillow.

But by morning the heartbreak was over, it belonged to the small secret hours; by breakfast time Mildred had come through her sorrow and her sleepless night and emerged a giantess.

Mildred was not stupid in that she was able freely to admit when she was in the wrong and philosophically set to work to put right the wrong. 'A common gutter-snipe——' Ivy had said; where had she learned such language? But that is just what Chad was; Ivy had been perfectly right; they had been awed by the fact that he was a Quest. There was only one way to treat someone of Chad's calibre and that was with a very firm hand indeed. He should never have been allowed to see so much of Ivy. Well, it was easy now. Mildred saw quite clearly that she and Ivy had come to the 'parting of the ways' as she put it. Ivy should be sent away, to London or anywhere else, Mildred would 'wash her hands' of her and if, by any chance, Ivy should get herself into serious trouble before she reached the age of twenty-one it would no longer be any concern of Mildred's; Ivy had proved herself to be intractable.

Ivy floated down to breakfast in a cotton house-coat, looking extremely lush and mature. Her golden curls were tied into a knot on the top of her head. Mildred did not look at her as she mumbled a 'Good morning' but as she got up to attend to the toast she saw the back of Ivy's white neck with the tendrils of golden hair curling in the nape. How often, when Ivy was tiny, had Mildred kissed that darling spot; tears sprang to her eyes; how often had it been kissed since? And by whom?

When she spoke her voice came more loudly than she had expected and with a harsh note. "What are you doing today, Ivy?"

Ivy stretched herself. "I dunno."

Mildred opened her mouth and closed it again. This was not the moment. She felt that if she were to tell Ivy now that she was free to go to London and do what she pleased from now on, Ivy would leap out of the room with a whoop of joy and without a backward look. But if she chose her moment, Mildred thought, Ivy might realize the significance of what was happening; she might, *might* realize what it all meant to Mildred and, in the midst of her rejoicing, spare her foster-mother a kind word. So she closed her mouth.

After breakfast Mildred made two telephone calls. The telephone was in the dining-room with an extension in Mildred's bedroom. Mildred always knew when Ivy was listening-in at the extension. Hitherto it had been one of the many sorrows she had to bear but now she accepted it as a matter of course. When Ivy heard the ping of the bell as Mildred lifted the receiver to dial the number she required, she would lift the receiver at the extension so that the click it made would be drowned in the sound of the ringing tone at the other end of the phone; but when the receiver was off at the extension Mildred always noticed a metallic sound to her own voice which was not there when the receiver was down.

This morning she simply said coldly: "Ivy, put down the receiver, there's a good girl." Such a thing had never happened before. Ivy was shocked into obediently doing as she was told but the surprise caused a warm red flush to spread over her neck and chest. She flounced back to her bedroom and banged the door.

Mildred was ringing up her school friend Dorothy who spoke fluent French. She asked her to put off the luncheon arrangement for today. "I can't explain now," Mildred told her, "but I will when I see you." That was all right. Dorothy was not too surprised; she hoped that there was no trouble of any sort—meaning, of course, Ivy.

But Mildred briskly rang off and left her to make her own conclusions which were only a little less lurid than the truth.

Then she rang up her bank which had a small branch opening three times a week in the village of Rivington. The manager had not yet arrived at work. Mildred went on with her household chores and by the time she again sat down at the telephone and dialled the bank's number Ivy had got over her fit of sulking and now fully dressed, she stood outside the dining-room door and heard every word that Mildred said.

Mr. Brown was being asked if he would allow Mildred a small overdraft. Though Mildred was a valued customer of long standing, Mr. Brown adhered to the instructions he had received from his head office: that new overdrafts were not to be allowed without the most careful consideration, preferably not at all.

So Mildred did not have an easy time. Mr. Brown did not ask her point blank but he would have liked to know why she required the fifty pounds for which she was asking. As a confirmed reader of detective fiction he formed the instant conclusion that she was being blackmailed because she required the money in notes.

"It is only a month off quarter day," Mildred pointed out, "there will be dividends coming in which will amount to more than the fifty pounds I am asking for."

Yes, indeed, but that money would be needed by Mildred for her ordinary living expenses.

"My living expenses are going to be drastically reduced, I promise you," Mildred said wildly. "I can't explain now but won't you trust me, Mr. Brown, after all these years——"

Mr. Brown would have trusted Mrs. Rollright implicitly if he did not know something about Ivy. From blackmail his alert mind leaped to illegal operations. It must be either one or the other. Fifty pounds, in notes, on the nail! What else could it be?

But Mrs. Rollright had securities; she should have her fifty pounds, bless her, and he, Mr. Brown, would have the fun of finding out before he was much older how the money was to be used.

"Oh, thank you," Mildred said with relief. "I'll come in for it this morning. I'll make out a cheque payable to 'Self'. No, I shan't need to see you. No, I assure you, it's quite all right, I won't waste your valuable time. Thank you, Mr. Brown, thank you. *Good-bye*——"

Mildred replaced the receiver, sweating. She had done a great deal for Ivy in the past but nothing she hated doing quite so much as this.

*　　*　　*　　*

181

Mr. Brown the bank manager was not the only one to spring to conclusions as to the purpose for which Mildred required fifty pounds in cash. Ivy also had her ideas and they differed considerably from those of Mr. Brown. It was not, in fact, ideas in the plural but one single idea. Mildred wanted the fifty pounds to give to Chad, to set him up in some sort of work. Ivy had no doubt at all on the subject. She had, in fact, seen it coming. She had seen her foster-mother looking at Chad with a puzzled frown many times in the last few days; she knew that Mildred was deeply sorry for him, bereaved of his dearly loved mother and amongst strangers in a country to which he was not native and of which he could not speak the language. Oh, yes, Ivy was certain that Mildred was going to do one of her impulsively generous acts and give Chad fifty pounds.

Angrily she banged her powder puff against her face and slashed her lipstick across her mouth.

Only Chad wasn't going to get that fifty pounds. Not he! If Mildred knew that Chad, as well as being a Quest, was a thief and a gutter-rat, a Cockney crook who had been up to all sorts of crime she wouldn't hand over her fifty pounds so readily.

But what good was that going to do Ivy? No, she had a better idea than that.

* * * *

Mildred was glad that the arrangement had been made for Chad to come to luncheon. She did not want her Uncle Matthew to be in any way upset again after the various disturbances of the past weeks. She would call at the lodge, as she called every day, have her walk round the garden with her uncle and bring Chad away with her. Then she would have a little time alone with him; if he still wanted to come to the Rookery for luncheon after he had heard what she had to say, well and good, if not—well, Uncle Matthew need not know that they

182

had had any discussions at all—Chad would simply have been having a meal with Mildred and Ivy.

The Rookery, the lodge and the village being at the three points of a triangle, Mildred found it convenient to call at the lodge on her way to the village. The general was planting out lettuces. He stood up as Mildred approached: "My dear Mildred, are you feeling all right? You're not looking yourself this morning at all."

Nor was she feeling herself. "Yes, I'm all right," she said impatiently, "just a sleepless night."

"What about this luncheon party of yours? Can you be bothered to have it if you're not feeling well?"

"It's not a party," Mildred said, "and Mrs. Thing is there this morning, preparing the meal."

"Mrs. Angel's here, too," Sir Matthew said proudly. "I've been listening to the blessed music of the Hoover for the past hour."

"Where's Chad?"

"He's in the kitchen. You know, Mildred, whatever you may say, I still think that boy is interested in cooking. Perhaps we should have him apprenticed to an hotel; a great many young men are going into the catering business nowadays. It's a good line. The boy's trying his hand at new dishes. I saw him studying a cookery book just now."

Mildred sniffed. She had not meant to sniff, it came quite automatically. Hurriedly, for she was ashamed of her sniff, she changed the subject. "I was talking to one of my jobbing gardeners about that aconite last night. He's rather keen on the yellow one you chucked out yesterday, Uncle. I gave him the one I had, he's planting it today in that corner where that eucalyptus died."

"You'd better have the others I threw out."

"That is what I was thinking."

"I'll get them for you. I threw them on the compost heap."

"Better in my garden than on the compost heap," Mildred said, with a shadow of a smile.

But they were not on the compost heap.

"I know I put them there," Sir Matthew said. He poked with the trowel amongst the recent grass cuttings: "Where on earth could they have got to?"

"Are you sure, Uncle?"

"Quite positive."

They were interrupted by a curious noise from the house. Mrs. Angel emerged and came towards them brandishing a feather duster in one hand and a polishing rag in the other. Her cries were evidently those of some distress.

"General," she cried, "oh dear, sir! Where has that gold snuff box gone to?"

But the general was looking for tubers of aconite which were far more important than gold snuff boxes. He continued to poke in a bewildered way, into his compost heap.

"Mrs. Angel!" Mildred cried, "you don't mean the *gold snuff box*!"

"Yes, I do, I do, come and see for yourself, ma'am. It's gone as sure as my name's Alberta. It's gone, all right!"

Mildred never invoked the Deity, but now no lesser being was adequate to the situation. She stood stock still and said: "Oh, my God!"

Mrs. Angel was satisfied, at last, that sufficient attention was being paid to the situation. "Yes," she concurred. "You've 'ad the burglars at last. I knew it. Sooner or later, I've said all along, sooner or later. You can't have a valuable thing like that lying about for long without someone hears about it——"

"Do you mean the St. Chad snuff box, Mrs. Angel?" the general asked suddenly.

"Yes, sir. That's right."

"Oh dear, Mildred, what a pity! What a pity!"

"Have you had it out for any reason, Uncle?"

184

"Out of the display table, you mean? Certainly not, what should I have it out for? It can't be missing, Mrs. Angel."

"Come and see for yourselves——"

Mrs. Angel importantly led the way into the sitting-room. "You see," she said, proud of her discovery: "All the other things have been rearranged so that the space where the snuff box was didn't show. That's why you haven't noticed it. So we don't know how long it's been missing."

"Not that it would be really any help to know," the general said thoughtfully.

Wouldn't it? Mildred thought.

"We'd better get on to the police," the general said, "they may be able to do something——"

"Wait a minute——" Mildred distractedly ran a hand over her brow. "Don't let's do anything hurriedly, Uncle. We must have a very good look for it, we'll feel so foolish if it turns up when we have the police busy looking for it——"

"We'll also feel rather foolish not being able to tell them how long it has been missing," Sir Matthew added.

Mrs. Angel stood looking from one to the other. Really, they made you laugh, the way they carried on. She'd have something to report to her daughter. Here was a first-class emergency, one which required the immediate presence of the police, and there they stood, talking to each other about feeling foolish.

Mrs. Angel hid her amusement. Action was what was required. You never knew—suspicion was as likely to fall on her as anywhere. She'd been that busy with her daughter she'd lost a lot in the way of salary lately; who knew but what the police might suspect her of taking the snuff box herself?

"Well, sir," she said, a trifle indignantly, "beg pardon and all that but it's only right to get the police in at once. It's only right, sir——"

*　　*　　*　　*

Without any explanation, Mildred left Mrs. Angel and Sir Matthew standing beside the little table. She simply turned and walked hurriedly away, closing the door quietly after her.

"Looks like Mrs. Rollright's 'ad an idear," Mrs. Angel observed.

CHAPTER XVIII

GINGER was still stirring his sauce. He had found a double saucepan and had poured his mixture into the top half. He filled the bottom half with cold water and put the pan on the stove. When Mildred came into the kitchen he jumped so violently that he almost upset the pan.

Mildred stood looking at him. Chad's ability to converse with Ivy was one of the many discoveries she had made during the night. What a fool she had been with her attempts at speaking French!

"Are you ready to come, Chad?"

"Come where?"

"Out to luncheon with me; have you forgotten?"

Forgotten? Ginger ran a hand all over his face. He had neither remembered nor forgotten. "It's me nerves," he said, "me nerves is all wrong."

Mildred hustled him out of the kitchen, through the hall, sweeping him before her into the car without giving him time to comb his hair or even glance at himself in a looking-glass.

She was glad she was driving her car for she could talk to Chad whilst doing so without having to look at him which was better for him and a great deal easier for her.

She said: "I don't know why you have pretended all along that you did not understand English. You've made a fool of us all. Have you anything to tell me Chad?"

Ginger's face twitched. "Nope!"

"Nothing you would like to tell me?" Mildred sighed, not

at Chad's unwillingness to tell her anything but at her own inability to gain his confidence. "Well, I must form my own conclusions." Pause whilst Mildred negotiated the gears. "I don't suppose it would be of any interest to you to know what they are?"

Silence.

"You see, I'm not surprised you're what you are, being your father's son. What we have to do is to avoid making the same mistakes with you that were made with your father."

Ginger felt that same twisting in his stomach, that contraction of his guts, a mixture of surprise and fear, that he had felt when Ivy had first discovered that he was not a harmless French boy. It was unbelievable that they could still think him Matthew St. Chad Quest. And yet it was not incredible, for the power of Marie Céleste's personality could carry off anything; even after she was dead. Ginger was in no doubt at all that his successful impersonation of the Quest grandson had been due solely and entirely to herself. They believed implicitly that he was Chad, son of the black sheep of the family, and the worse the light in which he was manifest the more likely were they to continue to believe it.

It was clear that only if Ginger had appeared looking as though he had just left Eton then they might, conceivably, have had the faintest shadow of doubt as to his authenticity as Martin Quest's son by a French woman.

But the shoes of the dead Chad were proving much too uncomfortable. Ginger no longer wanted to occupy them, he only wanted the money that was due to Chad. That, and to be able to stop thinking, for thinking was a form of work and Ginger did not like work in any form.

"You took the gold snuff box from the table in the sitting-room, didn't you, Chad? Come on, confess it."

Now what? Ginger sweated.

"I don't think you have disposed of it yet. Won't you please give it back to us, to Sir Matthew? It belonged to your grandmother, it has been in her family for over a hundred years. It's an heirloom, Chad. You ought to be as proud of it as the rest of us. It belonged originally to your great great grandmother to whom it was given by a Queen of England."

"I don't know what you're talking about," Ginger mumbled.

"Yes, you do. A gold snuff box with a miniature painted in ivory on the lid. It's insured for four hundred pounds. What was that?"

Ginger had said nothing, he had only made an exclamation.

"It isn't the money that matters, the insurance company will pay it, of course; it's the sentimental value. It's the sort of thing that money can't buy nowadays. Now, here we are at the bank. I'll be about five minutes. Think it over, please."

Mildred was regaining a little of her lost self-confidence, she almost skipped into the bank to collect her fifty pounds.

Lips moving, but not in the least like a monk saying his breviary, Ginger swore. He used every oath at his disposal and called the second-hand jeweller in Birmingham a string of most picturesque names. Just let him wait until Ginger got his hands on him, he'd wring his bloomin' neck, he would. He'd regret the day his mother bore him, he would, that . . . His own mother wouldn't know him! (Mothers always figure largely in the language of crook to crook.) Mince meat, that's what he'd be!

* * * *

Mildred had plenty of time afterwards to think it all over and every time she thought the events over the scene most outstanding in her mind was that of herself coming out of the bank holding the bundle of notes she had been given. They were not even in an envelope; the clerk had handed them to her with a rubber band round them. Mildred was in a hurry to get away, she could see the top of Mr. Brown's head above the partition of his office; she was afraid he would come out to speak to her and there was nothing more she desired to say to Mr. Brown. Mildred tried to get the notes into her modest note-case but they would not go, so she hurried out into the street, still carrying them in her hand. As she stood by the car she opened her handbag and put the bundle, unfolded, inside it.

While Chad watched her.

That was what Mildred could not forget. She stood there stuffing the notes into her handbag watched by Chad. She did it automatically, her mind occupied by what she was going to say next to the boy but all the time he was watching her with wistful ginger-coloured eyes, like a spaniel watching its mistress break up its biscuit.

Mildred climbed back into the car. "I'd arranged to have my friend Dorothy to meet you today. I thought she could speak French to you and find out what you really want to do with your life. But I should have felt silly! She would have known at once that you have been pulling our legs about not knowing any English."

Pause, then Mildred said gently: "You've had a bad life, haven't you Chad? Things went wrong for you, didn't they? Did you quarrel with your parents and run away from home, or what? But no, you don't want to tell me, do you? Now, I'm taking you to the Rookery for luncheon because I don't want Uncle Matthew upset thinking there's something wrong. The poor dear is quite upset about the snuff box." He wasn't but anyway, Mildred considered, he *ought* to have been. "Mrs. Angel is talking about the police. We shall have to call in the police, you know." Mildred changed to lower gear as the car ground uphill. "It would be far better for you to tell me everything now. We will all be closely questioned, you may be sure. You too, Chad. You know what that means, don't you? They'll want to know something about you."

"If you want to know," Ginger burst out, "it was that Ivy of yours took it."

Mildred cleared her throat.

"She's a regular bad lot, that gurl," Ginger went on. "She—" his brain was working now, "she broke in last night."

189

"Broke into the cottage?"

"Yeh. I heard a noise and came down to see what was up. Caught her red-handed. Nabbed her."

Mildred stopped the car. She couldn't drive and listen to this sort of thing at the same time. She still didn't look at Ginger but kept her eyes straight ahead. "Why didn't you do something about it?" she asked in a strained voice.

"Do something? Why, she's your gurl," Ginger said with a burst of self-righteousness, "when all's said and done she's yours."

Mildred closed her eyes. This was by no means the worst blow of the lot, it simply underlined everything that had gone before.

"Where is it now?"

"Why, Ivy's still got it."

"What's she going to do with it?"

"She's planning to go to London. Reckon she'll sell it when she gets there."

Mildred nodded.

Then Ginger gave Mildred a piece of sound advice: "It's no good," he said, "trying to make a lady out of an alley-cat like Ivy."

Again Mildred nodded. She knew that, now that it was too late.

*   *   *   *

Luncheon was a macabre meal. It had to be eaten, however, in the presence of one of Mildred's daily women and the decencies must be preserved but all three sat in absolute silence each enclosed a shell of his or her consciousness, each occupied solely with his or her thoughts.

And Mildred's handbag hung upon the arm of the carving chair in which Mildred sat.

Though Ivy did not look at the handbag she could see it all the time. Did it or did it not contain fifty pounds in notes? Had

Mildred or had she not given Chad the money in the car on the way? Ivy had had a nasty shock when the car had arrived containing Chad as well as Mildred. How could she have reckoned on Mildred fetching Chad back with her? However, it was not too late. If she had already given the fifty pounds to Chad—he was still here.

And Chad. He, too, watched the handbag but he was not adept at the art of seeing without looking, like Ivy. He shot it nervous glances from time to time.

Mildred felt defeated; defeated and deflated. She did not want to talk things over with Ivy nor did she want to discuss his future with Chad. She wanted to go upstairs and lie down on her bed. She had not slept all night, nor did she feel she would sleep now, but she badly wanted to sink down into a blessed oblivion.

When Mildred was entertaining, coffee was served in the drawing-room. It was a brave gesture intended to keep up one's standard of living for it was nasty coffee, the silver tray was not clean and the drawing-room smelt a little dank and unused. Mildred carried her handbag with her into the drawing-room, it lay beside her on the sofa as she poured out the coffee. When the telephone rang Mildred took her handbag out with her, it was hanging on her arm.

Ivy had no ideas about the time for and fitness of her actions. She went straight across to Ginger and sat on his knee. Ginger immediately heaved her off on to the floor where she sat, undismayed.

"Why has she put off Dorothy? There's something up. What is it?" Ivy asked.

"She's not stupid," Ginger declared. "You've made a big mistake thinking she is."

"Why, what's up?"

"She knows a hell of a lot more than you think."

"Has she given you fifty pounds, Chad?"

"Me? Why the hell should she?"

191

"But has she?"

"Not bloomin' likely."

Ivy sucked her finger thoughtfully. That didn't mean anything, of course. He was more likely to be telling a lie than the truth.

"What would she give me fifty pounds for? She's not crazy."

"To set you up," Ivy suggested.

"Set me up?" She seemed to him to be talking nonsense.

"I'm going, by the afternoon train," Ivy said.

"To London?"

"Yes."

"O.K." Ginger said.

"I'll write you a line and let you know how I'm getting on."

Ginger said nothing, he had not the least desire to know how she was getting on. There was a pause whilst they both thought about Mildred's handbag.

It was Ginger who should have got the money. He was a pickpocket of some little experience and Ivy was the product of an English girls' public school. But where Ginger was assiduous Ivy was bold, where Ginger thought twice Ivy didn't even think once, she acted.

*   *   *   *

Acted was the word.

It was quite clear that whatever her future might hold Ivy would not remain long on a stage in a static pose, holding a Grecian urn. Though a full minute had elapsed since Ginger heaved, tossed is hardly the word, Ivy off his knee on to the floor, Ivy snatched at the opportunity almost as it passed out of her reach.

"Ow, ow!" she screamed suddenly: "You beast! You absolute beast, how dare you lay a hand on me." She beat Ginger with her fists, screaming hysterically.

It was not the first time Ivy had had hysterics. She often

192

used to have them when she was thwarted. Mildred recognized the opening notes. It was the vicar who had telephoned, she cut him short by simply putting down the receiver, and fled back to the drawing-room.

Ivy had had some grand scenes in the past but they were pallid in comparison with the one she now staged. Even Ginger was impressed.

The general theme was that Ginger had tried to assault her the moment Mildred had left the room. That the time and the place were not expedient for rape was neither here nor there, Ivy did not give anyone time to consider. She shrieked and screamed, she lay on the floor, flinging out her arms and kicking her heels just as she had done when she was six years old. The difference was that now she was five feet ten and a half inches in height and weighed over eleven stone. Vases, ferns, silver photograph frames, coffee tray and small tables flew about the room.

Mildred tried to hold her.

"Go for some water. Fetch Mrs. Thing."

Ginger collided with Mrs. Thing in the doorway. She had heard the noise and was bringing in a bowl of water which she poured over Ivy, causing a double-strength bout of yells.

"Oh, this is terrible," Mildred groaned, clasping her head in despair.

"Leave her to me, ma'am," Mrs. Thing said grimly and she proceeded to tackle Ivy as she tackled Mr. Thing when he came home recalcitrant on a Saturday night. (Or, to be accurate, as she *used* to tackle Mr. Thing; he now no longer considered it worth his while to celebrate.)

It developed rapidly into a first class fight with Mildred and Ginger standing by as seconds.

It ended in a fit of wild sobbing, real *fin de siècle* stage sobbery, a first-class performance and thoroughly nerve-racking.

Mildred and Mrs. Thing pulled Ivy to her feet. "We must

193

get her up to her room," Mildred gasped. "If anyone were to call——"

Mrs. Thing declared that she had never seen a fit of hysterics the like of this. They had better call the doctor. With a few very dark looks at Ginger she continued to insist that the doctor be called; it was only a step from there to the police and though she did not actually take that step Ginger knew that it was imminent.

He must get back.

Whichever way he turned now it was all up with him. He must get back to the lodge.

He went, and no one but Ivy noticed that he had gone.

Mildred went to the phone for the doctor and Mrs. Thing went to make a pot of tea for them all, for if this wasn't the right moment for tea she'd like to know what was.

*　*　*　*

Afterwards Mildred could not remember exactly where her handbag had been. Perhaps she had left it by the telephone in the dining-room, perhaps she had had it hanging on her arm the whole horrible time.

She remembered getting Ivy up to her room, she remembered Mrs. Thing coming upstairs with a cup of tea for them both. She remembered taking her own cup of tea downstairs because she did not want to remain with the still shuddering Ivy for another moment. She couldn't remember where her bag was whilst she sat on the seat in the hall and sipped her tea. She realized, then, that Chad had disappeared, but she did not care.

Struggling to retain some fragments of normality she did what she would have done in the ordinary way, she went out into the garden to talk to the gardener. They talked about the border.

They walked round the garden and talked about the roses.

194

"Oh, by the way," Mildred frowned. "I haven't forgotten about those plants I was getting from the general."

"Oh, the aconite. Yes, ma'am."

"They've been mislaid somehow. He couldn't find them this morning."

"I reckon it's too late to plant them now they're sprouting."

"But you'd like to try them, wouldn't you, Lyon? I won't forget about them."

She went back into the house. She had a splitting headache. She went into the drawing-room which looked as though there had been a minor air raid. She was too tired to start tidying-up now. She hoped Mrs. Thing would have gone home as her time was up, she couldn't face her now and see the reproach in her eyes that there should be such goings-on at The Rookery.

Mildred lay down on the sofa. When she had had a little rest she would go up to Ivy's room and talk to her. She would say everything that she had planned to say. She would give her the money she had for her—and her blessing too.

Remembering her money Mildred felt for her handbag. Yes, it was there, on the floor beside the sofa. She lay back. She was sleepy at last. Perhaps she slept a little . . .

*   *   *   *

The clock struck four.

Mrs. Thing had certainly gone.

Now, when they were alone in the house, was the time for her talk with Ivy. The fearful scene in the drawing-room after luncheon had facilitated Mildred's plan. There was now no need to think out a way of explaining to Ivy what had made her decide to let her go, there was no need carefully to avoid any reference to anything which might make Ivy suspect that she had got up and followed her to the Lodge the previous night. She would simply say that their lives together had obviously become impossible—and so on.

195

Mildred sighed heavily as she got up. The doctor would be coming soon; she would have to explain that Ivy had had one of her attacks . . .

But Ivy had gone. Her room was very untidy. Drawers were left open, spilling out their contents, clothes were lying about all over the room. But when Mildred looked more carefully she saw that Ivy had taken only her best clothes. There was no doubt about that. The clothes she had left were those she had worn at the Ladies' College, the poplin blouses, the good underwear, the excellent tweed suits, the flat-heeled shoes, the cotton stockings, the blazer. She had left her tennis racket, too, her pleated tennis skirt and the sweater with the school colours. And there was her hockey stick . . .

Mildred wept.

CHAPTER XIX

GINGER went back to Rivington Lodge very slowly. It can hardly be said that he walked back; he had never gone on foot so far in his life, he slouched along the road, cigarette hanging from his lips, his face puckered with the agony of having to think. Yes, it was all up with him now, once the police came on the scene he was finished. The only hope now was to take what money he could lay his hands on and run for it. He still had his passport and if he had the money he could get back to the Rue des Mauvais Garçons all right.

If. If. If. If only the old man were to die now before he learned, as he was bound to learn, certain things about his 'grandson'. If only . . .

Ginger could go off to Paris and in due course he would receive his share of the estate, whatever might be known about him by anyone else. The old man *must* be kept in ignorance; it was Ginger's only hope.

There was only one way of keeping him in certain ignorance. Ginger knew what that way was, the knowledge lay festering in a separate compartment of his mind; it was like a sore place and to think of it was like touching an inflamed wound.

For Ginger, it must be clear, was no poisoner, he was just a poor thing, bent by circumstances to perform a wicked deed, a deed which he himself would be one of the first to condemn.

* * * *

The general was in the garden, as usual. He was at the end of his garden spraying his wall-fruit. Ginger shouted "Hi!" to let him know that he had returned and the old man raised a hand in greeting.

Ginger went into the kitchen. The meat had come, Mrs. Angel had put it in the larder. Ginger placed it in the pan of vegetables he had prepared. He put on the lid and turned up the gas a little. He looked into the saucepan containing the horse-radish sauce. It was just as he had left it. He stirred it.

Then he went to the larder again and took down the brown carrier from the hook behind the door. His movements were slow and heavy like those of a sleepwalker. He found the grater and an enamel plate. Then he took out a root and grated it. The result did not look appetizing. He grated another. There was now about one third as much root as there was horseradish. He stirred it into the sauce. The mixture still looked the nasty greyish colour but once it was cooked, Ginger knew, it would become creamy.

He squatted on the high stool beside the stove. He lighted the gas below the double saucepan and his cigarette with the automatic lighter; he smoked and, from time to time, stirred the sauce but he was not thinking about his cooking. He was thinking about Ivy and the shocking scene he had witnessed. He could not but admire Ivy now, he had always felt attracted to people with more personality than his own. At present she

197

was too young, too inexperienced, but after being employed by Mr. Blubberstein she might be improved out of all knowledge. Once Ginger was safely back in the Rue des Mauvais Garçons, and a man of means, he might get in touch with Ivy. He hadn't been keen when she suggested it but now, thinking it over, he considered he might do a lot worse.

The general always drank a glass of sherry before his evening meal. He came in from the garden, knocking the mud off his feet against the wall by the kitchen door and sitting down on the doorstep to take his boots off. His house slippers were kept beside the door in readiness for him. He put them on and went through the kitchen saying: "Jolly good smell, Chad old boy," merely desiring to be pleasant, "makes me quite hungry."

Ginger said nothing; he sat on, a wisp of smoke curling up from the cigarette at the side of his mouth. There was no need to think now, he had just to keep an eye on the pattern . . .

*　　*　　*　　*

It was six-thirty before the doctor arrived. He was sorry to have been delayed but he'd had a confinement. Mildred was no longer weeping; she had been busy clearing up the drawing-room, picking up pieces of broken plant pot, brushing up soil, tending her poor wounded ferns, trying to wipe coffee stains off the carpet, setting small tables upright.

"Mildred, you're looking awful!" the doctor exclaimed, "what's the trouble?"

"Ivy has had one of her attacks."

"Drat that girl, we'll have you with an attack of something before she's much older. She wants a good spanking and I've half a mind to give her one myself. Where is she?"

"She—" Mildred swallowed. "She's gone."

"A damn good thing too. Do you mean—run away?"

"I think so."

"Well, let's hope it's for good this time. You're worn out, my dear."

198

"You don't understand. She's my child."

"Nonsense. You know perfectly well you'd never have had a child like that. Mildred, listen to me. That girl has been tearing you to pieces for years now. We've all seen it and been sorry for you. The best thing you can do now is to cut your losses, simply forget about her."

"I—I have realized that I have failed hopelessly with Ivy. I was thinking of giving her some money and letting her go," Mildred said shakily, "but she's gone on her own."

"I shouldn't bother about giving her money, she'll get on all right."

It was only after he'd gone, leaving Mildred feeling better, that she thought of looking inside her handbag.

The notes had gone.

And then Mildred, though she could not remember exactly where her handbag had been during the scene did remember that Chad had, sometime before it was over, left.

There was no doubt whatsoever in her mind that Chad had taken the notes.

Suppose he and Ivy had gone away together?

It was possible, of course.

But perhaps he had taken the notes and bolted alone? It was rather odd, however, that he and Ivy should run away separately on the same day.

Perhaps that was what they had both been planning the night before. Perhaps Chad had been lying to her about Ivy having stolen the gold snuff box.

Or perhaps she had taken the snuff box and Chad had taken the money and they had joined forces. Perhaps . . .

Mildred felt dizzy. She went to the telephone to ring up Rivington Lodge and find out if Chad were there, which, of course, he would not be.

But if he were—then Sir Matthew would simply be worried by her telephone call.

Then she must ring up the police. But what a hideous scandal that would precipitate.

Mildred's irresolution lasted for a matter of minutes and then her mind cleared.

She would go to Rivington Lodge now and if Chad were there she would ask for the money to be returned to her. If he did not return it she would telephone to the police. If he did return it she would then have a long private discussion with the general about him. She would tell him all she knew about him and together they would form some sort of plan. It would upset the general very much, of course, but together they might be able to form some sort of plan for his erring grandson that would be satisfactory all round.

*   *   *   *

The cottage orné was full of the smell of the meal which was ready. The smell was so delicious that it made the general feel hungry. He had a second glass of sherry and when Chad came in to lay the table for the meal his grandfather got up for another glass. He poured out some golden brown sherry and handed it to Chad with a smile. "A nip for the cook," he said whimsically.

Ginger carried his drink into the kitchen and smelled it suspiciously. If it were a *fine*, a *Calvados* or something of that kind he would pour it down the sink.

But it was wine. Ginger drained the glass.

Presently he hummed a little, quite tunelessly, as he banged the plates and dishes about.

Work was reduced to a minimum by the serving out of the food straight from the pans, without using vegetable dishes. The general did not like the habit but he put up with it because of the evident saving of labour.

Ginger sliced the meat, some for the general, some for himself. He put potatoes and vegetables on the plate beside the meat. He spooned a little of the gravy from the pan on to the potato. He took the pan of horseradish sauce and spooned a large helping on to one plate. He hesitated with the pan held over his own plate.

And then, suddenly, he was back in the Rue des Mauvais Garçon. There was exactly the same smell, and the food looked the same and Marie Céleste was swinging the pan out of his reach: "It is not for you," she had said, "not for you."

It was not for Ginger, it was for Chad . . .

*   *   *   *

For the second time in twenty-four hours Mildred stopped her car along the road and walked towards the lodge in her 'sneakers'.

*   *   *   *

It was Chad, the harmless idiot boy who, in life, had never done anyone any harm—or any good—who saved his grandfather from a painful death. It was the dead Chad who was directly responsible for saving his grandfather.

Whilst Ginger was serving out the meal in the kitchen the general sat down at the table, unfurled his table napkin and waited. He toyed with his knife and his fork, he moved the salt cellar, he cleared his throat and fidgeted with his wine glass. Chad was being a long time; the general thrust a hand into one of his jacket pockets and there encountered something which, for over a week, he had had in his pocket. He had fingered it a lot in the past week. He brought it out now and turned it over and over between his fingers examining it.

It was Chad's little wooden donkey; his only achievement in life; the little wooden donkey at which he had chipped for hours and hours. It had fallen from the dead hand of Marie Céleste as they lifted her on to the bed and the general had picked it up and kept it in his pocket ever since, wondering, whenever he touched it, why Marie Céleste had so treasured it.

It was a fascinating little creature with a great deal of character. It was clear that whoever had made it had been an artist. The general stood it up in front of him on the table beyond his spoon and fork.

It was a patient little donkey, yet with the shadow of a smile, the general smiled too.

And Ginger came in carrying the plate of food, putting it down on the table before him.

The general picked up his knife and fork and started to eat. Ginger did not move away. He stood beside him. The general looked up to see why Chad had not returned to the kitchen.

He was staring at the donkey with a very curious expression upon his face. The general returned to his meal. The meat and vegetables were excellent; horseradish sauce too!

Ginger was back in the Rue des Mauvais Garçons which it would seem he had never left. There was the little donkey standing on the table in front of Chad, and there was the great bulk of Chad nodding and smiling at his donkey and then lowering his loving eyes to shovel great mouthfuls of food into his mouth. Presently Chad would be very ill, he would vomit and he would sweat and he would cry with pain. He would yell with pain. And then his face would go a terrible colour. And his eyes would turn up. . .

"Stop, stop!" Ginger cried, "don't eat the sauce, it is not for you, not for you!"

The general sprang up from the table, knocking his chair over backwards. Had the boy gone suddenly mad?

And then Mildred came in. She had seen through the window that something unusual was happening. Ginger was looking quite mad now, he was shouting in a high Cockney voice: "It's poisoned, it's poisoned, I tell you. You'll die if you eat it. You'll have terrible pains——"

Mildred shook him in the way she had watched her daily

woman dealing with Ivy's hysteria. Ginger was crying now, great tears were streaming down his face. It was the pity of it that was making him cry, the pity that his plan had not succeeded, the shocking fact that he had not the courage to carry it through.

"What have you done to the food?" Mildred shouted.

"Poisoned. Poisoned."

"But what with, and why?"

Ginger did not tell her with what. He did not, in fact, know the name of the plant. Nor did he say why.

"Who are you?" Mildred asked urgently, "You aren't St. Chad Quest, are you?"

Ginger shook his head, moaning.

"Who are you, then?"

"Me? I'm a—I'm a cheap crook."

"Ah!" With a great cry Mildred turned to Sir Matthew. "You see!"

"But Marie Céleste?"

Ginger pulled himself together. He did not look at Mildred or at Sir Matthew. He looked only at the little wooden donkey.

"Marie Céleste was all right," he said, steady suddenly, "She was a good woman. Her son died. I made her bring me over here and pass me off as Chad Quest. She had to, if she hadn't I—I'd of killed her, 1 would. There was nothing wrong with Marie Céleste."

Sir Matthew took a firm hold of Ginger's arm. "Her son, St. Chad, died, you say?"

"Yes, he died. He was a good boy, too. He's buried——" Ginger made a big effort, "he's buried in the Cemetery at Ivry. You can see his grave there, it's in a long line of graves, a long line——" But he was wandering from the point. "He was an artist, like his father." Of course Chad had been an artist; an idiot, but something of a genius, Ginger could see that now with extraordinary clarity. "Yes, he was an artist, but he was a good boy, too."

"When did he die?"

But Ginger had done what was required of him, what *Marie Céleste* had required of him. There was only one thing left to be done and that was nothing to do with Marie Céleste. That he must do on his own. Stiffly he walked from the front room and out of the front door, leaving it wide open.

Mildred started to run after him but Sir Matthew stopped her.

"Let him go."

"But he's got my fifty pounds, and the gold snuff box——"

"Let him go, I tell you," the general shouted in a terrible voice, he had never spoken to Mildred like that before . . .

* * * *

I'm a cheap crook! Ginger lay on his back and stared up at the starlit sky. I'm a cheap crook. How had he come to say that?

* * * *

The jeweller saw Ginger just a second or two before Ginger saw him. He saw the expression on Ginger's face. He'd been expecting him back, of course, and, upon the whole, he was not surprised at the facial expression.

He nipped into his office and took out his Colt .22 automatic. In answer to the ping of the doorbell he carried it back into the shop, hidden below a newspaper and put it down on the shelf immediately behind and below the counter.

"Ah, good day to you——" there was no point in not being pleasant.

"That snuff box you bought off me——"

"Yes?"

"You're a cheap crook," Ginger said, it was satisfactory to use the words about someone other than himself. "You're just a cheap crook. You know full well it's wurf a lot more money than what you paid me. Four hundred pounds it's insured for. It's solid gold, it is, and historical."

"My dear sir," the jeweller said with a patronizing laugh; he spread out his hands to either side, very slightly. "A cheap bit of pinchbeck, if I remember rightly. I sold it to a young person who was looking for a present for her mother, for two pounds. So I made five shillings profit."

"You're lying," Ginger shouted. "I'm sure you've got it there. You're keeping it until you've got in touch with a proper fence. Or else you've sold it to a fence already." He thrust his chin forward trying hard to see the truth in the eyes behind those thick distorting lenses. "You'll hand it over," Ginger cried, "or I'll go straight to the narks."

The jeweller laughed: "That's rich, that is. You going to the narks! Where are you going to say you got it from, eh? Tell me that one, eh?"

Ginger did not lose his temper, he had no temper to lose, he felt merely an unbearable irritability. He took the jeweller by his string-like tie and pulled his face towards him.

But the jeweller was in no doubt at all that he was going to be murdered. This was just exactly the emergency for which he had been so long prepared. In less than a second he had the revolver against Ginger's heart—and had fired it. Once was quite enough but just to be on the safe side he fired it three times.

*   *   *   *

When the police were actually there he didn't feel quite so confident about it. There was a suggestion of a whine in his voice.

"It was self-defence, I tell you, it was either him or me."

"We're not arguing," the inspector said a trifle shortly. "Just a minute, just a minute, though. Turn on the light, Sergeant."

The inspector kneeled down and looked for a long time

at Ginger's face. Then he touched his hair. Against the parting and on both sides of it there was a thin line of hair of an unmistakable bright auburn.

"Wait a minute," the inspector said again, "I know who this one is." He frowned for a moment and then his brow cleared. "I don't remember the name but he was gazetted last fall, over that Great West Road tobacco job. The other two boys got three years but this one got away. Ginger they called him. And look at his hair, ever seen such a rich black? But that's what matters." The inspector pointed to the parting and looked up at the others for approbation.

"Well," he said, turning back to the corpse, "looks like fate's caught up with you, Ginger." He looked up at the jeweller. "Seems like you've saved us a packet of trouble with this one, mate."

The jeweller looked just a little smug as he picked a thread of cotton off his lapel.

*　　*　　*　　*

Ivy sat in the underground carriage and smirked at the man sitting opposite. Her skirt had risen considerably and the man was looking self-consciously anywhere but at Ivy. But Ivy wasn't grumbling, she was perfectly content. She had been very clever indeed. She was perfectly satisfied that even if the stupid Mildred were to suspect her of having taken the money she wouldn't do anything about it.

In her newly found independence, Ivy was determined that she was going to stand no nonsense from Mr. Blubberstein, nonsense, that is, of the kind referring to hours and conditions of work. She was in a position to dictate her own terms. Mr. Blubberstein had it coming to him if he didn't toe the line.

Ivy peeped into her handbag to make sure that the forty-nine pounds left after paying her fare to London were still there . . .

*　　*　　*　　*

206

"I'm glad we've got the snuff box back," Mildred said, "but I wish they had been able to trace the fifty pounds."

"Never mind that, Mildred, let us be thankful that we haven't been brought into it. Think of the trouble we might have had, reporters all over the place and our life stories in the Sunday papers." The general shuddered. "No, we've come out of this unpleasant affair very well indeed. If you've lost fifty pounds in the process I consider it's a cheap let-out."

"But—I was going to give it to Ivy. That's the point."

"She's a lot better without it."

"The poor child, all alone in London——"

"All alone?" The general simply raised his eyebrows and left it at that. "Talking about being alone, don't you think the time has come, Mildred dear, that we should join forces?"

"You mean share a house?"

"I do."

"But what about our gardens?"

"We have to sacrifice something. Let's take a sporting chance, Mildred. We'll toss a coin. If you win we'll live at The Rookery and if I win the toss we'll live here."

Mildred smiled. "Very well," she agreed. "Here's a penny——"

THE END

>>> If you've enjoyed this book and would like to discover more great vintage crime and thriller titles, as well as the most exciting crime and thriller authors writing today, visit: >>>

The Murder Room
Where Criminal Minds Meet

themurderroom.com